WARNING!

Adult Fiction

Sexually Exquisite

*If you are not eighteen or older,
do not, seriously, do not read this book.*

SEXCAPADES

Honey B

GC

GRAND CENTRAL
PUBLISHING

NEW YORK   BOSTON

Grand Central Publishing
Hachette Book Group USA
237 Park Avenue
New York, NY 10017

Visit our Web site at www.HachetteBookGroupUSA.com.

Printed in the United States of America

First Edition: March 2008
10 9 8 7 6 5 4 3 2 1

Grand Central Publishing is a division of Hachette Book Group USA, Inc.
The Grand Central Publishing name and logo is a trademark of Hachette Book Group USA, Inc.

Library of Congress Cataloging-in-Publication Data

HoneyB.
  Sexcapades / by HoneyB. — 1st ed.
    p. cm.
  ISBN-13: 978-0-446-58228-5
  ISBN-10: 0-446-58228-X
  1. African Americans—Fiction. I. Title.
PS3563.O87477S49 2008
813'.54—dc 22
                2007037696

Let Me Whisper in Your Ear

Date:

Given To:

Given By:

Personal Message:

*Dedicated with love and gratitude
to my editor, Karen R. Thomas, and
my agent, Andrew Stuart*

There may be a shortage of men but there is no shortage of SEX.

Introduction

Sex · ca · pades: wild and exciting sexual undertakings (not necessarily lawful)

Sexcapades is erotica at its best.

Prepare yourself for a sexual metamorphosis. This novel is tasteful, tantalizing, daring, and at times shocking. Get ready to hold on to your genitals because the sexual scenes in *Sexcapades* are sensuous, sizzling, and mind-blowing.

Before continuing to read this book, you are encouraged to take three deep breaths. Fill your lungs to maximum capacity, hold your breath for five seconds, and then exhale all of your inhibitions. Proper breathing during sex heightens your orgasms. You will want to cum just for fun by yourself or with someone else. Let your feelings and your fluids flow freely. Buy a leather whip. Take an exotic trip to a nude resort. Release your animalistic instincts. Hiss at your boss if you want to. Growl at your neighbor if you desire. Spark a sexual fire inside of you that heats up everybody around you. You don't need permission to be a sexual god or goddess.

Good sex is healthy and stimulating. Sex has healing powers. Did you know having sex two hundred times a year can make you feel and look up to six years younger? Now that you know, don't skip the quickies; every orgasm counts. Because it's difficult to find one person to fulfill all of our needs, multiple intimate partners are healthy emotionally and physically. Most men have experienced the benefits of multiple partners. After reading *Sexcapades*, women will decide how many partners they'd like to have and why.

Fuck responsibly and wrap that dick up.

Women, you don't have to be in a relationship to satisfy or explore your sexual desires. Masturbate or find a partner you enjoy having sex with. Ask the man or men that appeal to you, "Would you like to be my sex buddy?" Go back to the *Let Me Whisper in Your Ear* page and write your e-mail address and/or your number inside a copy of *Sexcapades* and give him the book. After he's read your personal message, and, trust me, he will, ask which chapters are his favorites, and why. Engage him in an open-ended discussion about sex and sexuality. Ladies, you should know what you want and expect from a man in and out of bed. Oh, and never suck his dick before he licks your clit.

Men, this novel is equally intended for you. You can say to a woman, "I'm in search of a *Sexcapades* babe and I was hoping that you could help me find her." Write your number and contact information along with a personal message inside a copy of *Sexcapades* and give her the book. Giving her the book is a safer approach than asking her to do the things you like that are in the book. If you've given the book to the right woman, she'll call you. If you're a good lover, she'll call you again.

For men who prefer men and women who like women, *Sexcapades* was written with you in mind. There are same sex encounters in several chapters. Irrespective of who's having sex, I want each reader to read between the thighs and the lies as if you were each character. What I'm learning is that every sexual community is plagued with sexually repressed individuals. A fifty-year-young good-looking lesbian disclosed to me, "I've never had a woman make love to me." Her words were sincere and important. In a relationship, no one wants to feel as though they're getting fucked.

Sex is boring when you don't know how to make love or at a minimum exhibit passion. If you're simply fucking every person you have sex with, lying dead like a fish, trying to knock the bottom out of the pussy, not squeezing the dick with your pussy, or wondering how long it's going to take the other person to cum so you can go, you're wasting everyone's time including your own. Sex is powerful when you are in touch with the erogenous zones of your body, and of your partner's body, and when you've mastered how to maximize your sexual energy. You must tune in to your partner's reactions.

It's time for Western culture to stop being so damn hypocritical about sex. Western culture thrives on paranoia. "It's wrong to have sex out of wedlock. It's illegal to have sex if you're under the age of eighteen. It's a sin to have sex with the same sex." Even within religions, ministers, preachers, priests, rabbis, etc. make their congregations feel guilty about sexual pleasures. Some religions go as far as to ostracize fornicators and refuse Communion to divorced couples.

There are preachers on episodes of *Dateline* television trying to have sex with minors. Politicians are on so-called private lists with madams. There are people who have sex with dogs and cows. Boys, girls, women, and men are raped more by family members and friends than by strangers. Individuals lie about their marital status to get laid. We've had a nationwide class-action lawsuit against dioceses due to priests molesting children within the Catholic Church.

These unscrupulous acts occur because Western society teaches us to suppress instead of encouraging us to embrace our natural sexual instincts. Some folks sneak, hide, rape, and commit sexual offenses because societal stigmas make them feel ashamed of wanting to have sex. Too many people are taught to believe that sex is dirty, it's wrong, it's sinful, etc.

I say, "Sex among consenting adults is wonderful."

I don't understand parents who tell their children not to have sex when what they should do is educate their children on safe and responsible sex. I don't condone minors having sex, but teenagers are going to have sex regardless of what their parents say. In most cases the parents did not practice what they're preaching to their children.

Like some of you, I started having sex when I was fourteen and ended up pregnant at fifteen because I had no adult to openly talk with about my raging hormones. Parents are disseminating old information to a new generation of sophisticated children and it didn't work then and it's not working now. Teenagers are being violated via the Internet by sex predators and pedophiles because their parents think their children are safe because they're at home on the computer. It's time to get real about sex and sexuality. Ignorance is worse than education. I want everyone to go to www.fam ilywatchdog.us and research the sexual predators in your neighborhood. You might be surprised.

The reality is abstinence is abnormal. What Western culture needs to do is develop a healthy mental attitude and approach toward sex education. God made us to procreate and mate. If no one taught us how to have sex, we'd do it naturally.

It's time for women to wake up and stand up and claim their rights to sexual freedom. Women need to start opening up and expressing themselves sexually without any consideration of males' opinions. Ladies, fuck 'em. When *you* want to. If you're single like me, you might adopt my motto. Until the right one cums along, "Take the dick and run."

Don't invest your time trying to make him a man if he's not already. I ain't tryna bring a man up or hold a man up and I tell him that when I meet him. Don't try to lift him up if he hasn't picked himself up. Don't try to upgrade his lifestyle if he's content. Dick is plentiful and free, so don't pay for it. Don't let him drop you off at work and keep your car. Don't give him keys to your house if he's not paying the rent or the mortgage. Under no circumstances should you ever let a man hit you. Ou, I have a zero tolerance for a man who lay hands on a woman and you should too. And when you finish fucking him, don't hesitate to put him out.

That's what some men do, you know. "Oh, just read this book and judge for yourself. And if you make it to the Essence Music Festival in New Orleans, just drive down N. Rampart Street across from Louis Armstrong Park at night and check out the sea of fine-ass black men. Yes, men. For blocks and blocks you'll see all men. If you lose track of your man, you might just find him over there ass up or ass out or on the corner with a dick in his mouth. Don't take my word for it. I ain't got to lie y'all."

Where was I? Oh yeah. When women deny men sex as a form of discipline, women are actually denying themselves sexual gratification. The male will either suppress his sexual appetite or feast someplace else; in an alarmingly increasing number of cases single and married men are mating with men to satisfy their sexual appetites.

Stigmatized promiscuity and gay bashing result in closet lesbians, men on the down-low, lovers who cheat on their spouses, and an increase in sexually transmitted diseases. If a woman knows her husband is bisexual, she can ask him to use a condom or she can ask for a divorce. If a man is aware that his lover contracted HIV from having an affair, he can protect himself during sex or he can end the relationship.

All this lying, deceiving, tiptoeing, and creeping by folks who are supposedly grown just to have sex has gotten the HoneyB fed up. Look in the mirror and be honest with yourself. Stop all the lying and double standards. You can't be everything to everybody, so stop trying. No one person will ever satisfy your every need. You will never own anyone's dick or pussy, so stop acting like you do. Do whatever you want but tell the truth. Many couples are miserable and too many married individuals are unhappy. Please realize that a person's sexuality is not a measure of their character. And a grown person does not need your permission to be an adult.

Society should embrace all types of sexuality: homosexuals, heterosexuals, lesbians, and, in my case, try-sexuals. I'll try most things once. If I like it, I'll do it again. If I don't like it, that's it, I'm done. But at least I know, based on my personal experiences, what appeals to me. I don't give credence to society's predetermination of what's morally correct. I say, "Screw society because the people making up the rules sure as hell aren't living by the rules." Like the individuals in Jena, Louisiana, who incarcerated Mychal Bell and charged several African American teens in 2007 for defending themselves against several white guys while the white guys were never ever charged. And it all started because some African American teens wanted to sit under a tree designated for "whites only." I'll stop here because injustice against any race upsets me. Back to my point, it's my prerogative to enjoy sex with whomever I choose.

Other cultures understand the healing powers that are exchanged between couples during sex. And there are so many ways to have healthy sex without penetration, like mental stimulation, cuddling, foreplay, masturbation, cunnilingus, and fellatio. The best sex occurs prior to orgasms, which last only a few seconds. The human touch is powerful and healing. Try it and see for yourself. Hug, caress, or stroke someone. Lovingly play in their hair and watch their body spontaneously relax. Rub their feet. Kiss the nape of their neck in public. Massage or lick their nipples and observe their reactions.

Sexcapades is about your personal journey to freely explore your sexuality. If particular scenes arouse you, allow your mind to engage in the sexual moment and stimulate your senses. Masturbate if you want to. Then think, write, or talk to a friend about how the sex scenes made you feel. Be honest with yourself. This is your opportunity to grow spiritually and sexually. After you've assessed your sexual feelings, embrace your new discovery.

As seen on *The Oprah Winfrey Show*, 51 percent of all women are single and 75 percent of all African American women are single. I agree with Oprah when she said, "That's a good thing." Women are choosing whether they want to become wives or have children, realizing that they are not defined by having a man or a husband. Personally, I never want to get married again. Sure I could, but what I prefer is compatibility, compassion, love, sex, affection, intellectual stimulation, and friendship, none of which requires a legal commitment.

Marriage today is way overrated in my opinion. Most married couples don't effectively communicate with one another. Millions of married people are having extramarital affairs. And way too many people are simply married on paper to maintain their financial status. So I give one thumb-down to married couples who are unaware of their sexual power and two thumbs-up to sexually liberated singles. You know the singles I'm talking about. They're always walking around smiling, happy, and energetic and they have lots of stories to share about the people they're dating or places they've traveled.

So, ladies, for those of you in search of Mr. Right, enjoy sex with Mr. Right Now until you find the man of your dreams. If you're like me, make new friends around the world and have fun wherever life takes you.

Most important . . . if you don't remember anything else I've said, "Honey, be safe, don't get stung. Fuck responsibly. Wrap that dick up!"

SEXCAPADES

Sexcapade 1

Nick

I'm gonna make you cum, with my mouth . . . Is that okay?"
Every word she spoke was exhaled faintly above a whisper.

Eagerly he nodded, causing his forehead to bump her nose several times.

Reclining until his back meshed flat against the bed, Nick interlocked his fingers behind his head, generously spreading his lean, muscular thighs nice and wide, professing, "This big banana dick is all yours, lovely. Open wide and proceed with caution."

The long sweet swerve of his hard-on curved into a perfect hook that he knew could hit the corners of her pussy with the same precision that his Bentley mastered the curvaceous mountainside of Highway 1 in San Francisco.

The plush pillow-top mattress snugly fitted with a black satin sheet sucked in his entire body like an undercurrent drawing a mannequin beneath the sand of the ocean floor. Clearly Nick realized it wasn't the mattress making him weak. It was how she'd said what she said that caused blood to rush to his dick and harden, yearning to have her plump, juicy lips anywhere on him. Right now, any set of her sensuous lips against his inferno flesh could make him shoot cum all over her titties.

The image of Natalie's gorgeous face—hovering two inches from his—shielded his view, yet he knew directly above the bed was her mirrored ceiling. Oh how badly he wanted to watch her seduce him. Being able to see her wrap those luscious cherry-stained lips around his thick dick made him . . . damn, he had to suppress his urge to explode all over the curly pussy hairs twirling between his fingers.

Brushing her mouth against his ear, Natalie gasped, then exhaled, "Umm," exuding her sexual energy. "Ou, baby. Looking at your sexy body," she said, pausing to circle her fingertip atop his erect nipple, then continued, "is making my pussy *sooo* wet. I love it when you make my pussy juicy. Do you like that too?"

Anxiously he nodded, glad she'd slid over to the adjacent pillow, allowing him to become both a voyeur and a participant. Staring at her reflection in the ceiling, he found her more beautiful, inside and out, each time they had intercourse. Regretfully he'd promised not to break agreement number two: never to fall in love with her, and since he was a man of his word, he focused on the overwhelming pleasure invading his six senses.

Natalie's touch was feathery. Her taste, sweet and sticky like rock candy slowly melting in his mouth. Her smell, the light fragrance of his favorite sundae topping, warm melted caramel drizzled atop rich brown sugary pecans, with the whipped cream of her cherry spread across his face. The sound of her voice made his dick ooze with precum but beholding the beauty of her heavenly body was orgasmic foreplay. With all things considered, nothing or no woman could match the spiritual magnetic energy that attracted and bonded him to her.

"You with me, daddy?" she asked, planting a delicious kiss on his mouth.

Nick's lips pressed together as his eyes shifted away from hers concealing his love for her.

While he was motionless, she stretched her thigh wide across his chest, then wiggled her hips, inserting his middle finger inside her vagina.

Probing for her G-spot, he said, "Oh damn, you're hot and wet."

"Um, hmm, told you so," she moaned, gyrating on his finger. "Deeper, daddy, go deeper for mama."

Enjoying the seduction, he watched her slow motions as she held her outer lips, then spread her pussy apart exposing her long stiff shaft and shiny protruding clit. Gazing deep into his eyes, she confirmed, "This good pussy is all for you." Then she squirmed onto his finger until his knuckle damn near disappeared into her hot fleshy hole. Slowly moving his hand, Natalie amazingly sucked all of her cum off his finger using her vaginal muscles.

"Fuck!" Nick yelled to himself.

This should be the day he asks to fuck her in the ass. No, no, not today. Asking might ruin the moment. He didn't want to do anything to make her unhappy. If he played along with her, would she eventually change her mind and marry him? He'd better hold off on anal sex and save that for their honeymoon.

If any more blood cells detoured to his dick Nick would definitely bust a nut from his gut through his balls, splattering her pussy with his seeds. That was, if he didn't pass out first. Exhaling, he tried to relax a little, glancing at the picture of them on her nightstand as they casually hugged at the company picnic. Everyone at the corporate headquarters of Dons and Divas Restaurants was clueless that they were sex partners.

They weren't a couple, or dating. Sex for them was initiated out of convenience. Nick didn't have time to court and wait until a woman was ready to have sex only to discover after several dates what the woman really had was sexual hang-ups and insecurities about her body. "I'm not sucking your dick or licking your balls, so don't ask. Oh, and just so you'll know, I have sex only with the lights off." Nor did Nick want to experience a bad fuck that would force him to ditch her and call the next woman on his long list of names gathered from speed dating.

His fantastic fuck partner had her own reasons for blowing him on the regular. Natalie didn't want to have sex with a different man every night but when she'd confessed that she had to have at least one orgasm a day to relive the stress of her demanding job, Nick quickly volunteered to assist her. Being that she was his counterpart, he completely understood and willingly accommodated her requirements for sexual fulfillment.

Now that they were deep into their uninhibited sexual relations, Nick wanted all of Natalie—mind, body, soul, and her hand in marriage. But she'd warned him that making such a request could risk everything, including the million-dollar promotion. They were competing to manage the company's new Dons and Divas Restaurant in Paris, France.

With all of their concerns, nothing was more significant than rule number one: no matter what they'd always remain best friends. The last and final rule was sex every day, even if for only fifteen minutes. So far, over the past three years, not one of their rules was broken.

"Damn, you make mama feel real nice," she whispered, circling the tip of her nail around his giant mushroom head. "Can I thank you by sucking your dick, baby?"

This time Nick's eyes rolled to the top, disappearing behind his eyelids. Propping himself on his elbows, he inhaled deeply, then exhaled long and slow into the air, "Whoa. Goddamn, woman."

She stroked his dick, then moaned, "I take that as a . . . yes?"

"Hell ye-ye-yes," he stuttered, reaching for the red lace bra concealing her voluptuous heart-shaped cleavage. With his dick throbbing against her firm grip, he palmed her lovely titties with both hands, then squeezed her nipples.

Tenderly Natalie's hands covered his as she whispered, "Uh-uh. No, daddy." Loosening his grasp, she continued, "This is your moment. Live in it. Cum all over my face in it. Bask in it. You fucked me so good I wanna show you how much I appreciate this big-ass dick," she said aggressively, pushing him against the bed. Yanking both of his legs downward, she commanded, "Lay flat on your back. Now scoot your ass to the foot of the bed. I'm controlling this dick. Relax and listen to me. No, you don't need this," Natalie said, slipping the black satin king-size pillow from his grip. "Not yet, anyway. Yes, yes, baby, let your feet hang toward the floor, lay just like that for mama. You comfortable, handsome?"

Exhaling, Nick mumbled, "Yeah, I'm good," gnawing the hell out of his fist.

She could've twisted his dick like a pretzel and his response would've been the same. What if he ignored rule number two and told her the truth? *Natalie, I'm in love with you.* Would his heart be broken? Would she really leave him? Would she string him along for his big dick? He wouldn't dare ask her to be his wife and have his baby knowing that they were both married to occupations that they had more passion for than sex. But the thought of her having his child made him smile on the inside. Perhaps one day they'd be a family.

Patiently Natalie traced her finger down the crease in his bare chest, then over his smooth abs. He admired her immaculate French-manicured nails that were now dancing in his pubic hairs as she grazed her fingertips over his dick, from the base to the head, making it rise like a puppet, except there were no strings attached.

"Fuck!" Nick yelled into the air.

Merciless Natalie cushioned her nose into his nuts, separating his seeds, then inhaled. "Your natural musk is my all-time favorite fragrance. Ever wonder why I have so many sandalwood candles scattered about my bedroom?"

Not only had he never wondered, right now he didn't give a damn about any candles unless she was going to drip hot wax all over his body. Ou, how he loved the dissipating burning sensation of drops of melted wax clinging to his nipples, chest, balls, and inner thighs.

Softly, Natalie moaned, "Ou, yes, I love your big nuts, baby."

Her exotic whispers drove him to the brink of snatching her straight black hair that was neatly aligned with her chin on one side of her face and her cheekbone on the other side. Oh, how bad he wanted to ram his dick down her throat and fuck her tonsils until she swallowed them along with his sperm. His legs rattled. He shook his head, then rubbed the aching stiffness of his dick.

"Because the manly scent reminds me of you. You, my magnificent lover, are all man and I love that shit. I prefer not to light them. You know, the candles. I warm the jars on hot plates and let the wax melt from the bottom. Like sexing you. I like marinating your seeds inside your balls before making you cum. I go wild with pleasure getting whiffs of your masculine scent whenever I whisk by one of the candles."

Nick said to himself, "What the hell is she talking about? Shut up and suck my dick."

Instinctively Natalie inhaled like she was reminiscing fond memories of him. Hopefully she'd add this moment to their list of adventures. He knew he would. But what he couldn't figure out was how she'd mastered making each time she pleasured him seem like their first time together.

"Fuck!" he yelled, curling his fingers into his palms. His fists trembled uncontrollably. Desperately he wanted to cum.

Delving her nose between his nuts again, she inhaled long and slow, pressing her lips against his balls. "See. Look. Look at how hard you made my nipples," she said, inserting her pointing fingers inside her red lace bra, freeing her plump titties, setting them atop the underwire. "This happens to me every time I inhale you. Every time I smell the candles that remind me of you. Give me your hand, daddy."

Climbing on top of his stomach, she raised her hips, then dipped his thick middle finger into her pussy again. This time she humped a few times, then moaned, "Ummmm," smoothing back her hair while arching her spine.

Gripping her ass he said, "Keep this up and I'm gonna bust this big-ass nut for sho'."

He removed his finger, then opened his mouth wide. Slurping on his finger, he relished the taste of her juices. "Um, um, um. Sweet rock candy. Damn, woman, you taste delicious."

"Let me see," she said, leaning into his mouth. Stirring her tongue like a straw in a lump of whipped cream, she said, "Ya know, you're right. I am tasty."

Natalie resumed, picking up where she'd left off, trailing her hands over his thighs, his knees, his legs, finally caressing his toes as he tucked them between the mattress and the red leather footboard.

Listening to her seductive moans kept his erection firm and unbelievably hard.

"Have I ever told you, you have *very* succulent nipples for a man? My pussy is dribbling just watching 'em. I love the way your nipples stay hard. Mind if I lick?" she asked, slithering out her tongue.

She'd mentioned before the way she liked how his nipples resembled two Sno-Caps. Like someone had set the chocolate candy dots atop his muscular chest and had forgotten to come back and get them.

"Do your thang, girl," Nick muttered, yanking lightly on his long thick dick.

Softly she kissed his button-size nipples, then straddled the red fiberglass stool at the foot of the bed. "This chair is cool but my pussy pressing against the seat is hot and juicy. Close your eyes and relax while I squeeze the pulsating muscles inside of my saucy pussy. Just for you, daddy."

Nick struggled to get comfortable while she patiently waited. Inhaling deeply, Natalie moaned, "Oooooou." Exhaling into the crown of his dickhead, "Aaaaah," she blew into his pubic hairs. "Next time I inhale, I want you to exhale."

Oh God, I can't take another minute of foreplay. Just suck my dick, please, Nick thought. All of his sexual energy rushed to his groin. "Okay," he mouthed, but silence escaped his lips.

After each inhale, she exhaled softer, and softer, moving her lips fractions of an inch from the tiny opening in his dickhead. After the third exhale into what he considered his fourth eye, she whispered, "Focus all your energies throughout your body. Feel the tingling sensations from your toes to your ass," raking her fingernails over his tight ass as she continued, "to your groin, to your navel, to your nipples, to your ears . . . ummm, yes, daddy, yeess." Her nails dug deep into his cheeks, making him want to cum.

Nick cried inside, "I don't need dick meditation. I need your sloppy slobbering lips sliding up and down my dick."

Natalie licked her lips, then softly pressed them onto his

swollen head. "Um, hmm," she hummed lightly, easing the tip of her tongue along the underside vein.

He moaned, gripping the sheets to keep from grabbing the back of her head.

Seductively she whispered to his dick, "I'm ready to make you cum with my mouth . . . Is that okay?"

This time he yelled louder, "Suck me. Fuck!"

Impatiently Nick nodded but he didn't have to because his remaining blood cells charged his overstuffed erection, creating an extra rise of his dick, signaling that Natalie unequivocally had his undivided attention.

Leaning into his balls she licked his nuts, then kissed them. "Umm. Sugar. You taste so damn sweet."

Dipping her fingers into a crystal bowl sitting on the tray beside her bed, she stirred her nails, then she eased her finger between his lips.

His mouth suctioned off the juices savoring every drop of her special homemade concoction: pineapple juice with a few pieces of fruit mixed with raw honey, a touch of brown sugar, and a few dissolved peppermints.

Gliding a mint deep into her pussy, she moaned, "Oh, the sensation breezing throughout my vagina is sending chills throughout my body." Removing her finger, she slid it under his nose. "You know what this scent is?"

Nick's hand grabbed hers gliding it into his mouth covering her knuckle. He moaned, grunted, and moaned some more, wanting to chew Natalie's finger because it tasted and felt so damn good.

With her finger lingering in his mouth, hungrily she kissed

him before moving to his nipples. Swirling the honey mixture onto his chest, her lips suctioned his Sno-Caps until they shriveled tight like raisins. He felt the precum seeping from his dick trickling onto the underside crevice of his head, saturating the satin sheet.

"I want you to place your feet at the foot of the bed. Scoot your ass to the edge, bend your knees, and spread your thighs like a butterfly," Natalie instructed, patiently waiting for Nick to cooperate.

Bowing between his thighs, she sucked the precum off of his head, then moaned, "You taste sweeter than honey."

She ran her juicy tongue down his shaft, over his balls, then stopped at his hot spot beneath his balls. His ass automatically tilted upward when she French-kissed the fuck out of him, then licked his asshole several times.

"Aw shit!" Nick yelled, which was followed by a sudden, "Oh my God!" as a burst of precum unexpectedly squirted out.

Quickly Natalie braced her hands to prevent his thighs from closing in on her ears. Moving back up to his balls, she tea bagged them into her cool mouth. Inhaling, exhaling, she moaned, "Hmmm," vibrating his nuts like an electrical massager.

Gradually Nick's knees drew closer to her shoulders. She pulled them down, then pushed them back open. "This will feel better if you relax and keep your legs apart. You know what I'm doing, don't you?"

"Besides driving me fucking insane?" Nick's chest rose and fell rapidly.

"I'm tasting you before basting you."

With his ass on the edge of the mattress, Natalie retrieved

a pineapple chunk from the bowl. Circling the million-dollar hot spot underneath his balls, she massaged his asshole, then picked up the bowl, trickled juice on his dick and his balls, and delicately rubbed the stickiness all over his groin.

"Whoa! That's too cool!" Nick responded. "That's enough. Feels like my shit is outdoors in a blizzard."

Natalie whispered, "You know what I'm doing? Right?"

Surrendering without answering, he simply shook his head before collapsing onto the mattress.

"I'm getting ready to heat up your dick before making you cum in my throat," she said softly, blowing on the peppermint sweetness of his erection.

Natalie delved in. Wrapping her fingers around the base of his dick, vigorously she slurped the juices from his nuts.

"Mmmm. I wish you could experience how damn *good* you taste."

She sucked his balls, then eased her hot hungry tongue all over his dick. He felt the throbs pressing against the walls of her mouth as she suctioned tighter while bobbing up and over his head.

Slowly Natalie stroked him with her hand twisting his shaft. She dipped her other hand into the bowl, covered her fingers with more juice, then massaged his dick while placing a fresh peppermint at the back of her throat until it dissolved. Moments later she began feasting again. Her head rose, his hands pushed her down. She rose again. He plunged her head back down again.

She needed to quit playing and go on and suck his dick for real.

With the bottom of his feet heel to heel and toe to toe, Nick's ass humped to her face, then fell to the bed. When his feet slipped toward the floor, he knew she had him right where she wanted him, defenseless. Natalie pressed his hips into the mattress, urging him, "Damn you! Grab the back of my head."

He tried but he couldn't. She'd made every part of his body limber including his arms. Nick exhaled as heat oozed from Natalie's throat onto his throbbing shaft.

"Yes," she moaned. "Yes, yes, yes, daddy. Fuck me."

She was doing all the fucking with her beautiful mouth riding his dick. The faster she bobbed, the hotter his dick got. Precum seeped from the tip clinging to her lips.

Nick had to focus. He wanted to cum so badly he didn't want to fuck up and let little nut beat the big nut.

"Daddy, my pussy is so damn wet," Natalie said, trembling and stroking his dick faster. "I want to jump on this dick and ride the shit out of you but this orgasm isn't about me . . . it's all for you. You're the best lover I've ever had. Ou yeah, I can taste the tartness oozing from the pores of your shaft, so I know you're ready to blast off like a rocket." Natalie eased up a little, then said, "It's time for me to make you cum with my big juicy lips . . . you ready?"

Nick nodded, then said, "Hell yeah."

"I'm gonna ease your dick to the back of my throat . . . and when I do, my throat is gonna be really hot . . . when I come up, you're gonna cum."

"Fuck!" he screamed as she slowly eased her mouth over his shaft. Wiggling her tongue she nestled his head into the cushiony roof of her sizzling mouth.

Continuing to navigate his head pass her tonsils, he closed his eyes, feeling the rising temperature in the back of her throat. Uncontrollably his body began to rattle.

Suctioning her jaws around his shaft, Natalie began slowly yanking upward with her esophagus like she was trying to swallow him whole. She suctioned hard along his underside vein, drawing the sperm from his nuts as if she were sucking in a long stand of spaghetti through a straw.

Nick yelled, "Oh shit!"

He pressed his hips harder against the bed; Natalie's lips were now midway up his dick.

His legs rattled uncontrollably as he yelled, "Oh fuck, woman!" His body sprang forward.

Slow and steady, her mouth cupped his head as she suctioned one last very long and firm draw.

"Oh my God, Jesus!" Nick shouted, repeatedly ripping the black satin sheet away from the mattress.

Natalie watched him watch her in the mirrored ceiling. Then she swallowed every single sperm before licking her lips. Nick collapsed backward lying motionless.

Gently she kissed his lips, then said, "Thanks, daddy, for letting me suck your beautiful dick."

If Natalie could've read his mind, she would've heard him say, "What in the fuck did you just do to me?"

Whenever Nick recovered, which wouldn't be anytime soon, he was definitely wearing her clit the fuck out.

Natalie

Mind-blowing sex with Nick was great but what Natalie really appreciated about Nick was his intellectually stimulating conversation in and out of bed and the fact that he was a pleaser. Nick actually cared if she was sexually satisfied. Relocating from New York to San Francisco thus far was one of the best decisions she'd made. Keeping her business relations separate from her personal life by discreetly fucking Nick was another wise choice.

Natalie grew tired of dating corporate men with big paychecks and small minds hiding behind their material possessions because they didn't know how to please a woman. Those were the ones who needed to invest $5,000 into a lifelike blow-up doll that could suck their dicks without complaining, pay for sex without a woman having to ask him for money, or jack off.

Placing Nick's breakfast plate in front of him, Natalie sat at the dining table. "So, how do you think Flint is going to make his selection? Do you think the partners entrusted the decision solely to him? I sure wouldn't if I were them," Natalie said, using her fingers to shove aside the blueberries and blackberries as she picked a fresh raspberry from their shared fruit platter. Her tongue eased out and the raspberry vanished behind her glossy lips.

Motioning for Natalie's hand, Nick closed his eyes, bowed his head, then prayed, "Heavenly Father, bless this food. Bless the hands and heart of this beautiful woman who prepared this meal. I ask that you impart nonjudgmental wisdom in the words we speak and allow us to be impervious to the criticism of others. Amen."

Nick tossed his silk tie onto the back of his chair to keep it clean. Loosening the seventeen-inch collar circling his neck, Nick unfastened each button, exposing his smooth muscular chest. The tail of his lightly starched pale green long-sleeved shirt hung beside his thighs. His rippling abs descended toward his thirty-six-inch waistline above his immaculately tailored forest green slacks. He watched Natalie gently place her big toe inside his sunken belly button. Slowly she trailed her foot to his crotch, then tapped his dickhead, making his lips and his dick curve with pleasure.

"Curious." He paused, then continued, "Not that I agree but why wouldn't you let Flint choose?" Munching on a toasted whole wheat English muffin loaded with garlic herb schmear and lox, Nick added, "By the way, thanks for making me the happiest man in the world. Man oh man, that blow job last night was unforgettable."

Casually he removed a small white box from his pocket, then slid it from his side of the table to hers. "I can't pay you for keeping me happy but here's another expression of my appreciation of your attentive affection. Thanks for always making me feel like the man. You know how much I care about you, so I won't go there."

Gulping his coffee, Nick washed away the lump forming in his throat.

Eyeing the box while savoring the last raspberry seed on the tip of her tongue, Natalie knew exactly how much Nick loved her. The watery glaze of softness in his eyes told her he wanted more. She did too but instead of getting emotional, Natalie pondered Nick's question. There was a list of reasons both of them could give like the fact that Flint was an undereducated know-it-all who didn't have any college degrees. Nick had a master's in finance with a BS in communications and Natalie held a doctorate in accounting, a master's in business administration, and a bachelor's in business marketing.

Clearly Natalie understood that holding any number of degrees didn't make anyone more or less successful or guarantee they'd acquire common sense. Feverishly holding on to her dream, maintaining her financial independence, remaining single until she was ready to get married, believing in herself, and striving to attain her goal of owning several restaurants motivated Natalie to excel at everything she'd done from quickly advancing in her professions to creating an image that men and women admired, but more important, Natalie had developed a reputation that others respected.

Her business, Divas Galore, would uplift women. Natalie would host the ultimate dining experience where women could arrive before their dates and receive a captivating makeover that would make each woman a confident diva on the inside while looking stunning on the outside. Dining at Divas Galore would become a journey of self-discovery not just a destination for a meal one would soon purge from their body.

Natalie's patrons could eat healthy and shop wisely at the same time. Sexy models—male and female—would strut along a runway maze modeling the hottest shoes and trendiest fashions. Waiters would wear high-end jewelry and designer clothes. Diners could purchase diamond bracelets or watches right off their servers' wrists and present it to their lovers.

One thing Natalie had learned about service-oriented businesses was if sophisticated, confident, and sexy women were there, the men would happily come. Every night she would give ladies a discount on all cocktails and dinner menu items, saving them or their dates enough money to spend more money. Even when Natalie's eyes were closed at night, she never fell asleep without thinking about how to get closer to achieving her goals.

Tracing the edges of the cardboard box with her finger, she focused on Nick's full succulent lips going in for another bite of his muffin. Slowly Natalie inhaled, welcoming the sexual energy tingling inside her breasts as the creamy topping settled in the corner of Nick's mouth. Wedging his tongue in the crease, Nick licked, then swallowed as his eyes settled on the front page of the *New York Times*, which signaled he wanted a moment to read his favorite paper, so Natalie quietly focused on her life.

After graduating at the top of her class, Natalie never envisioned working in the restaurant industry. She'd hoped that Coleman Investment Group would become the go-to firm with the highest rates of return on her clients' portfolios. She'd planned to become the first black female billionaire with a software program, a Web site, and business workshops that taught women around the world how to achieve and maintain their financial independence even if they were married. Glancing at Nick, Natalie realized in order to succeed at any business she had to find loyal partners who shared her vision.

Lifting the lid on the box, Natalie smiled, then removed the diamond and tiger eye earrings. Nick loved shopping for her. His belief was gifts were best received when least expected. But gifts didn't prove loyalty, people did. And as much as Natalie loved Nick she wasn't sure he'd ever agree to work for her.

"Consider them a good luck gift on getting my promotion," Nick replied. His eyes hovered above the newspaper staring into hers.

Removing her amethyst studs, Natalie put on the O-shaped tiger eyes with a diamond X embedded in the middle symbolizing Nick's love. His statement wasn't worthy of a direct response. Smiling, Natalie leaned forward, then said, "Thanks, daddy. They're lovely," gesturing for a kiss.

"Just like you," Nick commented, snapping open the business section.

Nick thrived on evoking her emotions. Easing back in her chair, raising her brows, Natalie thought, Was he seriously claiming her promotion? All righty then. While Nick read, Natalie resumed reminiscing on her past.

Growing up in the fourth-largest city—Houston, Texas—Natalie believed relocating to a larger city after grad school would provide higher-paying job opportunities and require only a few minor lifestyle adjustments. She was wrong. Nothing she'd done prepared her for New York City.

All of her life she'd never learned how to swim and moving to the Big Apple felt like she'd jumped into the Atlantic Ocean without a life preserver. From hailing taxis in the sleeting snow, to struggling to get the next promotion, to trying not to get crushed between closing subway doors or sandwiched between employees who were trying to fuck their way to the top, there was too much fierce competition to stay ahead of her conniving coworkers while staying out of the path of everyone else, especially the reckless out-of-state drivers attempting to navigate directions on their iPhones during rush hour. If Natalie didn't move out the way, she was forced out of the way.

Natalie saw day trading in her sleep and stock options flashing in the middle of her wet dreams. The day she fell asleep on the subway, missed her stop at Grand Central Station, then ended up in the Bronx, she quit her job, hired a headhunter, and accepted her first job offer at Dons and Divas.

Taking the position initially offered by Samantha Sexton, the president of the corporation, would've defeated Natalie's reasons for quitting her other job. Without reservation Natalie declined the New York position and agreed to pay her own relocation expenses. One week later, she moved from the largest to the fourteenth-largest city, San Francisco.

Watching Nick open and close his thighs while reading the paper, Natalie said, "We both know the only reason Flint is CEO is because his wife, Samantha's father owns fifty-one percent of the company."

Mr. Sexton, a seventy-year-old priest, crept through the office a few times a week, seemingly to give himself something to do or someone to preach to in between quoting Bible scriptures and standing behind his pulpit on Sundays. Natalie avoided religious debates with Mr. Sexton, while Nick initiated conversations about the Bible with him. Placing her faith in God was sufficient for Natalie. She didn't need Mr. Sexton to audit her business expenses alongside the contents of her heart. Natalie treated others the way she wanted to be treated and she didn't need to sit in a pew for a pastor to tell her right from wrong.

"I love your hair like that. You should wear it that way more often," Nick said, washing down the last bite of his muffin with a gulp of homemade brewed Starbucks breakfast blend coffee.

Whenever Nick complimented her in the middle of her trying to initiate a serious conversation, it was best she didn't respond. One of the things Nick knew Natalie couldn't stand, whether it was business or sex, was routine. A man could tell a lot about a woman based on her physical appearance, the way she walked, even how she moved her hips, her hands, her tongue, and her lips, especially how she ate her food.

Natalie made it a point to change her hairstyle every day. Today, she'd worn the wet look. She'd washed, then coated her dark hair back with a light layer of holding gel, then used a wide-tooth comb to form sexy S-shape waves and let it dry. Natalie was in a jovial mood, so she wore her long eyelashes and lightly stroked-on chocolate lipstick, dabbed with a teasing hint of glittering gloss in the center of her bottom lip.

Pushing his chair away from the table, Nick propped his ankle across his opposite knee and asked, "Come on, Natalie, do you really want me to believe that all of sudden you're concerned with the lack of Flint's educational background? You and I both know that Flint married Samantha for her multi-million-dollar inheritance. Her dad has had two open-heart surgeries, so he has got one foot in the grave and she's the only heir to his estate. From the ghetto to the trailer parks to Wall Street to Hollywood every minute men say, 'I do,' not for love but for financial gain. Hell, I would've married Samantha if I'd had the opportunity. If Flint is fucking her good enough to call the shots at home and run her daddy's company, there's nothing you or I can say to change that. Now, look at me and tell me what's honestly bothering you, sweetie."

Nick knew her well and he was partly right. There was nothing Natalie could *say* to change the fact that Flint was their boss. Sipping her Kombucha—antioxidant, never get a cold, immune booster—tea, which her girlfriend Lola had introduced her to, Natalie said, "But you must admit there's something not quite right with Flint. He's not trustworthy."

Tightly pressing his lips together, Nick sat staring at Natalie, then said, "He's rich, so who gives a fuck. Are you going to tell me or am I wasting my time?"

Instead of answering the question, Natalie asked, "Baby, you remember agreement number one, right?"

Exhaling, Nick flatly said, "Sure do. Will never forget. Best friends no matter what."

Natalie continued, "All right, I have to know. Will you be upset when I get the job?"

Nick's foot fell to the floor like a brick. His mouth gaped open as he bellowed deep from the pit of his stomach, roaring with laughter, then said, "Of course not. What kind of silly assumption is that?"

"Stop laughing at me. I'm serious, Nick. Whatever. Thanks a lot for nothing. Are you——"

Chuckling, Nick said, "Sweetie, calm down. We both know there's no way old man Sexton would allow Flint to promote you or any other woman over me. Just look at the structure. All of the partners are males. His daughter doesn't have her name on any of the corporate docs. Flint is running the business in San Francisco, not Samantha. She's all the way in New York. Let's face the truth. Like it or not, I can bring onboard sponsors that will refuse to meet with you simply because you are a woman. But I tell you what. When Flint announces that I have the job, I promise"— Nick crossed his heart—"to take you to Paris with me and make you my assistant."

Clearly Nick didn't outrank Natalie in degrees, so like most men he had to try to tear her down in order to build himself up. But did he honestly believe that his balls made him more qualified for the job? Natalie may have not been born in New York City but she'd spent enough time there to learn some valuable polislicks. Nick's underestimation of the power of the pussy was common among men and his overconfidence would be the source of his demise or the harsh reality of his compromise.

Coldly staring at Nick, Natalie replied, "Assistant, huh? Is that right? The day that I become your assistant you might as well have Flint start sucking your dick. What makes you so sure anyway?" she asked, removing her napkin from her lap.

Cupping his dick and balls, his eyes, lips, and forehead shrinking, in his deepest voice, Nick protested, "Don't say no homosexual shit about my dick, Natalie. I will beat any man's ass if I thought he was thinking about thinking about my dick!"

Calmly Natalie said, "Nick, we live in a city that has performed same sex marriages. I'm shocked that after all the years I've known you you're still paranoid about gays. What if Flint's wife, Samantha, is a transsexual and used to be Sam?"

Nick shivered, then said, "You are so adorable when you're frustrated. And you, like most women, you, my love, are irrational. Let's just say, I can't tell you everything I know. Changing the subject, you mind blowing me right quick to take care of this hard-on you've created?"

Hard-on, huh? What part of their conversation got his dick hard?

Natalie thought about Nick's request for a moment, then decided why not. The last thing she wanted was to allow their thriving sex life to become tainted by their ultra egos, money, or a promotion. Curling her pointing finger toward Nick, she scooted her chair away from the breakfast table, unbuckled his belt, then unzipped his slacks.

Reaching inside she pulled out the most beautiful curvaceous dick, then firmly wrapped her hand around his shaft licking his frenulum until the vein on the underside of his dick bulged. Maintaining her grip, slowly she eased her shiny lips over his head and began gently sucking his corona while massaging his balls through his silk boxers.

"Aw shit yeah." Nick's eyes fluttered as he moaned, "Damn, that feels so good. I'ma go on and bust this nut right quick, baby."

Nibbling on his crown, Natalie gently scraped her teeth around his hole.

Nick shoved his dick, trying to force his entire head between her teeth. Natalie let him struggle for a moment until he begged, "C'mon, baby, let him in. Suck him for me. Please, baby, please."

Who was in charge now?

Nick was at her mercy. Natalie looked up at him. His eyebrows buckled, his head leaned back, and his mouth parted. She thought unless Nick could suck Flint's dick better than her, Nick could forget about getting that promotion. Natalie had sucked quite a few dicks, all for less than earning seven figures, including the one in her mouth. Sucking the right dick the right way could make any woman an instant millionaire.

"Oh yeah. Here it comes, lovely," Nick said, squirting cum shots.

Holding his seeds in her mouth, Natalie stood. With his dick hanging over his zipper, Nick removed the dishes from the table and placed them in the dishwasher. Natalie went to the bathroom, released the semen from her mouth, brushed her teeth, and rinsed with a mouthful of hydrogen peroxide and warm water to kill any lingering germs and sperm. Vigorously swishing the mixture for five minutes, Natalie watched Nick take the world's fastest shower, then put on a crisp camel-colored suit.

"Hand me my keys," Nick said, stretching his arm toward her as if she were his assistant.

Natalie refused to let Nick's demand creep into her psyche. She counter commanded, "Get me my purse."

Exchanging his keys for her designer bag, they headed directly to the garage. His squared-toe brown leather soles thumped alongside the clicking of her stilettos as they raced across the kitchen's tan-colored travertine floor. Nick's elbow pressed against her shoulder as their bodies jammed along opposite sides of the doorway.

Stepping back, Nick extended his palm with a slight bow. "After you, shorty."

Natalie might have been five foot five with her heels on but she had undeniable presence. Nothing and no one was going to keep her from securing that promotion.

"Whatever you do today, don't do me any favors. Give it your all 'cause when I do get the job, and I will, I don't want you to have any excuses," Natalie said, then hopped into her fire red Corvette with the license plate RGASMIC. Waiting for her garage door to fully retract, she let down her convertible top while sliding on her sunglasses.

Nick plunged the accelerator of his platinum Bentley, revving up his engine, then sped out of her driveway. The roof of his car barely escaped the edge of Natalie's rising garage door. Racing beside him, Natalie paused at the four-way stop sign alongside his car, winked, then just as his car moved an inch, she cut in front of him and yelled, "Where's your manners, baby? Ladies, first."

The minute that Justin Flint had announced the new position, Nick and Natalie began competing for every little thing inside and outside the bedroom. The rivalry excited the hell out of her. Who would get accolades and a bonus for saving or making the company money? Who would get to work first became a daily race. Who could make the other pass out or give in during sex? Who would read and analyze Flint's morning reports first?

Everything between them had become an award-winning sport where they were the only two spectators. Who would remain in the office and work the latest had become a ridiculous standoff. One night the janitor turned the lights off while they were both in the office well past midnight on a fucking fest to see who could last the longest.

Glancing in her rearview mirror, Natalie saw clouds of smoke but when the dust cleared, Nick's car was nowhere in sight.

"Damn it!" Natalie said, fearing he'd take the side streets, make it to the office first, and read the entire Monday morning report before she'd have a chance to lay eyes on it. Zooming through a yellow light, Natalie zipped onto the freeway. She was rushing at a smooth ninety miles until . . . screech! She slammed on her breaks to avoid rear-ending a pearl-colored Mercedes SUV.

"Shit! Where in the hell did this traffic jam come from?"

Swerving into the emergency lane, Natalie cruised for six miles. If she could maneuver her way over to the next exit without stopping, she should be ahead of Nick by about five minutes. Merging off the shoulder into the creeping flow of the fast lane, she noticed a police car behind her whirling red and blue lights. Natalie prayed he wasn't signaling for her to pull over. Not today.

Should she ignore him, pull over and get a ticket, or . . . she smiled quickly crossing two lanes, then exiting the freeway onto the street, praying he'd keep going, but he didn't. Parking curbside one block away from the courthouse on Bryant Street, quickly Natalie retrieved her silver bullet from her purse, parted her legs, then eased her miniature vibrating egg under her mocha-colored thong, positioning it against her clit.

When the officer walked up to her car, he asked, "Do you know why I, um——"

In the middle of his sentence, Natalie held up her hand and moaned, "Give me just a minute, Officer. Give me your hand. My pussy is sooo wet. Can you help me, oouuttt . . . damn, it's too late. I came without you." As she lowered her hand between her legs, her body jerked.

His mouth hung open as she removed the vibrating egg from her pussy. "Whoo! Excuse me. Thanks for waiting. Morning orgasms are better than coffee and doughnuts, wouldn't you agree, Officer? Mind if I reach into my glove compartment for a cum wipe?"

Shaking his head, the officer smiled.

"Yes? No?"

"Sure, lady."

Removing, then opening the moist towelette, Natalie dabbed her pussy, handed the tissue to the officer, exhaled, then said, "Thanks for being so patient. How may I help you?"

Knowing he couldn't charge her with indecent exposure because she had on all her clothes, Natalie sat there slowly licking the tip of her silver bullet.

"Wanna feel my bullet, Officer?" she asked, spreading her thighs before turning on the vibration.

Debating on whether to drop the towelette on the ground or hold it, the officer pretended it slipped out of his hand. Fumbling in his pocket, he pretended he was searching for something but looked more to Natalie like he was choking his hard-on trying to make his big-ass dick shrink.

"Nice-size dick," Natalie complimented, handing the officer a Magnum condom and her business card. Natalie smiled, then innocently asked, "Am I free to go, Officer?"

Scanning the card, the officer stepped away from her car, saying, "For now, yes. Drive safe, Mrs.———"

Shifting into first gear, she corrected him. "That's Ms. Coleman," Natalie said, plunging her accelerator.

Merging into street traffic, Natalie was mad as hell and damn near thirty minutes late. Technically she didn't have to arrive until 8:00 a.m. but it was already 7:15.

Driving to California and Stockton, she parked in the garage next to Nick's car, then texted her girlfriend Lola: *Nick and I can't make it to the swingers set tonight. Gotta work late. Tell your fine-ass husband I'll suck his dick next week.*

Lola and DeVaughn were Nick and Natalie's swinging partners. They'd been couple swinging for about a year now. Natalie introduced Nick to them because she thought if Nick could fuck sexy-ass Lola his feelings for her wouldn't be so strong. But Natalie was wrong. Nick wanted her more but DeVaughn wanted Natalie more than Nick and DeVaughn made certain all of them knew how he felt. DeVaughn admitted how their get-togethers gave him something new to look forward to because just like with Nick, DeVaughn never knew what Natalie would do to him.

Taking several deep breaths as she entered the crowded elevator, Natalie composed herself. Walking through the glass double-doors of Dons and Divas West Coast corporate office, she greeted Jonathan, the office assistant.

The entire office was accented with large Egyptian papyrus-like paintings of the goddess Isis, King Tutankhamun, and even Anubis, immaculately framed and strategically hung on every wall. Contemporary fixtures with columns of varying heights upheld head and shoulder busts of Nefertiti and Cleopatra. Irregular-shaped vibrant-colored vases four feet tall all filled with fresh pink lilies, Matsumoto asters, and white roses were flawlessly arranged at the entrance. The common area office furniture comprised of onyx tables with cherrywood trimmings, high-backed leather rolling chairs, and tall mahogany doors kept each office private from clients awaiting a meeting.

"Great, the beautiful woman has arrived. You're just in time," Jonathan said, handing Natalie her report. "Flint wants to meet with you and Nick in the conference room in exactly twelve minutes."

When Natalie first started working for Flint, Jonathan had

mentioned how she shared some basic commonalities with Nefertiti. Like Miles Davis's *Nefertiti* instrumental recorded the summer of 1967, where the horn section repeats the melody while the rhythm section improvises reversing the traditional role of the rhythm section, Natalie was smooth and unpredictable. Jonathan knew very little about Natalie and that's how she preferred to keep things. He could assume but Natalie had discovered the hard way that it was best to keep her promiscuous sexual lifestyle separate from her business partners. Everyone except Nick, that was. Natalie couldn't resist having Nick's naked body next to hers every day.

Natalie repeated, "Twelve minutes?"

"Yes. Flint said it was urgent. I'll bring you your peppermint tea in two minutes. Now go, Nefertiti," Jonathan said, fanning his hand backward.

Damn, what was the urgency?

Passing Nick's ajar office door, Natalie noticed his feet propped up on his desk and the *USA Today* newspaper sprawled over his face. She'd bet his ass was smirking but she wasn't going to be outdone early on a Monday morning.

Closing her door, Natalie scanned her report as Jonathan entered, set her teacup on her desk, whispered, "Five minutes, beautiful," then quietly closed her door. With two minutes remaining, Natalie had to utilize one of her Diva cards. Divas made the rules; they didn't play by them. Tossing her report on her desk, Natalie dipped her finger inside her pussy, dabbed her juices behind her ears, headed to the restroom to wash her hands, and made it to the conference room on time.

Whisking by Nick and sitting next to Flint, Natalie politely said, "Good morning, gentlemen."

Nick sniffed, squinted, then discreetly kicked Natalie under the table as Flint said, "Natalie, you smell . . . fresh."

Interlocking his fingers atop the conference table, Nick chimed in, "Yeah, Natalie, I agree. You do smell extremely *fresh.*"

That wasn't all Nick was going to have to agree with after Natalie would become his boss.

Clearing his throat, Flint said, "Well, we're not here to talk about the scent of a woman. What I need from each of you by next Monday morning is your best marketing plan for the Dons and Divas grand opening in Paris——"

Interrupting Flint, Nick questioned, "Did you mean one *week* or one month?"

"I know your concerns," Flint said.

Unless Flint was setting both of them up for failure, any CEO with business sense knew there was no way in hell to detail a successful business plan in one week. Natalie added her opinion, "We need more than a week. What about location, media, new partners, and new——" Natalie became quiet not wanting to give any of her ideas to Nick.

Flint interrupted, "Mr. Sexton has decided to do a test run of both plans." Nick winked at Natalie as Flint continued, "Your plans will be implemented at the Dons and Divas here and in New York. Natalie your plan will be a go two weeks from now and we'll leave it in place for thirty days in New York with Samantha overseeing the progress while Nick's plan is simultaneously implemented in San Francisco and I'll oversee that.

Then we'll switch for another thirty days. Nick the following month your plan will be in place in New York and Natalie's yours will be in effect in San Francisco."

"That's ludicrous. Who came up with this uneducated concept?" Natalie questioned.

Flint smiled, then said, "Nick. He didn't tell you?"

What the hell?

Nick's voice wavered, "Yeah, but I didn't think you were going to run to Mr. Sexton with my idea so soon. I was thinking out loud when I made those suggestions. I haven't had time to put my plan together."

That dirty dog. He was trying to sneak his way into the job. That's okay. Natalie was going to make sure Nick's plan blew up in his clean-shaved, monthly facial'd, pimple-free face.

"Whosoever has the best overall combined response will get the promotion to open up the Dons and Divas in Paris," Flint said.

Natalie was speechless and couldn't even stomach looking at Nick without her blood pressure rising.

"Natalie, I know this is news to you. Stay for a moment. Nick, thanks. You can leave," Flint said. "Oh, I almost forgot. One more thing, Mr. Sexton has given you a hundred-thousand-dollar budget."

"What?" Nick protested. "Didn't he leave off a couple of zeros? That's not enough money."

"Well, is this enough? The budget is split fifty-fifty. So in actuality you have fifty thousand dollars each. The plan is designed to make both of you work together but remember you're being evaluated separately. Samantha and I will have fifty percent input on the selection to Mr. Sexton and collectively the partners will make the final selection."

Nick stood, looked down upon Natalie, and then narrowed his eyes. His long black curly lashes froze as his lips tightened.

Holding up his hand, Flint said, "Oh, one last detail. Nick you will work on site at the restaurant overseeing Natalie's plan and Natalie will do the same for your plan. That way I can see if your plans were well thought out."

Nick pivoted, then stormed out of the conference room without saying a word.

Flint looked at Natalie, sniffed in her direction, then asked, "What's that smell? My goodness. Maybe I should have you come up with a fragrance for Dons and Divas."

That was one freebee idea for Natalie. "It's my special scent. Now, tell me why did you and Nick make this agreement without consulting me?"

"Nick had a great idea. But I didn't ask you to stay so we could discuss Nick. Look, what I have to say could land you this job before you ever complete your plan."

Natalie sat staring into Flint's devious eyes.

"Natalie, I'ma be direct. I've wanted to fuck you for a long time. I want to fuck you every night that I want until you leave for Paris. That gives us about three months."

Was he serious? Natalie was speechless. Fuck Flint? She was highly educated and wasn't about to try to suck sense into a dumb dick whenever he said so. Once or twice maybe but three times max, plus Natalie needed her promotion in hand first not some false promise from a corporate pawn 'cause if

Flint did some devious trickery and ended up giving Nick the job after she'd blown him she'd have to bury Flint alive with the largest sexual harassment lawsuit ever.

Flint was fine but he seemed so square, so boring, so corporate, so heavy starched white collar. There always appeared to be a plot behind his comments. Just looking at his tie centered perfectly in his collar, his hair neatly trimmed along his forehead, his sideburns evenly aligned with the middle of his ears, his hairless face, his perfectly arched eyebrows, his manicured nails, tailor-made shirt and suit, his watch, and that mysterious wedding band that symbolized a commitment to an invisible wife that everyone heard of but no one had talked to except via telephone. And all this time Natalie thought Flint was living an invisible life like that Basil character she'd read about in E. Lynn Harris's novels. Was he serious about fucking her or initiating some sort of sadistic mind game to determine how far she'd go to get the promotion?

"You don't have to answer right now but if you want this job, Natalie," Flint paused, then said, "or I can convince my wife to give the job to Nick."

Sarcastically Natalie replied, "Then let Nick suck your dick."

Raising his eyebrows, Flint said, "Hmm, why hadn't I thought of that. That could be an option."

In Flint's dreams. Even when Nick and Natalie partnered with Lola and DeVaughn, Nick would fuck Lola, eat their pussies too but Nick always made sure his dick and DeVaughn's dick never bumped heads and nobody's finger was allowed to penetrate Nick's ass. Nick Thurston was undoubtedly 100 percent heterosexual.

Natalie was almost certain that Flint had told his wife and the partners that Nick's suggestion was his brilliant idea. *Bastard.* Flint was trying to manipulate both of them. But why? Natalie stood, then looked down on Flint like Nick had just looked down upon her. Natalie propped her stiletto on Flint's thigh, dipped her finger deep inside her pussy, swiped her finger under Flint's nose, and left.

Flint

Having all the luxuries some people would kill for didn't necessarily mean Justin Flint was financially, sexually, or emotionally fulfilled. Did he have an insatiable appetite to acquire the finest things in life? Yes, but not at others' expense. Was he ungrateful for what he had? Not at all. Was his heart suffering from marital remorse for making a lifelong commitment to the wrong woman? Absolutely. There were irreplaceable advantages that dissipated the second the words "I do" escaped his lips like his twenty-four-hour access to sex, his independence, his freedom to come and go as he wanted, his masculinity, and his self-identity.

Flint never consented to an arranged marriage to Samantha exclusively for her money but everyone outside of their marriage had arbitrarily labeled him a loser and a user. If they only knew his truth, they wouldn't judge so harshly. Maybe if their childhood virginity had been violated and a dick rammed up their ass against their will they could sympathize with him. Strangers didn't seem to care much about tragedies that didn't affect them directly.

When Flint was introduced to Samantha she was an all-inclusive young, scintillating, sexy, sizzling package presented to him sort of as a hush gift from her father, who'd demanded all of them keep quiet about the taboo hidden incidents that happened in the privacy of their homes. Walls couldn't talk to people who wouldn't listen.

Each time Flint quietly sat alone in his home not watching television or tuning in to the radio or turning on the CD player, he heard the silent screams that streamed down his face trapped inside his tears. "Somebody help me please. God, please stop him from raping me." The one time Mr. Sexton's wife walked in on them, Flint's pants were down around his ankles and Mr. Sexton was on his knees sucking Flint's ten-year-old dick.

"What on God's green earth are you doing to this child? I'm calling the police," Mrs. Sexton protested, hurrying to the telephone.

Before she could dial a single digit, Mr. Sexton called the hospital. "Yes, this is Reverend Sexton, my wife is having another nervous breakdown. Can you send us help right away before she harms herself?"

Within moments, the only ray of sunshine that could've ended Flint's molestation vanished never to return. Years had gone by and the older Flint got the lining of his anus adapted to the situation. Now his pain was emotional and no longer physical.

Seven years ago Flint loved his wife and could hardly wait for her to come home but nowadays Saturdays were the only days they spent together. When Samantha flew home from New York, Flint would spend hours staring at his wife trying to figure out if she still loved him or if she considered him just a house sitter for her ten-thousand-square-foot mansion with the included responsibility of caring for her golden and Labrador retrievers.

Strolling alone around their empty-ass place six days out of the week was driving Flint insane since Samantha had banned his menagerie of friends from what she'd considered freeloading. "They eat up all my food and drink up all my alcohol, then leave their filthy trash all over my recreation room." If Samantha was home more, his friends would be there less.

If Samantha only knew the details about what happened in their house during her absence she'd probably drop dead immediately after killing him. His old neighborhood friends from high school were more trustworthy than the online strangers Flint sporadically invited into their bedroom to keep him company. Practically living alone, Flint needed excitement in his sex life and Natalie was the one woman other than his wife that he wanted to fuck.

Ordinarily Flint wouldn't consider himself dumb enough to make the same mistake twice by pursuing another fine-ass educated woman who definitely had the mind-set of a man, but the way Natalie strutted around the office in those sexy heels with her glossy lips and her waxed legs shining with oils, Flint couldn't resist letting his imagination travel up her skirts all the way to her pearl, wondering what her pussy would look like sprawled across his face. Desperately Flint had to know what Natalie taste like. He dreamed about how his dick would feel inside her pussy. Was she sweet? Tight? Could Natalie work her vaginal muscles like she did her brain in the corporate meetings or would she screw him the way Samantha had when the lawyer drew up a prenuptial? Quick and to the point.

According to Mr. Sexton's attorney, if Flint left Samantha, he'd have to leave with just the possessions he'd brought to the marriage and that was basically his naked ass because Samantha didn't own anything outright. If Samantha divorced him, Flint couldn't afford to sue her nor did he have enough evidence to blackmail her father.

At least Samantha used to care about his dick. His feelings. His needs. They used to travel together for business, making each trip pleasurable. But after they married, Samantha changed and she'd changed him. Samantha started traveling to New York every week without him. She'd emphatically said, "If you're going to live in my house, you have to earn your keep."

Flint didn't want a CEO position in her daddy's company. Flint barely knew what the hell he was doing operating a business. But he couldn't admit it even if Natalie did sense his insecurities and his ignorance.

There was something sultry about Natalie that clearly elevated her above other women including Samantha. Natalie was a cat-dog—possessing a half-male part-female attitude that quietly intimidated the males and females around her. Confidently she had control of her yin and yang sexual energy, gliding throughout the office graceful as a kitten, yet her mere presence could silently dominate any situation. Women like his wife who verbally demanded power all the time killed a man's sex drive.

Instinctively men wanted to fuck all the time. If Flint wasn't fucking, he was thinking about fucking. He wanted to cum morning, noon, and night, not just once or twice on Saturdays at ten o'clock at night or whenever Samantha decided to crawl into bed waving her black leather cattails whip.

Samantha rationing out her pussy as though there was a shortage left Flint no choice but to fulfill the doggish sex drive he had before he met and married her, and unbeknownst to Samantha she had her father to thank for his promiscuous behavior. Flint strolled outside to feed Samantha's pets. The cool breeze whisked across the wet spots on his face where the dogs had licked him. Flint didn't like animals but the dogs were playful and kept him company when his wife wasn't here.

Ding-dong. Ding-dong.

Inhaling deeply, Flint abandoned the dogs, headed back into the house to wash his face and hands. Finally, the person he'd been waiting for had arrived. Flint hurried to the foyer, blew into his moist palms, and slowly opened the door.

"Hey, good to see you. Glad you could make it," Flint lied, closing the door behind his lover.

"Yeah, me too."

Flint led the way into what he considered his house whenever Samantha wasn't home. Lounging in the living room, Flint handed his guest an ice-cold beer, then took a sip from his bottle. Flint liked drinking beer straight from the bottle for the same reasons most men took beer drinking to the head. Most beer bottles were shaped like dicks. The top resembled the male's corona. Flint opened wide, wrapped his lips around the head, and guzzled repeatedly until there was nothing left. The neck of the bottle replicated the shaft. The base of the bottle contained all the flavorful contents men ejaculated from their nuts. In a few moments, Flint would squirt the heavy load of semen weighing his balls down against the hot leather couch all over his lover's ass.

"You had a good weekend?" Flint asked, turning on Monday night football to create background noise. The television was a welcomed diversion for Flint when he didn't want to look at or talk to the person seated next to him.

"Always, but I am a bit stressed. Help me out here, will ya?" his lover said, patting the leather cushion between them.

Moving closer, Flint sat thigh to thigh beside his lover, then exhaled. Obviously his lover's male enhancement drug had his lover's dick poking a circular imprint in the black cotton pull-up sweatpants. Flint slid the elastic waistband over his lover's erection, exposing a rock-hard six-inch dick. Their routine was in motion and for the next hour Flint would fuck the shit out of his lover while barely speaking a word.

Slowly Flint removed his lover's white T-shirt, bit his nipples, then grabbed his balls. Tossing the naked man's clothes beside the sofa, Flint kissed his lover's neck and shoulders, then pressed his lips against his lover's ear and whispered, "Turn over, bitch."

Easing his own pants below his ass, Flint removed all of his clothes, then tossed them into a pile on the floor on top of his lover's. Doggie style, Flint's lover's knees sank into the sofa as Flint positioned himself behind him. Flint's dick instantly got hard but not from thinking about the dirty bastard who was moaning underneath him.

Flint wanted to cum so bad he didn't care who his dick penetrated anymore. If he weren't afraid that Samantha's dogs would bite his dick off, he would gladly let them lick his dick until he'd cum instead of fucking this man in the ass. Flint strummed a condom up his shaft as he fantasized about Natalie's glossy lips sucking his dick until he came all over her face. He bet she could fuck him the way Samantha used to before he'd said, "I do."

Flint squirted several ounces of lubrication in the crack of his lover's ass. Automatically his lover spread his legs and began massaging his dick with the excess lube streaming over his balls.

"Leave my dick alone, bitch. You my 'ho tonight. I'm getting ready to fuck the shit out of you," Flint said, rising up. Grabbing the black leather paddle off of the end table . . . *whack!* Flint spanked his lover's ass while watching his team score a touchdown. The routine was scripted to the point Flint could've kept his eyes closed.

His lover's entire body stiffened. Flint felt him stroking his dick faster. His lover's dick seemed humongous when he'd molested Flint years ago. When Flint was the one on the bottom and not the top, Flint wanted nothing more than to end their relationship. But he couldn't. Then Flint was too afraid; now he was too ashamed that he'd allowed this to continue for so long.

"Relax," Flint said, hitting him again and again until his lover whimpered like a dog into the decorative pillow. Flint's brain told his trembling hands to wrap his hands around his lover's neck and squeeze the life out of him. That way they'd all be free—Flint, Samantha, and Flint's grandmother. Surely everyone would understand. They said the truth shall set you free.

Tonight Flint's yang energy was extremely volatile and explosive and thanks to Samantha he had lots of sexual frustrations to release. He bet Natalie could be explosive in the bedroom when she wanted to be fucked really good. Massaging his large dickhead into his lover's ass, Flint stimulated his lover's prostate by pressing his dick downward inside the dirty bastard's loose asshole. After about a half hour of dirty talk and penetration, his lover squirted cum all over the sheet underneath them while Flint came at the same time.

When Flint pulled out, his lover stumbled to the shower, returned to living room, and quickly dressed.

"You're leaving early tonight?" Flint asked, thankful he didn't have to pretend any longer than necessary that he respected a man that he desperately wanted to kill.

"Yeah," he answered. "Got a late meeting with a deacon." Standing in the doorway, he spoke his routine parting words,

"If you ever tell anyone, I'll kill you and your grandmother."
Quietly closing the door, he left.

Cleaning the sofa, wiping off the leather paddle, and picking
up his clothes, Flint headed to his bathroom. As many times
as he'd contemplated committing suicide, he could live with
his lover's threat of killing him. But the thought of him harming his grandmother made Flint want to shoot him in his head
right between the eyes or, better yet, shoot him in his ass.

The brain was ultimately responsible for the fucked-up
things people did. Flint's lover was so deranged that years ago
he'd had his wife committed to a mental institution. No one
had heard from her since. Was keeping a secret more important than a person's freedom? Maybe this ordeal wasn't about
Flint at all. Maybe somebody else's child could've played the
same role, especially if he had a guardian like Flint's grandmother who was so rooted in the Bible she couldn't separate
religion from reality.

Stepping into a steam-filled shower, Flint allowed the tears
pouring down his cheeks to wash away his emotional pain
once again. He was filled with mixed emotions. He wasn't
a faggot, bisexual, or heterosexual but he realized stimulation of the male prostate—by a woman with her finger or
another man with his dick—was healthy and having his dick
in a man's ass felt so fuckin' good that was the only time his
entire body experienced the orgasm. Licking his lips Flint
imagined what Nick's dick would taste like?

Flint often wondered if an increasing number of men
turned to men for sex because men understood what women
didn't. Consensual sex between individuals created sexual

energy that rejuvenated the mind, body, and soul. Sex was healthy and healing but society was so screwed up that the immoral implications associated with sex had damn near everybody walking around suppressing their desires to have orgasms for a multitude of reasons.

Flint was a naive adolescent who'd fucked his way into money and got fucked in the process. If either one of them ever divorced, Mr. Sexton would cut both of them out of his will. Flint's wife, Samantha, used to comfort him in her arms, convincing him that he was heterosexual every time she sucked his dick. Now Flint had to pretend he was fucking Nick just to get through the moments of fucking Samantha's seventy-year-old father, who was born the same year the Golden Gate Bridge opened.

Now that Flint looked back on all the "son-in-law this and son-in-law that," he believed Samantha's father's main purpose for having him marry his daughter was so he'd have somebody to fuck him and so Flint wouldn't come forward and destroy the popularity of his upstanding public image.

At the age of six, Flint was instantly homeless the moment his mother took her last breath. Where else could a once poor boy from Alabama like himself who'd moved to San Francisco to live in the overcrowded low-income Geneva Towers housing project with his grandmother acquire such an elaborate lifestyle, immaculate home, and a bottomless bank account? Flint was cool except for the few times Samantha's father had fucked him in the ass, or requested that Flint suck his sagging dick and balls.

Flint's life was fucked up. People who were financially

challenged weren't free to do simple things that cost money like dine out whenever they wanted or fill up their tanks whenever they stopped at a gas station. "Let me get five on five." Flint never wanted to be that poor again. Which was more valuable? Freedom? Or money? Flint had every intention of making Natalie Coleman and Nick Thurston answer those questions before determining who would earn the promotion in Paris.

When a man gets bored, his dick gets hard, and shit happens.

SEXCAPADE 4

Nick

Next time, think before you speak, Nick scolded himself.

Sitting in his office at 9:00 p.m., Nick regretted having Natalie find out about his suggestion to Flint in the middle of their meeting this morning. Certainly there was a roundabout way he could've shared his idea with Flint but Nick wanted to receive full credit for his concepts and have an edge over Natalie. Flint should've kept Nick out of his mouth. Nick hadn't given him permission to disclose his recommendation in front of Natalie.

Nick had dedicated the majority of his time to this company for six long years and that gave him two years of seniority over Natalie. On her first day working at Dons and Divas, Nick noticed Flint occasionally staring at Natalie the same way he'd done. Difference was Nick wasn't married,

Nick was Natalie's counterpart not her boss, and Natalie wanted to have sex with Nick.

Once Natalie came on board, the office assistant Jonathan upgraded the decor in the lobby and conference rooms. There was something about being around Natalie that made people want to please her. Mr. Sexton started spending more time in the office too. Guess the old man didn't have anything better to do with his time but Nick certainly did. After hours Nick enjoyed countless blow jobs and quickies with Natalie in both her office and his. Natalie stimulated and satisfied every part of his mind, body, and soul. What man could ask for more than getting good pussy and a paycheck in the same place?

Out the window from the thirtieth floor, the full moon glowed over the stream of lights atop the Bay Bridge while a cluster of stars lit up the Golden Gate. It was a perfect night for uninhibited lovers like Natalie and Nick to have sex at Fort Point Lookout. But they'd stopped fucking at the Golden Gate Bridge the night they saw somebody being coaxed out of jumping 220 feet to his death. At the documented speed of seventy-five miles per hour, it would only take four seconds to hit the shark-inhabited Pacific Ocean.

In some ways, Natalie had the same effect on Nick that the Golden Gate Bridge had on the thirty-four people who committed suicide last year—fatal attraction. How could a woman so beautiful be so lethal? More suicides occurred on the Golden Gate Bridge than on all the landmarks in the world combined. More men went after Natalie than Nick had ever witnessed looking at other women in all the countries he'd traveled to. And when they encountered Natalie, they became either speechless or babbling idiots. But like with the jumpers from bridge over troubled water, few survived. Nick was the longest-lasting lover Natalie had but he wasn't sure how much longer he could hold on to her before letting go. Nick was ready for a wife and kids.

Torn between his passion for his job and his love for Natalie he couldn't wrap his head around devising and implementing any type of business plan with fifty grand. Not without investing his money. Nick had a decent 401(k) and a stock portfolio valued at $1.5 million. He was determined to get the position but he didn't want to risk losing Natalie's friendship, so he picked up his phone and dialed her extension to offer what she deserved, an apology.

Nick shivered at the thought of Natalie spreading his thighs and sucking the cum out of his dick last night and her servicing him again this morning . . . That's it! . . . Just like he'd spent lots of money to keep Natalie happy, he'd have to spend his money to make money and this promotion was well worth it. If Nick invested up to $1 million, he could recoup his investment in one year.

"Why didn't I think of this sooner?" Nick could put his own money into developing a plan that would blow everyone's mind, and make Natalie congratulate him on getting the promotion. But he still couldn't see himself relocating to Paris or any place else without his Natalie.

"Hey, Nick. What's up? Or should I ask what are you up to?"

Excitedly Nick said, "Natalie, look, baby. I'm so sorry. Can you come to my office? I really need to see you right now."

"I'm on my way out."

What? She was leaving without any intentions of letting him know? That was a first. She was bailing out before midnight, knowing they had only one week to get their plans together.

"Please, don't make me beg, I feel bad enough. If you must go, just drop in and see me for a minute. Please."

Natalie sighed heavily. "Fine, Nick," she said, then hung up the phone.

Minimizing his computer screen, Nick stuffed the hard copy outline for his plan inside his desk drawer and waited for his baby. Five, ten, fifteen minutes went by. Don't call her back, she'll be here any minute. Tapping his foot on the merlot Berber carpet, he swiveled in his chair. Twenty, twenty-five . . . finally thirty minutes later Natalie walked in looking—damn! Nick wanted to lift her onto his windowsill, raise her dress over her succulent protruding nipples, and eat her pussy until the sun came up.

Natalie's lips were freshly painted and her makeup retouched. She'd changed from the mocha-colored jacket and skirt she'd worn this morning into a candy apple red baby-doll dress that barely covered her ass, but she hadn't changed the tiger eye and diamond earrings. Glancing at her feet, when he saw the clear stilettos, Nick wanted to cry. Those were her favorite special occasion fucking shoes he'd bought her for their first anniversary and she'd only worn them for him. Her hair had thick tubular curls flatly aligned neatly in vertical rows from front to back and she smelled incredibly sweet like melted caramel. Blood rushed to his dick; he hoped Natalie would either blow him or let him taste her sweet sugary pussy.

The diamond solitaire he'd secretly slipped into the purse he'd handed her this morning wasn't anywhere on her hand. Natalie noticed everything, so she had to have seen the small box. Nick would never propose to her but he figured what harm would it do to give the woman he loved an unofficial engagement ring. If she loved him, she'd proudly wear it on the appropriate finger without him having to ask her.

"Hey, Natalie. You look great," Nick said, moving from behind his desk. He sat on the edge of his desk spreading his crotch nice and wide toward Natalie's face. She sat in the black leather cushioned chair, placed her elbows on the cherrywood arms, crossed her legs, and stared deep into his eyes.

Don't you see this big dick in front of you? Nick squirmed, hoping to redirect her attention.

"Hey, Nick" was all she'd said.

"Baby, I apologize if I offended you. That was never my intent. You know me better than that. I lost it for a second. I never should've shared my idea with Flint without including you but the conversation with Flint came up unexpectedly and one thing led to another. It was sorta like we were brainstorming."

Baby, don't you like the way my dick is bulging into a camel hump inside my pants?

Nick knew Natalie had to see his erection. And they hadn't

had sex all day, so he knew she was horny as hell too. Her pussy had to be on fire.

"Baby, I promise you, it won't happen again. Would you like to get started on our plans? I have some great ideas and I can order our favorite Japanese meal and have it delivered right quick," *while giving you this big dick.* "That is, if you're hungry for food," Nick casually suggested.

No matter how brilliant his plan was, there was only one position, so he couldn't reveal everything he'd come up with. Nick's objective was to find out what Natalie was planning. Take what he needed and leave her with the rest. Knowing Natalie, he was sure she was up to more than teasing him. After their morning meeting she stayed in her office with Flint for hours probably trying to convince Flint to give her the job. Nick wanted to cum so badly in Natalie's mouth that his dick started pulsating.

Natalie flatly asked, "Are you done with your little reverse psychology apology? Nick, you spoke from your head not your heart. And the only reason you apologized is because you don't want to lose this," Natalie said, parting her silky thighs all the way up to her curly-haired pussy.

Oh God. Where was her thong? She always wore a thong! Fuck! She was serious. Nick had really fucked up.

His heartbeat pounded in his dick, throbbing all the way to his aching heart. He loved this woman so much but he didn't know what to say to make things good between them again and he definitely wasn't ready to let her walk out on him looking hotter and tastier than his favorite Krispy Kreme doughnuts. The tightness in his chest took away his breath, his lips locked, and the excitement in his eyes dissipated into sorrow. Idiot. Idiot. Idiot. You messed up bad this time. That's okay, don't worry. Give her some space tonight. She'll get over her temper tantrum by tomorrow morning.

"Are you done?" she asked again.

"No, no, I'm not *done*. Natalie, I don't want to lose your friendship because of this simple misunderstanding. Remember our rule. Best friends no matter what. Baby, please tell me what I can do to make things right between us. I . . . I . . . I'll do anything you say," Nick pleaded, staring at the soft hairs on her pussy, longing for a lick as the words "I love you" trickled down his throat. He wondered where his diamond ring was.

He feared that Natalie sensed his desperate dick, so lip-synching the words came out of his mouth as he waited with baited breath for forgiveness and, if he was lucky, head.

Natalie stood and wrapped her arms around him. Nick exhaled with the warmth of her gentle womanly touch. Her cherry-colored lips kissed his lips ever so caringly. Natalie gazed into his eyes, held his balls, massaged his dick, and replied, "There's nothing you can do for me, Nick." Then she let his erection go and strutted out of his office, jiggling her booty.

Nick probably would've felt better if she'd slammed the door, cursed him out, or slapped his face, but she hadn't. She was a complete woman about the situation.

There was no way he was going to run behind her like she was a dog in heat. Locking his door, Nick unzipped his pants.

Lowering the waistband to his ankles, he squirted warming massage oil into his palm and began stroking his shaft.

Removing a photo of Natalie's pretty pussy from his drawer, Nick laid it on his desk. Considering porn and sex were the top income-generating businesses on the Internet, Nick could sell pictures of Natalie's pretty pussy and make enough money to pay for his business plan. But a true friend wouldn't do that. Or would he? Wasn't as though she'd take him to court. What proof would Natalie have to defend herself? Sit on the witness stand displaying exhibit A by showing the judge and jury her pussy?

Straddling his legs into a shape of an upside-down letter V, Nick moaned, "Ou yeah, baby. Spread your pussy for daddy. Daddy's gonna cum all over his hot beautiful pussy. You ready for this heavy load?"

He imagined Natalie's voice penetrating his ears, "This good pussy is all for you, daddy. Shoot your best shot of thick juicy cum all over mama's sweet pussy and you'd better not hold back or I'ma have to spank that ass."

Natalie had a way with the way she articulated her words and she'd had her way with him every day. This was their first disagreement and the first time she'd denied him sex. "Oh damn, mama, here I cum!" Nick yelled, blasting off on the five by seven laminated print of Natalie's pussy.

Cleaning up the mess he'd made, Nick hoped Natalie would get over what had happened today and call him tonight. Rechanneling his energy, he sat ass naked in his chair, brainstorming about what added features in a restaurant would make diners stand in line for over an hour in hopes for a seat at one of his tables. It had to be more than the food and more than the ambience.

Dons and Divas. Who were they? What defined them? What made them special? Who would pay $1,000 to eat? A few patrons, but who'd pay $1,000 to dine in privacy, meet celebrities, dance all night while swinging, swapping, and having sex in a restaurant while enjoying aphrodisiac delicacies? Or watch a live sex show while sipping expensive champagne? That's what Nick needed to find out. Legal or not, his plan would turn a six-figure profit per day based on the membership fees alone.

Typing in a few ideas, Nick eased on his jacket, pulled up his pants, straightened his tie, and headed to Natalie's office in search of her business plan.

SEXCAPADE 5

Natalie

Fool me once, shame on you. Fool me twice, shame on me.

Natalie loved every part of Nick from his heart to his wide smile that shone from the inside out, to his masculine scent, to his broad shoulders and his tight round ass, to how he randomly gave her expensive sentimental gifts. She knew, yes she knew for a fact, he loved her too but this wasn't about their love for one another or the four-carat princess-cut diamond solitaire inside the black ring box inside her purse. If Nick hadn't crossed her, she would've proudly worn his ring. Natalie's standoffish attitude was about her inability to trust the man that she was in love with. The man she wanted one day but not anytime soon to marry and father their children.

Lowering her convertible top, Natalie exhaled. Driving along Van Ness Avenue, she let the midnight breeze blow in her face.

When a man blatantly lies to a woman, deceives a woman, or mistreats a woman, a woman's gotta make him understand how she feels. Natalie knew if she said, "I'm upset with you," but still cuddled underneath Nick in front of the television, he'd assume all was forgiven. Natalie refused to send mixed signals confusing her man. No matter what she said, her actions would speak louder than her words.

Natalie wasn't one of those types that would say to a man, "You're gonna pay for that one," because she didn't have to. The best way for a woman to get back at a man was for her to fuck every man she wanted except him, but she had to make certain he knew about it without her having to tell him. And if he complained about her having sex outside of their relationship, the best thing for the woman to do was to ignore him. Change the subject. A woman should never argue to prove her point when her man was the one who was wrong, because a man, right or wrong, always strives to control his woman. Natalie wasn't oblivious to Nick's stiff tongue longing to lick her pussy or his hard dick dripping with precum inside his pants. But he had only himself to blame for not being able to slide his swollen dick deep inside her pussy.

Natalie was just getting started and by time she'd be done with Nick, he'd be just like a starving dog . . . happy to get whatever scraps she'd give him. Natalie faithfully treated Nick with the utmost respect and she genuinely enjoyed his company every day. How could he stab her in the back? She dared not tell Nick, "I love you," but she did love him . . . still. That was why her heart ached so badly.

Sure Natalie could've easily forgiven Nick, let him lick her pussy, and slept by his side tonight but the respect she held for herself was more important. If she didn't respect herself, why should Nick or any other person respect her? Sex, Natalie could get that anywhere but what she couldn't get was the electrifying energy that Nick and she exchanged during intimacy. Nick knew exactly where to touch her body without her having to tell him, he matched the intensity of her spiritual and sexual energy, and he sincerely cared about her. Something as simple as finding someone who genuinely cared about her had taken too many years and Natalie prayed God was not about to make her start over again. She wasn't letting Nick go anywhere but she had to make sure he understood, or at least try to make him understand, he'd broken their trust bond.

To release her sexual frustrations, Natalie decided to keep their date with Lola and DeVaughn. Arriving at the swingers mansion in Park Presidio, she left her Corvette with the valet parking. Thankfully she was a regular, otherwise they wouldn't have let her in without a partner. Once inside, Natalie immediately spotted Lola and DeVaughn at the bar laughing and drinking.

"Hey, guys! How are you?" Natalie said, kissing Lola on the lips first then DeVaughn.

Extending his tongue into her mouth, DeVaughn squeezed Natalie's ass and said, "Much better now. Damn, it's good to see you. Lola told me you guys couldn't make it tonight."

Involuntarily Natalie's pussy twitched. She squeezed her muscles tight and her body jerked with intense pleasure, so she let her pussy relax before she made herself have an orgasm. Taking a deep breath, she simulated the motion as if she were going to contract the entry point of her pussy but she didn't. Staying on the verge of contracting without actually doing so radiated chi energy from her pussy to her navel to her stomach, resonating to her heart, her throat, her neck, and up and out of the crown of her head.

"Yeah, it's good to see my favorite couple too," Natalie said, smothering DeVaughn's face with kisses, then exhaling, "Ahh," intentionally fogging the lenses of his chocolate-framed sunglasses. Her nipples tingled and hardened when she lightly brushed them against DeVaughn's muscular chest.

Lola glanced over Natalie's shoulder, hugging Natalie from behind. Lola's breasts nestled beneath Natalie's shoulder blades as she teased Natalie's nipples. Lifting her satin skirt, Lola brushed her pubic hairs on Natalie's butt cheeks. "Where's my Nick? I'm thirsty for Thurston," Lola moaned, kissing the nape of Natalie's neck.

"Oh, Nick's not coming tonight. He decided to stay in the office and work . . ."

Before Natalie finished her sentence, Lola stepped back, grabbed her cell phone, and speed dialed Nick's number. Natalie leaned into DeVaughn, thrusting his dickhead against her pussy. His strong hands cupped her face. DeVaughn licked his lips, pressed his lips against Natalie's, then he opened his mouth. Working his tongue into her mouth, he spread his legs on the stool pulling her closer.

A magnet couldn't have drawn more energy from a piece of iron than what DeVaughn's body was generating from Natalie's entire body. Lola sensed their intense attraction and started speaking loudly, "Nick, you need to get over here right now and I'm not accepting no for an answer. I need my partner."

DeVaughn ignored Lola and said, "Natalie, I swear I don't know what it is about you that drives me fucking nuts but I love your ass, your pussy, oh my God, I love you, woman. We need to do this more than once a week. It drives me insane to wait seven days to taste you." Leaning back to view Natalie's entire body, DeVaughn inserted his middle finger in her pussy and continued, "There's something different about you tonight. Fiery. Lethal. Whatever it is, I want all of it." DeVaughn sucked his finger. "You are so damn sweet."

Natalie felt a tap on her shoulder. "Here," Lola said, handing her the cell phone.

Natalie knew exactly what Lola wanted her to do. Convince her fuck buddy, Nick, to get his ass over here now. Natalie couldn't blame Lola, considering the way DeVaughn had greeted her. Unexpectedly Natalie was instantly drawn to DeVaughn tonight. Whatever sexual energy they generated Natalie did not want Nick to diminish or ruin.

Smiling, Natalie wondered if Nick's deception actually drew her closer to DeVaughn. It didn't matter. She needed sexual healing and DeVaughn was her next best dick. Damn, DeVaughn was oh so divine.

Natalie's body jerked into DeVaughn's as she moaned into the receiver, "Hey, there, Nick." DeVaughn held her tighter. She felt DeVaughn's possessive animalistic nature marking his territory for the night.

Angrily Nick hissed in her ear, "You are so wrong for this shit, Natalie. Why didn't you tell me you were hooking up with Lola and DeVaughn? You felt how hard my dick was. How could you walk out on me like that? I would've never done that to you. You know I would've gone with you tonight. And why didn't you tell me you'd almost finished your plan?"

Men were so damn predictable.

Nick had taken her bait. Natalie figured he'd sneak into her office and wouldn't leave until he found her business plan. What he didn't know was that was not her plan at all. That was a mock plan that Flint had given her, saying, "This is what Samantha does not want to see." Now she wondered why Flint hadn't given Nick a copy too.

DeVaughn took the phone from her hand and said, "We'll catch you next week, man. I'll take care of our girl really good tonight," then handed the phone to Lola. "Natalie, let's go upstairs."

Natalie hoped Lola didn't react to the fact that DeVaughn had dismissed her but at the same time she didn't care. Tonight, Natalie was to be the only one riding DeVaughn's big dick all night long.

"You two go ahead," Lola, disappointed, said. "I'd rather not participate without Nick."

DeVaughn didn't hesitate, tossing Lola the keys. "Here, baby. Take the car. Natalie can drop me off at home later. Text me when you make it in but don't wait up."

One of the reasons the members loved this swingers club so much was that the sexcapades didn't end until the members said so. Natalie had a feeling DeVaughn wanted an all-nighter. Considering he was in between professions and Natalie had to work tomorrow, tonight she'd decide when their time was up.

Natalie's pussy was so wet she felt moisture streaming down her inner thighs and she didn't care about anything but the orgasm percolating between her hot pussy lips. "Lola girl, I'll make sure your hubby gets home safely. Nick will be here next week. Trust me, Nick'll need you more than he'll want me," Natalie said, praying that was not true.

Allowing Lola to kiss her with those succulent lips that Nick loved so much, Natalie waved as Lola exited. DeVaughn and Natalie went upstairs to a private room with a large viewing window. Voyeurs could look in but DeVaughn and Natalie couldn't see them standing outside the window. Natalie was so sexually charged she didn't care who watched them. DeVaughn locked the door, signaling to other couples not to disturb them, and then said, "Natalie, tonight, I want to fuck you in your ass. Is that okay?"

Yes! He was going to fuck her in her ass and she didn't have to ask. A woman's anus had the second highest concentration of nerve endings in the body, many of which were connected to the vagina, and Natalie was ready to experience the most explosive orgasm of her life.

Natalie firmly answered, "Yes, DeVaughn," then whispered, "I'm all yours, daddy."

SEXCAPADE 6

Nick

Nick stood outside the window watching them in disbelief.

For years, he could never figure out why he hadn't asked or attempted to fuck Natalie in her ass. Maybe he equated it with homosexual tendencies. Nick wondered, Was this her first time? Was this their first time engaging in anal sex with one another? Maybe he never tried because he assumed Natalie wasn't into anal sex, or perhaps he wanted her to ask him, or, like some other men, he found anal sex gross and couldn't imagine anything going up in a canal that had a primary function of excreting shit.

Whatever his true reason was didn't matter right now. Where was his partner Lola? She could've prevented all of this from happening before his eyes. Nick stood outside that window in his camel-colored suit. Loosening his tie, he stretched his neck. The quick sharp breaths barely supplied enough oxygen to his brain to keep him vertical. Nick opened his mouth to scream Natalie's name . . . but he couldn't.

Didn't every man want to be the first to slip his dick into his woman's asshole, especially a woman that he cared about? Nick believed that finding a female of legal age who was a vaginal virgin held slimmer odds than hitting the lottery. He imagined the chances were much greater for him to meet an anal virgin and he was right when he'd met Natalie. But what difference did any of that make at the present moment when he'd done every freaky act of nature with Natalie except fuck her in the ass. If she were truly an anal virgin, in a moment she wouldn't be.

A camel-colored hump curved his zipper as he watched another man's dick joyfully smear precum onto Natalie's mesmerizing cantaloupe-shaped ass. He knew her body well and he knew right now her pussy was soaking wet.

Unzipping his pants, Nick held his swollen dick in his hand while he watched them fuck. The way DeVaughn had handled business in the front door let Nick know Natalie anxiously wanted that man to slip his dick in her ass. DeVaughn was gentle at the right times, swift at the right times, agile all the times, and he knew just when to fuck the shit out of Nick's woman . . . yes! . . . at the right times.

"Fuck!" Nick shouted to himself.

Week after week he pretended he was okay with another man touching her, kissing her, and fucking her, but he wasn't. He participated in swinging and swapping because he'd do anything to please Natalie. Nick placed his hand against the glass window. Right now nothing hurt Nick more than knowing there was nothing he could do to change places with DeVaughn who was getting ready to fuck Natalie in the ass, so he tucked his dick inside his pants and left before he'd end up doing something else he'd regret.

$\int$EXCAPADE 7

Natalie

Natalie felt Nick's energy reverberate in her ear, create a mirage of his statuesque image within her third eye, pierce her heart with Cupid's arrow, then vanish from the other side of the window. She sensed his dejection and she'd be lying if she said she didn't care about his feelings but he was the one who'd disrespected her not once but twice in one day. Because of his disloyalty, Nick was the last man that Natalie would completely trust.

She could never erase him from her mind, so she pushed all of her thoughts of Nick into her subconscious while she submitted to DeVaughn for hours of heavenly foreplay and fornication. Lying on her stomach sizzling with sexual heat, Natalie rested her head on a pillow. DeVaughn's strong hands caressed her sweaty back, moved down to her spine, then squeezed her ass. After separating her cheeks, one of his fingers probed her pussy while another explored the opening of her ass testing its tightness. Simultaneously maneuvering in and out of both holes, he gently kissed her clit.

"If I weren't already married," he whispered between her wet thighs, "I'd definitely marry you. I'm surprised he hasn't proposed to you. It's been what, three years now?"

DeVaughn's comments reminded Natalie of the diamond ring inside her purse. First opportunity she had, Natalie was giving Nick back his ring. She wasn't interested in being any man's wife right now. That's why she implemented her own rules. DeVaughn would be wise not to talk himself out of fucking her in the ass before sliding in the back door. Softly, Natalie replied, "I don't want to think about him right now. You just make sure you don't put that shitty finger in or near my pussy."

"Baby, baby. This is our first time, not my first time," DeVaughn reassured Natalie. "I know not to crisscross in the two holes so you won't get an infection."

"All I want is for you to make me feel good all over. Can you handle that and take my mind completely off of Nick?"

"Be careful what you ask for." DeVaughn whispered in her ear, "Get ready to cum again. This orgasm is going to blow your fucking mind."

Natalie prayed the anal experience wasn't overrated and that DeVaughn could back up his words. If this man made her cum again, she was gonna have to kidnap him from his wife for at least a week. She'd forget about her business plan, her ex man, and her boss competing for her time. Tonight all she wanted to do was shower her womanly juices until her secretions were exhausted.

"Mmmm," she moaned, tilting her ass upward back onto DeVaughn's finger.

Carefully DeVaughn removed his finger from her ass.

Natalie's face lifted from the pillow in protest. No, she thought. What was he doing? That shit felt so damn good she wanted him to continue. Squirming, she hiked her butt in the direction of his dick and for a split second Natalie wished DeVaughn were Nick.

Why did Nick have to screw things up this morning? Forget Nick. I don't give a damn about him! Natalie lied to herself. A part of her wanted to cry but she suppressed her feelings and her tears for Nick.

On previous occasions Nick had attempted sticking his finger deep inside her ass doggie style. Reluctantly she'd stopped him each time because of the sudden urge to lose her bowels all over the sheets. What was different about how DeVaughn pushed his finger all the way inside her? Maybe it was her present attitude toward Nick that allowed her to submit to DeVaughn.

Reaching over her body into his toiletry bag, DeVaughn retrieved a tube of water-based lube, squirted the solution onto his fingers, then methodically massaged the cool gel inside her asshole. He resumed probing her ass in and out. Slowly he twirled while inserting the first notch of his finger inside her. Then he eased in a little more.

Reaching for a condom, DeVaughn peeled away the edge using his teeth, removed the contents, plopped a drop of lubrication inside the condom, then placed the latex over his corona like a helmet, rolling the rubber up his shaft to the base. Since the anus did not emit secretions like the clitoris, G-spot, and cervix, DeVaughn retrieved the lubrication again and saturated the outside of his condom.

"Spread your legs," he commanded matter-of-factly.

Straddling Natalie from behind, he pressed the head of his slippery dick inside. Automatically her body tensed.

"Wait," Natalie said, staring at him over her shoulder while gripping the edge of the mattress.

"You want me to stop?" he asked, pausing with the tip of his head inside her ass.

Natalie shook her head.

"Take a deep breath and relax. Trust me. I know what I'm doing," DeVaughn reassured her.

When Natalie exhaled, DeVaughn gently pushed. Again and again Natalie wished DeVaughn were Nick. It wasn't too late to ask DeVaughn to stop and go home to Nick.

"Oh, wait," Natalie said, sinking her face into the pillow.

The familiar shitting sensation crept upon her. Natalie kept breathing to relieve the pressure. Fortunately she'd had a good bowel movement earlier. The two tablespoons of flaxseed oil she consumed daily lubricated her intestines and made her waste slide out smoothly, so as soon as she stopped thinking about Nick, DeVaughn's dick would have no problem gliding inside of her anus.

"We don't have to do this if you don't want to. We could do something different. I want to please you. I don't want to hurt you."

His compassion helped put her at ease and Natalie was determined to show Nick who was in control of their relationship. She exhaled, then said, "Okay."

"Okay, what?"

"Don't stop," she said, burying her face back into the pillow.

This time when DeVaughn pushed, she felt the head pop in deeper and her entire body tensed again.

"At this rate we'll be here trying all night. Turn on your side," he said.

Holding Natalie's hips, DeVaughn moved with her careful not to pull out. Once they were on their sides in a spoon position, he said, "Don't move. Let me do the work. All I want you to do is relax and take deep breaths. If you relax, this won't hurt. I promise."

I know that, Natalie thought. But this wasn't the time to prove how educated she was, so she did as DeVaughn requested.

Gently he moved in half-inch strokes, pausing whenever his head hit a wall of tissue. After a few moments, he continued his groove, stroking and pausing. His hand massaged her thigh and her ass. When his hand moved toward her vagina, quickly Natalie caressed her pussy. She didn't want to wonder if he'd remembered which finger he'd stuck in her ass earlier.

"The inside of your ass is like a strand of connected S's, so like with driving, each time I hit a curve, I have to slow down or stop and give you a chance to regroup, that way it doesn't hurt. I'm almost in, baby. Turn back on your stomach."

Natalie knew all of that too.

Feeling his dick inside her ass started arousing her, making her forget about Nick.

"I want you to rock with me," DeVaughn said, slightly increasing his rhythmic movement. "That's my girl. You're so beautiful. You're doing fine."

And fine she was until she heard him say, "Now on the count of three, I'm gonna push. I need for you to rock your hips back into mine and relax."

Natalie's entire body, ass and all, became tensed again.

"No, baby, relax. You're doing good. You want me to stop?" DeVaughn asked, this time seeming a bit frustrated and anxious at the same time.

Gazing at his reflection in the mirror on the wall, Natalie thought DeVaughn was gorgeous. Muscular arms, thick with definition, his hairy chest, and his sexy shapely lips and warm brown eyes excited her. Lola was one lucky woman to have a husband with a big dick who knew how to work his stick.

Since Nick had missed out, Natalie was pleased DeVaughn was the one who'd claim her anal virginity. This was a special day and even if it did hurt just a little bit, she'd enjoy the pain and pleasure of giving herself to DeVaughn. Natalie fantasized DeVaughn was hers. Well, he was for the night but Natalie was glad she didn't have the headaches that accompanied having a husband.

Staring into his eyes, Natalie said, "No, I'm okay. Don't stop."

"Stroke your clit and rock with me. It'll feel better," DeVaughn instructed, continuing his groove once more.

His hands balled into fists pressing into the mattress as he rocked his dick inside her ass.

"I'ma go a little deeper."

Preparing for the unknown, Natalie exhaled, trying to relax her legs, back, and arms. When DeVaughn rocked forth, surprisingly massaging her clit made her thrust her ass toward him. When he rocked back she rocked forward. Keeping pace with his rhythm she began enjoying the sensation each time they met halfway.

"I'ma go a little deeper."

"Um-hum. Yes, go deeper, daddy," Natalie moaned, becoming more aggressive with the depth of DeVaughn's dick.

"That's my girl. Back that ass up on your dick. That's it. You got it, girl. Ride this dick like you want it."

Natalie did. Holding on to the headboard, she enjoyed him ramming into her backside striking like lightning. Her pussy quivered.

"Now that I'm in," DeVaughn whispered, "I'm about to do a three-sixty in your ass. Don't move. Let me work this sweet pretty ass."

"Oh shit!" Natalie said, wrapping one arm around the pillow while massaging her clit faster.

DeVaughn turned sideways, forming a small letter "t," then humped. When he rotated his face above her feet, DeVaughn grabbed Natalie's ankles and stroked faster.

Whatever nerve he'd hit made her shout, "Oh my God, I'm cumming!"

"That's my girl but I ain't done yet," he said, moving to the side, reshaping their bodies into the "t" again, only this time he faced the opposite side of the bed. Natalie's body lay vertically atop the mattress while he stretched horizontally. Slowing his rhythm, DeVaughn curved his pelvis above her ass, lowering his body with wormlike movements.

Glancing over her shoulder, Natalie was amazed and turned on watching DeVaughn fuck the shit out of her. Sweat dripped from his forehead as he wiped his face with the white sheet.

"I want you to cum, again." He paused, then continued, "But give me a minute 'cause I don't wanna cum just yet. I want you to cum again without me. Damn, this ass is good."

Continuously looking over her shoulder, Natalie wanted to see DeVaughn's expression. His eyes were fixated. Not on her. On the inside of his lids. A tight frown drew his eyebrows closer. His bottom lip was clenched between his teeth. When he opened his eyes then his mouth and looked at her, Natalie's ass instinctively humped, pushing onto his dick.

"Fuck me harder, DeVaughn!" she yelled, calling out his name repeatedly.

With his body rotating head to head atop hers, together they formed the perfect number one. "Talk dirty to me. Tell me." He pounded her ass, collapsing her against the bed. "Don't move, damnit. Tell me you want this big-ass dick to come out your damn throat."

Natalie moaned into the pillow. "My God, that feels good!"

"Look at me. What feels good?" DeVaughn asked, continuously pounding his dick like a hammer into her ass.

"Your big strong black Mandingo dick feels so good inside my ass, daddy . . . fuck me like you own this shit."

Long, deep, slow, and easy strokes penetrated Natalie's ass as

DeVaughn said, "You'd better not give my ass to nobody, you hear me. This is my ass."

Gently DeVaughn massaged her back, stroking deeper and a little bit slower. He kissed the nape of her neck and whispered, "You feel so good, mama. I'm ready to cum. Cum with me, baby."

The deep gentle strokes in and the long passionate strokes almost but not quite all the way out made Natalie scream . . . "Yessss! Yessss! Yesss!" Gasping, she could hardly breathe as she came. Trembling. Shaking. Her fingers clamped onto the pillow.

DeVaughn paused and she felt the waves pulsating inside her ass as his cum released into the condom. Natalie felt each of his spasms. His sweaty body collapsed on top of hers. DeVaughn whispered, "You're not a virgin anymore. You lost your virginity and you came on the first try. Not many women can do that."

How in the hell did he know it was her first time? She'd never confessed that to him.

Natalie's entire pelvis felt breezy like chimes blowing in the wind. The more she'd relaxed the less pressure she'd felt. Actually, unlike vaginal sex, anal sex the first time didn't hurt nearly as much. It felt more like pressure than pain. Natalie realized it was DeVaughn's level of experience and coaching that had made her comfortable but she'd never admit that to DeVaughn. The fact that he took his time in the beginning, navigating around the curves of her ass until he reached the straight and narrow road into her intestines. The fact that he knew not to pull all the way out at any time until they were done kept her cuming.

Yes, this ass is definitely all yours tonight, she thought, laying her head on his chest.

Occasionally Natalie enjoyed being totally submissive. This was her first time one-on-one alone with DeVaughn but it wouldn't be their last. Natalie wanted him to see a different side of her. What she didn't expect was the stronger bond they'd formed.

DeVaughn's arm drew her near as he lowered his chin on the top of her head. "Just don't forget," he said, kissing her forehead.

How could she ever forget?

SEXCAPADE 8

Nick

Nick's dick was playing tricks on him.

His dick had become the all-time prankster, award-winning joker, incredible magician transforming Nick from a lion into a rabbit. Nick's dick had made a plum fool out of him. Nick wished like hell that were true. A needle filled with Novocain piercing his chest would've had the same effect or an IV filled with anesthetics trickling into his veins. Nick's entire body was numb. His rapid heart rate was uncontrollable. His short breaths were the only things keeping him alive.

He never should've showed up at the Park Presidio Playhouse or at Natalie's place last night, because after she didn't come home, in that moment, another part of him died. Nick would never love Natalie or any other woman the same. And it wasn't his dick's fault. It was mostly his fault.

Natalie had this weird invisible guardian angel protecting her, 'cause if she had shown up at her house last night, Nick was so angry, only God could've shown her mercy.

Pivoting in his high-back chair, Nick glanced out of his office window overlooking Union Square. The time was now eight o'clock Tuesday morning and Natalie hadn't arrived to work. This was uncharacteristic of her. Nick began to worry if she was okay. Had she been involved in an accident? He'd feel awful if anything horrible had happened to her while he was sitting there agonizing over his own stupidity being upset with her.

Trying to concentrate on the copy he'd made of her business plan, Nick couldn't focus his thoughts on anything except Natalie. "Fuck! I just wanna get my dick sucked," he cried into his palms.

Why did she have to let DeVaughn fuck her in the ass? That was his ass and she knew it. Nick had done every sexual act imaginable with Natalie. Didn't she realize he was saving anal sex for a superspecial occasion like their honeymoon or the grand opening in Paris? They could've hid away in one of the wings of the Louvre and made love in front of the *Mona Lisa* painting. But the chances of getting away with having sex in front of the well-guarded Leonardo da Vinci were slimmer than sneaking a feel on Natalie's ass in front of an eye-level masterpiece of Mary Magdalene.

The risks of having sex in public places were what made Natalie so fiery, irresistible, and sexy. Mary Magdalene and

Nick shared one thing in common—being ostracized and torn away from the love of their lives. Unlike Mary Magdalene, Nick wanted revenge. Last night he could've accepted Lola's offer, gone to DeVaughn's house and had sex with Lola, but he was so angry he would've torn Lola a new asshole or made her bleed profusely from trying to drill her back out with his dick. The unfortunate part would've been Lola's being innocently victimized by Nick's misdirected anger.

Tap. Tap.

"Just a moment," he said, staring in the mirror. Puffy, red, sleepless eyes with sagging bags reflected back. "Come, in," Nick said, swiftly gathering then aligning the stack of eight-and-a-half-by-eleven papers before shoving them in his drawer.

"Hey, Nick . . . oh my. Um, good morning?" Natalie said, standing in his doorway at nine o'clock. Avoiding eye contact, she glanced at the diamond watch on her left wrist that he'd bought her and continued, "You wanna get together and work on our plans at ten?"

Glancing at the princess-cut diamond ring glistening below her watch, Nick asked, "Can you come in and close the door behind you?"

"Sure, what's up?" Natalie said, wedging her tongue in the corner of her mouth. Closing the door, she backed her ass into the knob. Her eyes beamed above Nick's head out the window into the sunshine.

Tightening his jaws, Nick pressed his top teeth against his bottom teeth so hard his gums hurt. "What's up?" he repeated Natalie's words without parting his teeth.

She stood there with one hand behind her back grabbing

the knob like he was going to attack her or something. She did deserve a cruel response but Nick would never hit a female no matter how angry he was.

"Yeah, you asked me to come in, right?"

Nick countered, "But I didn't ask you to knock on my door. Obviously you have something to say to me. Right?"

Natalie looked ravishing in her vibrant turquoise suit. The plunging V slightly revealed her cleavage. The short skirt gently caressed her curvaceous hips. Nick stared at her silky legs, praying she couldn't read his thoughts of wanting to break them in half, creating his own version of the movie *Misery*. At the same time he wanted to say, "You got a minute? I really need to get my dick sucked. I deserve that much."

Natalie's cinnamon-highlighted hair extensions flowed mid-way down her back. Her bronze lipstick highlighted her earth-tone eye shadows. Every day Natalie personified perfection from her hair follicles to her French pedicure. How did she find time to always look so damn beautiful?

Exhaling, Nick lamented, "Did you have to let him do that to you?"

That was the last damn question he wanted to ask but the first one he needed an answer to. Nick knew he didn't own or control Natalie but he felt they had an unspoken agreement not to allow anyone to penetrate their bond.

"Do what?" Natalie asked, tucking her hair behind her ears to expose the tiger eye and diamond earrings he'd bought her.

"Nothing, Natalie!" Nick yelled, then lowered his voice. "Ten is fine. I'll meet you in the conference room," he said, opening his desk drawer.

Natalie smiled warm and bright. "Don't cut me any slack. Whatever you do today, Nick, it'll behoove you to think first," she said before turning to walk out.

Behoove who? What? Clearly Natalie was fucking with his heads. Did Nick deserve this type of treatment? Fine. Whatever. If that's the way she wanted it, then he could get on her ruthless conniving page. A revengeful man was more dangerous than a scorned woman. Before Nick opened his mouth, Natalie walked back over to his desk, removed the ring from her finger, and placed it before him saying, "I believe this belongs to you. See you in a few."

Nick definitely wanted his ring back but damn Natalie didn't give him the fucking pleasure of demanding it back. It was less than thirty days since his purchase, so he could request a full refund. For the next hour Nick redefined his plan, then met Ms. Coleman in the conference room.

Before Nick sat, Natalie crossed her legs and said, "Since you've got your plan and mine, why don't you show me what we've come up with."

Nick inhaled deeply through his nose, exhaled out his mouth, swallowed hard, then said, "Okay," frantically tapping his foot underneath the table. "Natalie, I want you to know that I borrowed your plan because of time constraints and because obviously you were occupied *all* night long. Otherwise, I would've never entered your office without your permission."

Natalie glanced over his head, around the room, descending her narrowed eyes into a blank stare focusing on the cherrywood table, tightened her lips, then said, "You've got two hours. If I were you, I'd invest every second wisely because exactly at noon, I'm leaving, so why don't you stay focused on business?"

That bitch. Natalie had never talked down to him like that before. She opened her purse and the crimson-and-gold thong teddy he'd bought her fell out. No "Oops or how did this get here?" Nothing. Who was this woman sitting in front of him? "Nata——"

Leaning across the table, raising her palm inches from his face, Natalie said, "Nick, please spare us both. Okay? I may be nice but I'm nobody's fool. Oh, in case you're wondering who I'm doing for lunch, it's DeVaughn. And the next time you decide to give me a ring . . . don't."

In order to get through the next hour without strangling Natalie, Nick pretended he was talking to a new company employee. Nick shared his thoughts of a dance club with high-profile guests, and private booths, but he intentionally left out the components about the sex rooms, dwelling on the thought that Natalie would be giving his sweet pussy to DeVaughn for dessert.

DeVaughn was married and needed to focus on pleasing his wife. Or maybe they should swap and Nick could call Lola up and see what she was doing for lunch. Her firm was a few short blocks away and Lola would gladly suck his dick with no questions asked. Or Nick could follow Natalie. DeVaughn's lucky ass married Lola for the same reasons that Flint had married Samantha and Nick had partnered with Natalie. Men, no matter what their past may have revealed, were the greatest pretenders. Regardless of their circumstances, they acted as though they were single but deep down inside men hated being alone. Even worse, men hated being lonely.

What the fuck are you crazy? Why are you dragging DeVaughn and Flint into your bullshit? Man, stop tripping off of Natalie. She's not all that.

"Your ideas are great, Nick, but how do you propose we implement the renovations with our limited budget?"

As Nick was getting ready to answer with a mock recommendation that they solicit sponsors, Flint entered the conference room.

"There you are, Nick! I was looking for you. Natalie, can you excuse us for a moment? Don't go too far, I need to see you immediately afterward."

What in the hell was Flint doing? Nick had an entire hour left to convince Natalie to suck his dick tonight.

"I'll be back from a business lunch in two hours. I'll see you at one," Natalie said as she stood, swayed her hair over her left shoulder, then winked at Nick before slowly exiting with the strap of the thong teddy dangling from her purse.

Liar!

When the door closed, Flint sat next to Nick. His thigh touched Nick's leg, so Nick scooted over as Flint asked, "How's the planning coming along?"

Tonguing his two front teeth like he had a strand of coconut wedged between them reminded Nick of Natalie's sweetness and her toughness. Not just her pussy, Nick meant all of her. Natalie's heart, her brains, and her sense of humor appealed to him. Every damn thing Nick did reminded him of Natalie. He hadn't realized how much she'd become an intricate part of his life until she'd just walked out the door.

Nick answered Flint, "Not as fast as I'd like. Natalie seems to be preoccupied with external affairs, so I'm not sure how well this collaboration is going to work out. Maybe we should work on our plans independently. Personally, I think she's going on an interview. She's secretly looking for another job."

Was DeVaughn meeting Natalie at the Huntington Hotel and Spa, where she and Nick had experienced their first champagne facials, then fucked to the tunes of the San Francisco cable cars going by as they timed their hourly orgasms to the chiming of Grace Cathedral's bells? Or had he reserved the penthouse suite with the Jacuzzi tub at the Nob Hill Hotel? With only two hours reserved, Natalie and DeVaughn had to be at some nearby upscale hotel like the Sir Francis Drake, where Nick and Natalie occasionally partied on Wednesday nights at Harry Denton's overlooking the city.

"Working independently is nonnegotiable. But I didn't come here to discuss Natalie," Flint said. "I came here to discuss how you could secure this promotion on your own."

Was Nick dreaming? Was his mind playing tricks on him for real this time? Was Flint serious? Yes! If Nick could seal the deal, he'd flip the script and have Natalie down on her knees sucking his dick morning, noon, and night. Nick didn't care what he had to do. Whatever Flint had in mind, Nick was all the way in there!

Flint said, "Meet me at my house Sunday evening at six o'clock sharp. Don't be late. I have an unforgettable plan designed exclusively for you. I've gotta run. I'll give you the details later."

Flint didn't realize how he'd saved Nick from phoning every hotel within a two-miles radius. Being back in control felt good but having his dick sucked would feel great. Sitting in the conference room alone, Nick picked up the phone and dialed Lola's cell.

"Hey, Nick. What's up?"

"You hungry?" Nick asked with a sinister grin.

"Famished," Lola said with a light chuckle.

"Perfect. I'll pick you up at noon," Nick insisted, then hung up and made a reservation at Huntington hoping they'd run into DeVaughn and Natalie.

Men were simple creatures. Women complicated men's lives. All a woman had to do to keep a man happy was suck his dick on the regular. Lola wasn't Natalie but Lola's luscious lips wrapped around his dick would get Nick through the day and if he were lucky Natalie would get over being mad at him and suck his dick all night.

SEXCAPADE 9

Natalie

Natalie bailed out of the conference room and headed straight to the ladies' room, and into one of the private stalls. Digging into her purse, she removed her douche bottle and placed it under piping hot running water for five minutes. Unscrewing the plastic cap, she sprinkled a healthy pinch of alum into the tiny hole, and then vigorously shook the bottle. Screwing on the nozzle, she removed her thong, squatted over the toilet, and inserted the long clear plastic tip deep into her pussy pocket. The warm water seeping into her vagina sparked an unexpected orgasm.

The tightening effects of the alum would drive DeVaughn crazy. Ninety-eight percent of what Natalie knew about sex, she hadn't learned from her mother or her father but from reading nonfiction books like *The Multi-Orgasmic Woman:*

Discover Your Full Desire, Pleasure, and Vitality; Blow Him Away: How to Give Him Mind-Blowing Oral Sex; The Black Woman's Guide to Sexuality; and *Healing Love Through the Tao: Cultivating Female Sexual Energy.* Natalie was totally amazed at how many women, including those with PhDs, knew very little about their bodies but expected men to figure out all of their desires. Since she took sex seriously, she kept some alum in a small vile inside her purse.

Alum, generally used for pickling, was a woman's best kept secret. After sexing Natalie for three years, Nick was still clueless that the magical seasoning, sold in the spices section of every grocery store, kept Natalie's pussy just-right-tight. All that ignorant bragging from men about how they could tell if some man had been fucking their woman's pussy didn't apply to a veteran like Natalie 'cause she'd say something like, "So what? What are you going to do? You want this good pussy or should I give it to somebody new." Most women underestimated their pussy power, but not Natalie.

Putting on her thong, Natalie washed her hands, then pranced by Jonathan, happily saying, "I'll be back in a few hours."

On her way out, Natalie greeted Mr. Sexton with a friendly, "Hello," as they traded placed on the elevator. Something about that old man was eerie. Always carrying a Bible in his hand to symbolize his closeness to God. It wasn't the Bible that puzzled Natalie, it was the lack of spirituality that resonated from within the old man's soul. Mr. Sexton never seemed genuine in his ministry. What was his real purpose for randomly showing up at the office? Thankfully he was Flint's visitor and not hers.

Men didn't control a damn thing and Natalie wasn't about to pacify any man into believing that he could be the man while she was paying the mortgage or paying the bills. If she wanted to drive a man crazy, she sprinkled a small amount of alum into her douche one hour before having sex. If Natalie didn't want her next man to know she'd recently fucked another man, she'd douche with alum in between lovers.

Until Nick, Flint, DeVaughn, and any other man Natalie dealt with found a way to turn their dicks into a pussy—like Natalie's red snapping man-taming pussy—she didn't need them to admit to what she already knew: Natalie Coleman was solely in control of her life.

Neither Nick nor Flint would lay eyes on her again until tomorrow morning. Natalie refused to succumb to their foolish testosterone-driven demands. Like hungry wolves lurking under a full moon, between tomorrow night and sunrise Natalie was going to make each of them howl her name until they passed the fuck out. But Mr. DeVaughn Davis would holler first.

Sashaying to her car, Natalie thought about Nick, the man she fell in love with three years ago. Up until yesterday their love was so strong they seemed emotionally and physically inseparable. If anyone had told her that Nick was going to cross her, Natalie would've laughed in their face. Their work ethics were the same. Their sex drives were a perfect match. Mentally they stimulated one another. And more important their respect for one another was mutual. Or so she had

thought. Why? Why did Nick feel the need to fuck her outside of the bedroom?

As Natalie cruised out the garage, the cold wind whipped
her hair across her face, the sunshine glared into her eyes,
blinding her as she quickly slipped on her sunglasses to regain clear visibility. Driving alongside the Powell Street cable
car tracks, Natalie maneuvered through traffic for the next
thirty minutes until she was on the Golden Gate Bridge. Exiting into beautiful Sausalito, the best smallest city outside of
San Francisco that catered to lovers, Natalie left her car with
valet parking at her destination, The Inn Above Tide.

Glancing around the lobby, she checked with the recep-
tionist to retrieve the room key DeVaughn had left at the
front desk. Entering the spacious penthouse suite, she saw
DeVaughn was already naked and waiting with open arms
in the white porcelain tub that sat adjacent to the floor-to-
ceiling window. A bottle of champagne surrounded by ice
sat in a silver bucket next to the tub.

Air bubbles raced around DeVaughn's abs, bursting against
his succulent shriveled nipples. The melody of "At Last" by
Etta James permeated soft, slow, and low as the sunshine
beamed through the windows. Sailboats floating upon the
cerulean ocean created the picturesque backdrop that Natalie and Nick loved so much. Smiling, DeVaughn was right
where Natalie needed him, naked and vulnerable.

Easing her skirt over her hips, Natalie rubbed her shoulder, then whispered, "I could really use a good massage."

"I got you covered," DeVaughn replied, retrieving a four-
ounce bottle of oil from the ledge of the tub.

Submerging her toes into the hot whirlpool, Natalie tilted her ass in DeVaughn's face, then slowly lowered her butt down his wet neck and over the bubbles covering his slippery chest. Settling into his lap, she squeezed his floating dick with her booty.

DeVaughn leaned over her shoulder, moved her hair aside, and meshed his lips into the nape of her neck. Natalie relaxed, wrapping DeVaughn's strong arms around her waist. It was time to get what she'd come for.

Laying the back of her head into his chest as she sipped from a flute of champagne, Natalie moaned, "Mmm," gazing at the sailboats bobbing along the ocean. "Baby, I need a huge favor."

DeVaughn didn't hesitate as he responded, "Anything for my Natalie," kissing her wet hair.

Moving the back of her head onto his shoulder, Natalie said, "That feels so good. First I want to thank you for making incredible love to me last night. I want to reassure you that you were my first."

Natalie felt the excitement rising in DeVaughn's penis. Men really were easier to manipulate than women. His body tensed, then relaxed as he regained his composure. "No shit. For real?"

"Yes, daddy. Seriously," Natalie said, stroking his leg.

"I thought you were trying to make me feel special. I was joking about being your first. You mean to tell me Nick never hit this?" DeVaughn said, thrusting his hips into her ass.

"He never tried, so I never offered. Anyway, what I need for you to do for me is convince Lola to use her marketing staff to devise a business plan to revamp Dons and Divas. But you mustn't let her know the plan is for me and I must have the final by Friday."

"Friday? Are you for real? I hear you but how am I supposed to get my wife to do that so fast without being honest with her? I tell Lola everything."

Raising her eyebrows, Natalie questioned, "Everything?"

"Yeah, she knows I'm here with you. Natalie, give it to me straight. What's going on with you?" DeVaughn asked, trying to scoot backward when his back was already against the wall.

"Nick and I are competing for a promotion. And the way I see it, if you can convince Lola to have her marketing and development team lay out my plan, we can split the fifty grand I got to develop the plan, and if you feel for me the way that I love you," Natalie lied, twisting her neck sideways to kiss DeVaughn, "you can relocate to Paris with me and we can leave Nick and Lola here."

"Paris? As in Texas?"

"Paris as in France. Look, all you have to do is tell Lola you're applying for the million-dollar position that Nick and I are competing for and she can't share any of the information with anyone, especially Nick and me. You're the man. What do you think, daddy?"

"Whoa, are you serious?" DeVaughn's voice escalated, "A million dollars? Damn. Y'all must be selling more than steaks and lobsters."

Natalie knew the price tag would interest any man in DeVaughn's unemployed situation. Facing DeVaughn, she scrolled her fingers between his chest and then from his right to left nipples as she kissed his lips and said, "Dead serious. Come with me."

"One million dollars?" he uttered.

"Yes," Natalie said, luring DeVaughn out of the tub. After toweling DeVaughn, Natalie led him to the chaise longue in front of the wood-burning fireplace and said, "I want you. All of you. DeVaughn, I think I'm falling in love with you."

DeVaughn's eyes shifted away from Natalie's. His voice trembled, "I love you too, Natalie. I have from the first time we started swinging together. You know this. But I'm in love with my wife."

"Ssshh," Natalie whispered, propping several pillows behind DeVaughn's back. "Sit up, bend your knees, and lean both of your legs to one side."

Natalie could've asked DeVaughn to crisscross his legs into an overlapping position and spread his thighs wide but she knew he wasn't as flexible as Nick. The soreness and fatigue from overlapping his legs would redirect DeVaughn's attention to his discomfort and away from her. If a man was uncomfortable, he'd focus on negativity. If he was happy, Natalie knew she had his undivided attention. If a woman could keep a man relaxed, she'd have a better chance of getting exactly what she wanted.

Facing DeVaughn, Natalie set her booty into the crevice of his lap, softly wrapped her legs around his waist and behind his back, gently circling her arms over his shoulders. Face-to-face they sat in silence exchanging breaths. Natalie embraced the back of DeVaughn's head bringing his lips to her mouth. Passionately they kissed.

Every movement, every stroke, every touch, every breath, had a deeper purpose. Natalie was soul mating with DeVaughn. And while he immersed himself into their spiritual connection, he had no idea of the long-term effect this would have on him.

They sat quietly until DeVaughn's penis went from erect to limp. Carefully Natalie inserted his limp dick inside her tight, hot, fleshy pussy.

"Aw damn, your pussy is supertight. When was the last time ole boy hit this?" DeVaughn asked.

Opting not to respond, Natalie was just getting started. In order for them to take their sexual energy to the highest level possible, Natalie had to take her time and make sure they never lost their connection. A break was fine, but if DeVaughn lost patience, she was in jeopardy of losing him.

"Don't move, daddy. I want to feel your powerful magnetic energy."

For thirty minutes they made love without having sex. Feeling DeVaughn's soft erection inside of her made Natalie's puckering pussy so juicy she used her muscles to gently push his dick out.

Without speaking a word, Natalie held DeVaughn closer pressing her clit down onto his head. She had to take him to a higher spiritual level. Her body trembled with pleasure. Slowly, she kissed DeVaughn's ear, his neck, collarbone, chest, nipples, stomach, pubic hairs, and then she eased his limp dick into her mouth.

DeVaughn's body began to tremble uncontrollably until a long stream of semen flowed into her mouth. Patiently Natalie waited until he was done before picking up her champagne flute. Pretending to take a sip, she released his sperm into the glass. DeVaughn was so relaxed with his head tilted backward that he never noticed she hadn't swallowed.

Gulp. Natalie moaned, "You taste so wonderful."

Tossing the pillows to the floor, Natalie placed her hands on his chest and nudged him until he was flat on his back. Straddling DeVaughn, she planted her feet on the floor then rotated her hips until his dick got rock hard. Suctioning him inside using her pussy, Natalie squirmed her hips deep into his pelvis, rounding up and down.

DeVaughn grabbed her ass and started rolling her hips back and forth. "Damn, Natalie, you're incredible. Ride the shit out of this dick, baby."

DeVaughn didn't have to ask twice. Natalie bounced so hard her ass started hurting but she was on a mission. "What's my name?" she asked, squeezing DeVaughn's dick with her PC muscles.

"Natalie," he exhaled.

She asked a little bit softer.

"Natalie," he said a little louder.

Pulsating her pussy around his dick, Natalie held his dick tight, refusing to let go, then whispered, "I can't hear you."

DeVaughn hollered, "Natalie! Natalie! Oh my God, Natalie!" until tears streamed down his face.

There were a lot of things a well-trained pussy could do to a man. Natalie knew all the tricks. Most women weren't skilled enough or patient enough to love a man properly. Women desperately wanted to be loved but didn't have an inclination about how to make a man fall in love with them. If Lola hadn't taken the time to spiritually bond with her husband on an intimate level . . . well, DeVaughn was her husband according to their license but from this day forth, he belonged to Natalie—mind, body, and soul. No piece of paper could define or dissolve their new relationship.

Kissing DeVaughn's tears into hers, Natalie moaned, "I love you, baby."

Concluding her stellar performance, Natalie collapsed onto DeVaughn's chest to bond and gain his full trust because what she was going to ask of DeVaughn next would make him her best friend or her worst enemy.

$\int$EXCAPADE 10

Flint

On the streets and back roads, in alleyways, parks, hot tubs, public restrooms, host homes, gyms, sex clubs, movie theaters, offices, stairways, nightclubs, pubs, dives, inns, hotels, pool halls, motels, bed-and-breakfasts, lovers' beds, and bathhouses of San Francisco, a man could get whatever his dick desired whenever and wherever he chose.

He could get a blow job, solicit a quick fuck, have a fist shoved up his ass, or participate in an orgy. He could have a dick in his ass while sticking his dick in an ass and when he was out of cum he could leave with reprieve or without repercussions. No whining or fussing or cussing or drama from some woman who must have forgotten he already had a mama.

Men fucking men had become a sport of sorts and anything was available by clicking on a dick online on Web sites like Power Men, Bang Bang Boys, Guys Go Crazy, and Fisting Central, and the orgasmic blitz of men in heat sucking dicks in bushes was spreading faster than California forests' wildfires, burning down relationships. Nationally and internationally bisexuality is eradicating heterosexuality and in reality in a few more decades the people who haven't died from AIDS will choose same sex marriages over women who are desiring to push babies in carriages.

Passing by Nick's office at eight o'clock, Flint raised his hand to knock, then changed his mind. Grabbing the knob, he opened the door but he wasn't prepared for what he saw—Nick leaning back in his leather chair, his dick on swole with his hand feverishly pumping up and down.

Nick jumped out of his seat and Flint got an instant hard-on when he saw Nick's thick dick curving sideways—and those huge nuts were unbelievable. Nick's dick was beautiful, and if Flint could drop to his knees and finish the job without Nick's protesting, Nick's dick would be halfway down his throat. Every man, including Nick, had a price that was right.

"Oh damn. Good night, man," Flint said, quickly closing the door, then hurrying back to his office. What Flint had to say could wait until tomorrow if he remembered. Inhaling deeply, Flint tried to keep his heart from pounding against his chest but he couldn't.

Damn, he had no idea Nick's dick was so huge. Flint had to move Nick up from Sunday night ahead of his wife's arriving home on Saturday. Hell, Flint might have to do Nick in the ass tomorrow.

Locking his door, Flint powered on his computer and logged on to www.GayDemon.com, checked out the new galleries, then downloaded a free video and pics of Ebony Shaft and the Black Seducer. Closing his eyes, Flint fantasized that he was seducing Nick. With Nick's knees touching his shoulders, Flint was on top penetrating deep inside his ass. Flint held that image while frantically pumping his shaft. Just when Flint was about to explode, right when his nuts started drawing closer to his body, he circled his thumb and forefinger around his balls, firmly yanking his nuts down. Holding his balls away from his body, Flint took a few deep breaths until his urge to cum all over his computer subsided. The orgasmic sensation was intense but masturbating wasn't getting Flint off the right way. He desperately needed the real thing and Flint knew just where to find the biggest Bay Area dicks.

Flint's dick wanted rough ass-pounding sex with Nick but his mind wanted to penetrate Natalie's pussy. Passing Nick's office, Flint noticed the light was out, which meant Nick had left. He was probably embarrassed that Flint had caught him jerking off.

Racing out of the garage, Flint parked his car curbside on California Street and phoned Natalie to find out why she hadn't returned to the office like he'd told her to. She wasn't the boss, he was.

"Hello, Flint," she answered, sounding super relaxed.

"Natalie, when I tell you to do something, I expect you to

do it. You have one more time to think your balls are bigger than mine and you're fired."

Natalie laughed while saying, "Balls are for dicks. And for confirmation, I do have my own," then she seriously said, "Flint, look. I can't be in the office and working on this plan for you at the same time. The contacts I need are outside of the office."

Hum, maybe she was right but he was still her boss and he was horny as hell. "Meet me at the Hot Tubs on Van Ness in thirty minutes."

"I'm too far away to make that happen tonight. Tomorrow is good."

Tomorrow? Deepening his voice, Flint asked, "Where are you?"

A deeper masculine voice resonated in the background, "Hey, baby. Come back to bed."

Women are such big liars. Flint got this kind of role playing from Samantha; he wasn't about to accept Natalie's manipulative behavior too. He commented, "Working, huh? Then who was that?"

"Hello, who was that?" Natalie asked. "Flint, did you hear that? That sounded like a man in your background. Was he talking to you?"

"Sounds like he was talking to you," Flint countered.

"Did you say something? I can't hear you. Hello? Flint? I can't hear a thing. We must have a bad connection. I'll see you in the morning. Good night, Flint."

That was a battle not worth fighting. Tossing his cell phone on the passenger seat, Flint couldn't get Nick's dick off of his mind. Flint's dick was so hard his corona could've driven them across the Bay Bridge, exited off of University, and parked on Fourth Street. Flint couldn't risk getting fucked in San Francisco and having Samantha or her dad find out he was cheating, and Berkeley was the next best city in the Bay Area for men to have sex with men.

Flashing his "men only" gym membership card and ID, Flint strolled passed the Jacuzzi. Man, with all the big dickheads floating above the bubbles, this was going to be a great night. Flint entered into a locker room filled with naked bodybuilder physiques. Black, white, Asian, and Latino men comprised a smorgasbord of dicks in a nice range of sizes. It had been a while since he'd been there but, man, he was in a jungle of dicks and ready to swing deep up in some ass.

Flint removed his shoes, suit, and shirt, and before he could step out of his underwear, a handsome, deep dark muscular Mr. Wonder Bar stood in front of him, untied the white towel wrapped about his waist, showed Flint his dick that hung damn near to his knees, and smiled.

Instantly Flint got a hard-on.

"Meet me in the Xtreme room in ten minutes," he said, walking away.

Damn, all Flint had time to do was shower. Instead of relaxing in the Jacuzzi with the dozen of naked men, he was off to the Xtreme room to have sex. Samantha was ignorant for believing her rationing out pussy once a week would make him appreciate her more. Sex in the city and surrounding areas of San Francisco was plentiful. But Flint had to admit his promiscuity had turned him into a certified closet bisexual freak who liked pussy almost as much as he loved dick.

When he opened the door, Mr. Wonder Bar was spread-eagle in the black leather sex swing. He rattled the metal chains hanging from the ceiling and demanded, "Come fuck me in the ass."

"Whew." Dropping his towel to the floor, Flint was relieved that he was a bottom because Mr. Wonder Bar was so fine he probably could've convinced Flint to let him take his adult male virginity. If women could reclaim their virginity, so could Flint. Easing on a condom, Flint reached for the complimentary tube of lube.

"You don't need that shit for me," he grunted. "I'ma real man."

The lubricant slipped from Flint's hand as he immediately circled the guy's asshole with his dickhead, then he shoved his dick inside the guy's muscular sunken asshole.

"Yeah!" was all he kept repeating before closing his eyes. The bass in his voice turned Flint on more.

Gripping the chains, Flint pumped Mr. Wonder Bar faster than the image of Nick jerking off. Flint was on the edge and glad it didn't take long for both of them to cum. When the guy was done, Flint picked up his towel, showered, and quickly left the gym.

Driving home to San Francisco, Flint decided to go through San Rafael and take the Golden Gate Bridge. The moon was full, the night was clear, and he was totally confused.

Fuck! Flint! Why do you do that shit, man? What is your fucking problem? You're not gay. You're not straight. You're trying to convince yourself you're bisexual but you're not. You should become asexual and keep your dick to yourself. After having sex with Samantha, you hate her fucking ass. After fucking her dad, you hate yourself. When you leave these bathhouses, you wish you were fucking dead. You love getting your shit off, man, but you hate everyone around you immediately after you cum. You're either going to kill yourself or somebody else.

Flint's subconscious was right. He felt the hatred raging inside of him. What made him so angry? His whole life was one big lie, and to top that, he had been bought by his wife and her dad. But, the oppressed become the oppressor. Samantha and her father had fucked him, so Flint planned on hurting Nick and Natalie because he had the power to.

Deep in his soul Flint felt it. He harbored the kind of hatred that could explode during road rage or over a too-sweet glass of lemonade served without ice on a scorching summer day. One day Justin Flint knew he was going to snap, lose his motherfuckin' mind, and strangle somebody to death in the midst of fucking them.

But why?

SEXCAPADE 11

DeVaughn

DeVaughn had never lied to his wife and he didn't plan on starting today just because a piece of ass gave him head and made him feel like the man. Yes, he was Natalie's lover but no matter how hard she tried to wedge herself between his wife and him DeVaughn wasn't falling for Natalie. So what if they swung on the regular, he'd never said, "I do," to her. DeVaughn wasn't trying to degrade or play charades or let an orgasm rain on his marital parade, but he'd be lying if he'd said, "I'm not afraid."

His wife was open to threesomes, foursomes, and then some but there was one thing Lola wouldn't do . . . strap-on. DeVaughn wanted to take his freakiness to the ultimate level but not with a man. He'd done everything imaginable with his wife, so he couldn't understand why she wouldn't do this for him. Maybe Lola thought they'd both end up being bisexual. Was it fair for Lola to enjoy being with another woman but deny him the experience of—not being with a man but—knowing how anal penetration felt? DeVaughn had no reservations about asking his wife but was sure there was no way he'd ask Natalie.

Natalie's unprecedented sexuality scared the hell out of him. It was like she could read his vibes but he couldn't read her mind. Not knowing what she'd do next excited him. Natalie had made love to him like no other woman, including his wife. But there was no way DeVaughn was fucking up his life or his lifestyle for chilling deep inside some good pussy. He was clear. He loved Lola. But he was no fool. If Lola questioned him, he'd plead the fifth. Or if she didn't question him, he'd pretend everything was cool but knew it wasn't.

Natalie's overt sexuality frightened him.

Before last night DeVaughn had never fallen to his knees and slept at the feet of a bona fide freak. Those luxuries were reserved for his wife. Lola was his college sweetheart. His confidante. His best friend. Lola's openness and honesty revealing to him her attraction to men and women made him love her more. He didn't have to sneak or cheat on his wife. She said, "DeVaughn, as long as you keep me first, I'll always keep you first. But if you ever put another woman or man before me, don't bother trying to explain, we're done."

Lola knew he didn't roll that way with guys but she never took anything or anyone for granted. Now DeVaughn questioned if he'd put Natalie before his wife by spending the night out. Lola only explained the significance of him always keeping her in the number one position once, but the way she stared into his eyes without blinking sent chills through his body. He never forgot the sincerity of his wife's words. Aside from honoring their wedding vows, keeping her first was the only thing his wife demanded of him.

Allowing his feelings for Natalie to escalate made DeVaughn nervous. Although he told Lola where he was going, he hadn't planned on staying all night. Had he crossed the line? How was he going to explain spending the entire night at a hotel with Natalie? Natalie was supposed to be a little something on the side not the main attraction.

The orange sunrise shimmering off the ocean and beaming through the ceiling-to-floor windows wasn't more beautiful than waking up and seeing Natalie. Damn, how did she do that shit? Nobody in real life looked that damn sexy when they woke up. She must've freshened up in the middle of the night while he was asleep or something.

Fluttering her eyelids, Natalie said, "Good morning, baby," then kissed his dick first then his lips. Natalie's breasts were perfectly round and it must've taken her months of wearing those large nipple suction cups Lola wore to create those perfect half-inch thimble-size nipples.

Quickly DeVaughn protested, "Oh no. Don't wake him up. Let him chill. I gotta get my behind home."

Ignoring his request, Natalie pressed her fingers deep into his moneybag—the indention directly in front of his anus that lead straight to his prostate—and said, "I thought you knew. Breakfast is the most important meal of the day."

She popped his dick in her mouth, sucking like he was a Super Blow Pop. All DeVaughn could say was, "Ou, baby, please." The remaining word "stop" crossed his mind but not his lips.

Natalie's finger slid from his moneybag inside his ass. Every time she strummed her finger, a lump lodged in his throat as he hummed, "Um, um, um."

DeVaughn watched her head bob as she slobbered on his dick with each lick. Damn that shit looked so delicious he wished he could lick his dick. Oh my God, that shit felt good when her hand tightened, then slid up and down his slippery shaft with her finger softly strumming inside his ass. Natalie's mouth was hot and each time her lips traveled south her hand stroked upward while her finger strummed his prostate. So much shit happened at the same time DeVaughn didn't know what sensation to focus on.

His eyes rolled toward the back of his head, his mouth gaped opened as his entire body trembled curling up his toes. The cum inside his nuts gathered into a bunch huddling inside them.

When Natalie's hand slid to the base of his dick nestling above his balls, DeVaughn said, "Aw shit." Natalie knew the ejaculation delay trick too?

Her thumb pressed against his underside vein, trapping his sperm inside his balls the same way he stuck his thumb into his garden hose to stop the flow of water. Natalie held her thumb there for a few seconds while she continued sucking and strumming, building the pressure inside his nuts. Just like water bursting through that garden hose, when Natalie removed her finger from his frenulum and his ass at the same time . . . "Oh my God! Natalie," DeVaughn yelled, blasting cum all over her titties like Silly Putty sticking to a window.

Massaging his cum into her breasts, Natalie smiled, then said, "Call me if you're free to be lunch."

DeVaughn thought, The hell I will.

Lying in bed, he let Natalie shower and leave first while he tried to come up with a story to tell his wife. Checking his missed calls, he saw that Lola had phoned five times. The more she called, the more nervous DeVaughn had become. He couldn't turn off his phone, so after the first missed call from her he silenced the ringer. Turning off the phone would've been a dead giveaway that he was guilty of whatever he was doing. DeVaughn couldn't return any of her calls last night because he was too caught up in Natalie's sweet tight pussy. And he refused to call his wife back this morning. Lola was a human lie detector and he was afraid she'd immediately sense the lying tone in his voice.

"Bye, baby. Call me later," Natalie said, strutting out the door in a fresh salmon-colored suit. Her hair had gone from halfway down her back to short and super curly.

DeVaughn's chin hung in disbelief. How in the hell did Natalie transform into a totally new look in twenty minutes? And when did she bring in that suit she had on? Women.

Taking a hot shower, he delayed the inevitable. Putting on the same clothes and underwear he'd worn the day before, he paid cash to the checkout attendant of the hotel to avoid having Lola see the charge on her credit card. Reluctantly he headed home. The drive was long but not nearly long enough.

Creeping up the hill to their home in the Grass Valley area of the Oakland Hills, where some of the professional basketball stars and football players, famous and once-upon-a-time media-ridden celebrities of the sixties and seventies lived, DeVaughn glanced out over the cliff to the Oakland Zoo in Knowland Park trying to conjure up a believable lie.

"Baby, on my way home last night a truck filled with almost a thousand gallons of gasoline overturned, exploded, and burned down the MacArthur Maze. I got stuck in traffic, so I stopped to have a drink, had one too many, and fell asleep in my car." Nah, Lola would slap his face, then kick his ass out for telling that obvious lie.

True the truck did crash, the fire did rage, and sections of the bridge actually collapsed at three something in the morning which was well after the 2:00 a.m. last call for alcohol in the entire state of California. Plus the news coverage showed there was no traffic jam and the only person injured was the driver, who allegedly had an extensive criminal record. One bad decision by that guy's employer to give that driver a chance to make an honest living may have cost the owner his company. DeVaughn prayed his poor judgment not to go home last night didn't cost him his marriage. He had to come up with something quick.

"Baby, I lost my cell phone." That wasn't good enough because she'd ask where he lost it and one question would lead to a series of other questions.

Cruising into their driveway, DeVaughn didn't see a deer, a raccoon, a wild turkey, a skunk, a snake, not even a rabbit. Where were those damn mountain lions when he needed them? If he were attacked, his wife wouldn't care where he'd been. Lola was scared of any kind of wild animal, so why she bought a big-ass house that could fall off of the cliff with a 5.5 earthquake and land in the tigers' cage at the zoo below was beyond him.

Entering the house through the garage, DeVaughn took a deep breath. He had to come up with something quick.

Lola was sitting on the edge of the bed putting on her shoes, getting ready to leave for work. If he'd waited another ten minutes he wouldn't have had to explain anything for at least ten hours. Damn, why hadn't he thought about that option? He could've stayed at the hotel and had a real breakfast.

Glancing up at him, Lola asked, "DeVaughn, you okay, baby? I tried calling you five times. Where's your phone?"

Every letter of the alphabet scrabbled in his head but if DeVaughn were playing Scrabble he wouldn't get points for even a simple one-syllable word. Lola stared in his eyes, then kissed his lips. That's what DeVaughn appreciated about his wife. Even when she had cause, she never doubted him.

Immediately his tongue shifted into gear without engaging his brain and DeVaughn started babbling, "Baby, my car broke down in the Montclair Hills, I had no reception. Had to knock on a stranger's door, use their phone to call Roadside Assistance. Roadside tried calling me back but the call kept dropping and they didn't find me, so I slept in my car all night. Baby, my back is killing me," DeVaughn said, pausing to rub his lower back, then continued, "When they finally showed up this morning and fixed the car, I was stuck in traffic on Highway Thirteen. Baby, you don't know what I've been through."

Lola took two steps away from him and said, "Um, hmm. You're right. I don't know what happened but I do know that wasn't it. I'll give you one more opportunity to tell me the truth. But next time I want you to think before you speak. I have to meet an important client in an hour. I'll talk to you when I get home."

"Baby, you just reminded me. I was so stressed out, I forgot to tell you. I got an offer for a job paying one million dollars!"

Lola laughed so hard her mascara streamed down her cheeks. "DeVaughn, stop it! 'Cause if I stop laughing, I swear I'ma hurt you. You must think I'm a fool. You spent the night with Natalie! You're taking this swinging thing to another level. Don't you say shit when I fuck Nick!" Brushing by him, Lola said, "Move out my way, I've got to go."

Blocking Lola's path, DeVaughn placed his hands on her hips and frowned, praying she wasn't serious about getting even. A strange energy resonated throughout his body. Had his wife been with Nick last night? Maybe he should've been the one questioning her. He knew the rhythm of Lola's body. Something about her hips felt different like she was slightly pulling away from him. Lola's body tensed as though she didn't want him touching her. Trying to shake it off, DeVaughn stroked his wife's breasts and she gasped, holding her breath three seconds too long.

His forehead shrunk. "Lola, do you see me laughing?"

Lola's anger escalated. "DeVaughn, do you see me laughing? I hope she was worth your lying to my face."

"I'm not lying. I have a good chance of getting this million-dollar job."

He heard Lola mentally calculating their monthly increase in income. "Are you serious? What company? Doing what?" Her eyebrows damn near touched. "It is legal, right?"

"Baby, yes. All I have to do is present the best marketing plan for this new restaurant and I've got the job. So I'ma need you to help me out."

Resuming her laughter, his wife kissed him on the cheek, retrieved one of those makeup removal towelettes from her purse, dabbed under each eye, and said, "I'll call you later. And make sure you answer your phone 'cause if this is the same marketing plan that Natalie needs, you might as well pack your shit and leave before I get home." Lola slammed the door to emphasize her point.

Was Natalie trying to break up his marriage? She'd sworn him to secrecy, knowing that Lola already knew.

Watching his wife walk away, DeVaughn didn't care how upset she was, Lola had a few too many happy dips in her hips to say he hadn't fucked her at all yesterday.

SEXCAPADE 12

DeVaughn

How could he have been so inconsiderate of his faithful wife?

A second thought, a simple, "No I can't make it," to Natalie, or regurgitating his well-rehearsed line, "I love my wife," could've kept DeVaughn home last night. After his company had downsized and let him go without severance pay, Lola provided his food, clothing, and shelter. She never complained about him not working nor did she make the classifieds the default home page on their computer. Lola was the woman who uplifted his manhood, stroked his ego, and sucked his dick any time he wanted her to. Wasn't her commitment to him enough for him to remain loyal to her?

Logically, yes. But the situation was more complicated than he'd initially imagined. Fucking a fine-ass wife every day, then having his wife's permission to lick another sexy woman's pussy opened the doors to making DeVaughn's wildest wet dreams come true. The enjoyment that overwhelmed him during anal sex with a woman other than his wife left him wondering if he could anonymously draw up a petition to legalize polygamy or adopt a concubine or advertise for a harem.

Why had Natalie deliberately chosen him as the first lover to fuck her in the ass? One thing DeVaughn knew was that Natalie knew, like with most men, he didn't have a clue. The aftermath of sex wasn't supposed to be more difficult than solving a riddle. Why hadn't Nick shown up Monday night? What was the real reason DeVaughn had sent Lola home alone that night?

Anatomically the vein on the underside of his dick had a pulse but obviously it didn't have a brain. In retrospect DeVaughn wished he'd stayed at home instead of making that hotel reservation without hesitation, jumping in his car, and driving more than thirty miles across the Bay and Golden Gate Bridges into Sausalito. At any point he could've turned around but his dick was on autopilot cruising to its destination . . . good pussy. Why was he tripping so hard? Lola wouldn't dare put him out for making one bad decision.

The promise of Natalie's lips slobbering on his dick rendered him unconscious. DeVaughn would do the dumbest shit to cum in a woman's mouth and most women, especially the one who'd sucked him senseless, knew that. Replaying the sequence of events that occurred yesterday, blood detoured to his dick. If only he could borrow that memory zapper used in the movie *Men in Black*, he could legitimately forget everything that happened. DeVaughn fought to erase the last regrettable twenty-four hours from his memory.

Zooming in his car, then shuffling his feet along concrete, DeVaughn raced all over Oakland, Emeryville, and San Francisco, buying things to aide in maintaining his wife's trust without having to make a confession. He prayed the monetary pacifiers would sooth her temperament long enough for him to hold her in his arms and make love to her. Methodically DeVaughn rendered forethought to each makeup gift on his list.

His first stop was Victoria's Secret in Emeryville. That crimson-and-gold thong teddy like the one Natalie had worn for him hung on a rack near the door. The one he picked up wasn't Lola's size, so he put it back, searching the tags on the remaining outfits but he didn't have any luck until an assistant approached him.

"Can I help you find something?" she asked, smiling generously.

"Um, yes, sure. I'm looking for a sexy outfit."

Raising her eyebrows, she asked, "For?"

Sticking out his chest, DeVaughn sternly replied, "My lovely wife."

The way the assistant said, "Follow me," made him feel she didn't believe him but this shopping ordeal wasn't about her.

The all-white thong teddy with beaded embroidered bra cups and the sheer ass-length robe was definitely a better choice for his wife. Heading across the street to ALDO's he charged the sexiest four-inch split-toe stilettos with decorative jewels. Striding over to Bath & Body Works, DeVaughn purchased two dozen white candles, six small heated oil lamps, three bottles of lavender oil, a bag of white tealight candles, then he stopped at Godiva for a chocolate-covered banana decorated with fresh strawberries.

On the way to his car DeVaughn couldn't resist buying two dozen white roses from Daphne's Flowers. Speeding downtown to San Francisco, he went directly to Macy's perfume counter, bought a bottle of her favorite perfume, Trésor, then dashed across the street to the garage. Stopping in front of the jeweler's window, the most hypnotizing onyx and opal anklet lit up DeVaughn's eyes, so he bought her that too. DeVaughn's last stop was the florist on Grande Avenue in Oakland. A quick purchase of a dozen of his wife's favorite gardenias completed his outing, so he headed to his car.

They say emotional spending can put you in debt. In this case, DeVaughn prayed his investment would pay off.

When his phone rang, he juggled the flowers to one arm. His car keys dangled beside his head as he pressed the cell phone to his ear, answering on the third ring, "Hey, honey, what's up? How's your day going?"

"You sound happy and winded. Still up to no good?"

"You'll see how good I am when you get home, woman. Did your meeting go well?"

"In fact, it was excellent. I got a lucrative job offer from one of my clients but I turned her down. If you get offered the job you told me about, then I'll reconsider her offer but one of us has to be stable you know."

Oh, his wife would be everything except stable when he laid hands on her. Anxiously DeVaughn wanted to make love to his wife, then fuck the shit out of her until she begged him to stop. He smiled from ear to ear, admiring himself in his car window. Undoubtedly he had the best wife. A woman who not only believed in him but supported him and never made him feel like he was less of a man simply because she earned more money. But there was no way he'd let her accept a job making more money than him. This was his first chance to prove he was the man without having to pull out his dick.

"What time are you coming home?" he asked.

"Actually, I'm on my way home now. I have to hop a flight to Las Vegas for a dinner meeting tonight with a VIP client."

"Oh, baby, that's perfect and so are you. I can't wait to taste you before you leave. I love you, honey, bye."

No sooner than he ended the call his phone rang again. "Yes, baby," DeVaughn said, laying the gardenias on the passenger seat next to the roses.

"Wow, did sucking your dick have that affect on you. Now I'm your baby?" Natalie teasingly asked.

"Oh, it's you. Sorry I thought you were my wife calling back."

Funny how DeVaughn emphasized the words "my wife" with such conviction. Wasn't like he had much of that dedication when Natalie sucked his dick. Reminiscing about the incredible blow job he'd gotten this morning, DeVaughn shivered as he inhaled the scented lavender oil that spilled from one of his bags. Lowering his four windows, he leaned against the door of his car facing the Washington Mutual ATM, then crossed his feet at his ankles.

"Did I catch you at a bad time?" Natalie playfully asked.

"For you, yes. For me, no. I want to thank you," DeVaughn said, reaching his hand inside the car window, rubbing the silky teddy between his fingers.

"Thank me? What for?"

His voice escalated, "For making a damn fool out of me, that's what!"

People passing by stared at him. He didn't give a damn. He didn't know them and they sure as hell didn't know him.

Calmly Natalie replied, "I have no idea what you're yelling about."

"Don't play that 'I'm so innocent' bullshit with me! You! Tried to come between me and my wife! You had me ask her to put together a business plan, told me to keep it on the under, knowing damn well you'd already told her."

Natalie firmly said, "No, you're wrong. I never said a word to her. I swear."

If it wasn't Natalie that told Lola, then the only other person who could've told Lola was Nick. Now the extra swing in his wife's hips made more sense. DeVaughn didn't care, either way he'd laugh last when he stole Natalie's job.

"Look," DeVaughn said, lowering his voice as he sat in his car, "I apologize. If what I'm about to try works, I'll have you to thank. I'll explain later. I've got to go."

Revving his engine, DeVaughn gave thanks to the Creator for blessing him so. After all he'd been through as a child, it was a miracle he was alive. His wife completed him. She gave him stability, nobility, and strength to hold his head high with dignity and pride when no one else believed in him. There was no way he could repay his wife for all she'd done. The only thing he had was his word, so he had to tell her the truth. Just not before she told him the truth about what she was doing. Then DeVaughn would have leverage to dismiss putting Natalie before his wife. Actually DeVaughn felt relieved believing their infidelity and dishonesty was equal.

When he got home, one would've thought DeVaughn was a human tornado the way he vacuumed the house, lit the candles and the oil lamps, neatly positioned Lola's lingerie across the bed, and filled their Jacuzzi with warm water.

When his wife walked in the door, he greeted her with open arms, a large bouquet of gardenias, and a hard dick.

"Ou, baby. What brought on all of this?" Lola asked, kissing him tenderly.

DeVaughn placed his lips over hers and held them there for a moment. Kinda like the way Natalie had done to him yesterday. Instantly he felt his wife's energy resonating throughout his body. This time her hips moved closer toward him. Damn, out of all the years he'd been married, why hadn't they made this type of connection before? Perhaps because before yesterday he hadn't known how to spiritually make love to his wife's mind, body, and soul.

Placing the flowers in her arms, DeVaughn carried Lola in his arms into their bedroom. Slowly he undressed her, then escorted her to the tub. He stepped in first, then extended his hand to her, tenderly leading her to him. Relaxing into the warm water, he rested his back against the tub, lowered her body in front of his, then handed her a flute of icy cold champagne. Surrounded by silence, he stroked her hair as they relaxed until their fingers and toes resembled dried raisins.

After drying her body from head to toe, DeVaughn toweled his body, then escorted his wife to the bedroom and dressed her under the fading sunlight beaming through their bedroom window. There she stood barefoot and beautiful in all-white lingerie. He braced his back against the pillows, folded his legs, then guided her hips atop his lap and waited until the erection of his dick subsided.

Slowly he pushed his limp dick inside his wife's pussy and they both felt the fireworks exploding inside of them. Her energy flooded his body as she moaned, "Oh, baby, I love you."

"I love you too," DeVaughn whispered.

And he did. More than she'd ever know. Sometimes doing the wrong thing led to doing the right thing, if only one could learn to forgive, not the other, but themselves. During their quiet bonding, DeVaughn loved his wife more than he loved himself. So much that he would readily give his life if it meant sparing hers.

He exhaled into her breath as she inhaled into his. He tried on his wife everything that Natalie had tried on him, and to his surprise it worked. Had his wife been with another man? In the moment, whatever his wife had done didn't matter. Soul mating intimately and sexually with his wife gave him the strength he needed to stay focused and keep his wife first. As for Natalie, she was still important to him and by no means did DeVaughn plan to stop making love to her. In a unique way, having sex with Natalie made DeVaughn love his wife more.

$\int$EXCAPADE 13

Nick

Over somebody else's dead body, today was definitely not going to be a repeat of yesterday. Nick wasn't angry enough to kill anyone. He didn't have that much hatred inside of him. But he was furious. Inhaling air, filling his lungs to their maximum capacity, Nick blew his frustrations into the fleeting clutter of papers on his desk, trying to figure out why women were so damn scandalous when things didn't go their way. One fucking slipup and he was supposed to kiss Natalie's ass begging her for forgiveness. Fuck Natalie.

It was Wednesday morning and Natalie sashayed by his office looking ravishing as usual. Her hair was in curly shoulder-length locks bouncing to the rhythmic sway of her hips. The light scent of Natalie's warm caramel fragrance invaded Nick's office. Her canary long-sleeve crewneck dress stopped midway on her thighs. A forest green zipper stretched along the center of her back from the nape of her neck to her thighs, separating her firm gluteus maximus. The lime and forest-colored, eel skin, open-toe sling backs Nick had bought her matched the bitch's outfit perfectly. Nick didn't mean to consider her a bitch. He had more respect than that for Natalie and himself but Natalie had stooped to an unexpected low.

The difference for Nick between today and yesterday was today he cared a little less about Natalie. Fucking DeVaughn outside their foursomes, Natalie was spreading herself too thin and it was just a matter of time before she turned into a slut. Nick didn't mind having a freaky woman. Actually Nick loved having an uninhibited woman who expressed her desires in and out of the bedroom but he was not going to fuck a slut. With his new position, Nick could hire any decent fuckable secretary of his choice and give her cash bonuses based upon how well she performed her other duties as assigned.

"Hey, Nick," Natalie said, smiling brightly, standing in the hallway outside his door. "You wanna work on our plan at ten?"

Firmly, Nick said, "No, you go ahead without me. Lola's flight just arrived from Vegas, so I'm meeting her for lunch again today to help me out. Call DeVaughn. Being unemployed and all, I'm sure he's got time to assist you with all of your needs. Take care."

Natalie's jaw dropped for a split second. Swiftly lifting her chin and cheeks into a contrived smile, she was speechless. Had Nick said something that . . . oh damn. Mentioning Lola's name rattled Natalie's nerves? Not nearly as much as him seeing his ring still lying on his desk where she'd left it. Natalie could tell him about her fucking or hooking up with DeVaughn but . . . hell yeah. She was concerned about him doing Lola. And they both knew Lola had the contacts, not DeVaughn.

Checkmate. Nick had Natalie cornered because he'd already warned Lola that DeVaughn would ask for a marketing plan for Natalie. Nick was relieved when Lola told him, "Nick, I won't do it. DeVaughn is my husband and unequivocally I love him. But woman to woman, faced to my face, the way Natalie kissed then dismissed me the other night when you didn't show up let me know that Natalie was down for Natalie. Not you. Not me. Not even DeVaughn. I'm not the type of woman to raise my voice. I say what I mean and I mean what I say. I can party all night with Natalie but if the ship is sinking and there was only one life preserver, I hope she knows the dead man's survival float 'cause I'd float by watching her drown in her own deception."

Nick laughed inside after Lola had said that. Natalie couldn't tread water or float, let alone swim. She'd joyfully lounge on the nude beaches they'd visited but she refused to let her hair get soaked with salty seawater or chlorinated pool water.

Today Nick was simply having a nooner with Lola but thanks to Natalie, in that brief moment of envy, he felt her pensive energy and her fears unraveling the ribbon that once wrapped her perfect plan.

Damn, Lola's timing was impeccable. Answering her call, Nick said, "Hold on just a sec," then told Natalie, "Please come in and have a seat."

Frowning, Natalie sat in chair facing Nick, then crossed her sexy legs.

"Hey, I was just thinking about you," Nick spoke into his receiver with a wide smile brighter than the sunshine beaming through his window.

"Oh, you were, huh? That's great," Lola said. "What were you thinking?"

"How we could spend maybe an extra hour or two at lunch today. I have something special for you." Moving his lips closer to his cell phone, Nick stared at Natalie as if he were talking to her, then he whispered to Lola, "You know how much I love to suck toes, well I have one of those purifying footbaths scheduled for you where they soak your feet for an hour to extract all the toxins from your beautiful body. When you're done, I'm gonna suck your toes until you cum. What do you think?" Nick picked up his diamond ring, eyed it for a moment, and then placed it back on his desk.

Natalie's breasts rose with excitement and fell with disappointment. Her legs grew closer together, wrapping her foot behind her ankle. Nick would bet money that if he finger fucked her right now, her G-spot would gush secretions like a water fountain.

Lola moaned in his ear, "Sounds sweet to me. I'll see you shortly."

"Oh, before you go, don't forget to bring my package," Nick said.

"What package?" Lola asked. "You're supposed to bring me the outline for your BP, remember?"

"I've got that but you know what package," Nick said, gathering his business plan papers in front of him.

"Oh, no problem," Lola said, still sounding slightly confused.

There was no package. Nick knew Lola would eventually conclude that he'd meant for her to bring condoms. They would need those too but his performance was intended for the one-woman audience seated in his front row facing him.

For once in the past forty-eight hours, Nick was in control. Jotting down his remaining thoughts, he prioritized the outline Lola requested for his business plan.

Clearing her throat, Natalie said, "And you asked me to come inside because you wanted?"

Shifting his eyes upward without moving his head, Nick said, "Oh, I'm sorry. There's nothing you can do for me, Natalie. I thought you wanted something. I'm done with you."

Squinting her eyes, stiffening her shoulders, and tightening her lips, Natalie did exactly as Nick expected, she stormed out of his office without a response.

Maybe he'd fuck Lola in the ass today to see if that would help expedite getting his business plan. Who was he kidding? The only reason Nick wanted to fuck Lola in the ass was because DeVaughn had fucked Natalie in the ass. At least then he'd feel even with DeVaughn.

Men were born territorial and competitive. Seemingly women were too. Slipping his iPhone into his jacket pocket, Nick cleared his desk, shutdown his computer, turned off the lights, and closed his door. It was time to let Ms. Coleman guess where he was all night when he didn't return until to-morrow morning.

Driving along Geary Street to the ocean where he and Nata-lie often went, Nick parked his car in front of the totem near the Cliff House. He couldn't resist revisiting the lookout point where Natalie had hopped over the barrier, stood on the cliff, removed all of her clothes, then beckoned for him to join her in broad daylight.

As he reminisced about the good old days, a smile crossed Nick's face as he inhaled the salty ocean breeze, watching the waves build momentum before crashing against the cliff and splashing upon the shore. That day when he'd jumped across that barrier to join Natalie, she pointed out over the water and said, "See, Nick. Isn't that beautiful?"

"What?" he'd asked her, squinting to see something other than sailboats.

"The horizon, silly. Isn't it great not knowing what's on the other side? It's like life, Nick. We can only see so far. Beyond what we can see, we must have faith. We must trust our in-stincts. That's what animals do, Nick. Animals don't read maps or ask for directions. They trust their instincts. If it doesn't feel right, we shouldn't do it. If it feels good," Natalie said that day, standing completely nude without a care, "we should allow ourselves to be free. Fuck me, Nick. Right here on this cliff, right now."

Since that was in the beginning of their relationship, Nick had had his reservations but he'd done it anyway. Not for him-self. For Natalie. Natalie was the one woman who could con-vince him to do anything and although he was pissed at her,

Nick still loved her. If he professed that he'd stopped loving Natalie overnight, he'd be lying to himself.

"Hey, Nick," said a familiar voice resonating from behind him.

Looking over his shoulder, he saw Lola frantically waving. Walking toward her, Nick passed the totem, opening one side of the double glass doors. He waited for Lola to enter, then he smiled at the grizzly bear statue in the doorway. With the entry to the restaurant surrounded by ceiling-to-floor clear glass, Nick still couldn't figure out how Natalie had sucked his dick in front of that bear without any one noticing.

"Nick, you're a typical Aries man. You're a big kid sometimes, you know that? I like it," Lola said.

Lola was simply gorgeous. Unlike Natalie, Lola didn't need all the clothes and makeup and hairstyles. Lola's smile radiated throughout his body. Inhaling deeply, Nick exhaled, then smiled at Lola. Motioning for the hostess, Nick held up two fingers.

Lola gently grabbed his bicep, "I already have a table for us overlooking that cliff you were out there standing on forever. That's why I had to come and get you. Before you fell over."

Lola was talking but Nick hadn't heard a word. They sat and as he glanced out over the Pacific Ocean, watching the seagulls swarm high in the air before settling on the water, for the first five minutes all Nick thought of was Natalie.

"Can I get you something to drink?" the waiter asked.

Ordering for both of them, Nick requested, "A bottle of your finest champagne, please."

"Certainly, sir," the waiter said, walking away.

"Natalie, I'm sorry, I mean Lola, can I confide in you?"

"Who me? Or Natalie?" Lola sarcastically asked.

Nick smiled without parting his lips, then said, "You know what I meant. Anyway, I have a million dollars to invest into my future and I want you to handle this for me."

"Nick, that's a lot of money, baby. Are you sure? I know you mentioned for me not to do a plan for Natalie under any circumstances but, come on, a million dollars? What if your plan isn't successful? Then what? Are you mentally and financially prepared to risk that much of your money? There's only one way investing a million dollars makes sense to me. Are you starting your own business?"

"Not really," Nick said, wondering whether he should go through with this.

"Not really. Hmm. So you'll invest a million dollars in someone else's vision? Nick, you're smart and totally capable of owning your own business. Take your million dollars and open your own restaurant."

Wow, Lola had confidence in his abilities. Nick wanted to own a restaurant but the responsibilities of hiring, firing, and trying to make sure his employees didn't steal from him or fake on-the-job injuries were ones he'd rather have for someone else's business. At least if Dons and Divas failed Nick could work for someone else. "You honestly believe in me or you're just saying what you think I want to hear?"

Lola asked, "Then why involve me?"

"Because," Nick paused, then confidently said, "I have faith in you."

Raising her eyebrows, Lola countered, "Nick, your faith is

misplaced. Are you sure you want to invest a million dollars into a business plan for somebody's business? If that's what you want I'll make sure you get an excellent plan. But I won't accept more than two hundred and fifty thousand."

Lola made Nick an offer so profitable he said, "Let's do it. We can go straight to my bank and I can hand you a cashier's check today for two hundred fifty thousand. But there are two things you must promise me. One, I will have what I need before Monday morning and, two, you won't share my plan with anyone, not even DeVaughn."

The waiter returned with a chilled bottle, poured two glasses of champagne, awaited Nick's approval, then left. Raising his glass, Nick looked Lola in her eyes and asked, "Deal?"

Lola's smile was wide as she answered with a hunch of her shoulders, "Deal," clinking her glass against his.

Nick assumed her hunch was in favor of him starting his own business but a man should never take on more than he's capable of handling, and right now Nick wasn't mentally ready to own a restaurant. Maybe in another two years he could partner in business with Lola.

They finished lunch, went to the bank, then straight to the hotel. Now that his business was in order, it was time for Nick to show Lola how a real man pleases a woman. All that straight fucking he'd watched in too many porn videos was for mindless jackasses screwing like rabbits. Thrusting deep inside a woman's pussy trying to knock the bottom out was straight amateurism and didn't require any fore- or afterthought, and surely any man busting a nut while not caring if the woman was satisfied wasn't worthy of him pounding his chest. In the end, neither the man nor the woman was totally pleased.

After Natalie taught him how to make love to her, Nick no longer watched those "ou" and "ah" videos with uneducated men shoving their dicks in women's pussies, assholes, and throats like they were fucking blow-up dolls.

While Lola was getting her footbath, Nick enjoyed a long hot steamy shower. Lathering up his dick, ass, and balls several times, he then rinsed thoroughly. Other than getting a prostrate exam, Nick had never let a man shove anything up his ass. But he was cool with twirling the first notch of his finger inside his own asshole to clean it out before letting a woman suck his dick, tea bag his balls, or lick his ass.

By the time Lola entered the room Nick had finished showering. Greeting her at the door, he held her in his arms asking, "How was your treatment?"

"Oh my goodness. I had no idea that cleansing your feet in minerals could extract so much dirt from your body."

Correcting her, Nick said, "Impurities."

"No, baby. You had to see all the particles floating in that water after I was done to believe it. Give me a moment to freshen up," Lola said, making her way to the bathroom.

While Lola prepared her body for him, Nick began working on his body for her. Sitting on the edge of the bed, he placed his hands palms up in his lap and inhaled deeply, then held his breath for five seconds. Gradually exhaling, Nick focused on relaxing his body in order to selflessly please Lola. He was executing another key element Natalie had taught him—a man has to give before he gets, otherwise his woman is not properly prepared to receive him. No two women were the same nor did women like repetition, so Nick centered himself in the moment to cater to Lola. With the last ten deep breaths, he began squeezing the muscles at the base of his dick to heighten the sexual energy flowing throughout his body.

A dick was merely fleshy tissue and could be lengthened by constant stretching but in order to strengthen his dick Nick regularly exercised the muscle he used to do dick curls. During the swingers sessions Natalie and Lola loved how his dick was as strong as a hammer.

When Lola finished showering, she emerged from the bathroom. Because he was used to all the foursomes they'd had, this was the first time Nick witnessed Lola's raw beauty. His energy raced to his fluttering heart, rising to his throat, choking his airway. This time Nick had to breath deeply. DeVaughn was one lucky man. So was he but the difference was Nick didn't have a beautiful goddess like Lola to go home to every day.

"You look amazing," Nick said, slowly twirling Lola around. Stepping close to her body, he held Lola, leaning her head to his chest.

Lola whispered, "Nick, this doesn't feel right. Our sexcapades are fun and all"—Lola's voice trembled—"but I'm not supposed to have these loving emotions for any man other than my husband."

"You're not alone. I feel the same way you do. Something this right can't be wrong but I never want to lose your respect. If you want to stop here, we can leave." Nick had already lost Natalie's respect. He didn't want to ruin his friendship with Lola too.

"No, Nick. Don't stop. I need to know if what I feel for my husband is real or if I'm committed to upholding my marital vows because society dictates that's what a good wife is supposed to do. I want you to make love to me, Nick. Can you do that for me?"

"Lola, if you were my woman, there's nothing I wouldn't do for you." In their moment of sincerity, Lola reinforced what Natalie had made him suppress. Nick wanted more than being a great lover. Nick wanted to be somebody's husband.

As promised, Nick laid Lola's precious naked body across the bed and slid his tongue between her toes. He reminded himself that the essence of foreplay was in the slowness and patience of his approach not in the hard erection of his throbbing dick. Kissing the arch of Lola's foot, Nick worked his way up to her big toe and buried it in his mouth while massaging her foot.

Relaxing on her back, Lola exhaled, "Umm, that feels so good."

Taking her other foot into his hands he kissed each of her toes saving the big one for last. Nick wanted to take his time with Lola. If DeVaughn wasn't on his job of fully pleasing his woman, she'd not only fall asleep in his arms thinking about Nick, she'd come back for more good loving. If she did, that two-fifty that he'd given her would become the best investment Nick had made into their future.

Being that he was the cunnilingus champion and Lola had the prettiest pussy next to Natalie's his tongue secretly hardened inside his mouth preparing to lick her clit dry. Waking up Lola's senses, slowly Nick kissed and massaged from her ankles to the back of her knees up to her legs, ever so gently kneading his fingers into her muscles. Working his lips up her thigh, he parted her pussy with his tongue. Lola's hips nudged toward him, silently indicating she wanted more.

"Nick, that feels so good, baby."

Reassuringly Nick groaned, "I'm just getting started."

Licking his middle finger, he slowly circled Lola's clit. Trading his tongue for the use of his thumb and finger, he massaged up and down her shaft. Moistening her pussy with his saliva, Nick watched Lola's shaft grow fuller. Pushing away the hood with his tongue, he sucked her clit. Lola's hips nudged toward his mouth.

Not wanting her breasts to feel abandoned, Nick traced her areolas, winding closer to her nipples. Twirling her engorged nipples between his thumbs and fingers, Nick kissed her clit carefully, sliding one of his hands between her wet thighs, then he slipped his finger inside her pussy. The sudden arch of her back along with her moaning, "Ou, Nick" indicated Lola felt real good.

With each gentle thrust of his finger, Nick sucked Lola's clit from underneath the hood and into his mouth. Lola's hips rotated on his finger so he thrust a little harder. Lola's body stiffened slightly, pulling away. Immediately Nick softened his strokes. She didn't have to tell him she didn't like the pressure. He was totally tuned in to Lola's body language.

Between the "ous" and "ahs" a man had to listen to a woman's nonverbal communications. Spiraling his finger along the outside of Lola's vagina, her hips and pussy lips came back home to him. The taste of her clit's secretions became more flavorful, letting him know she was ready to cum in his mouth. But Nick wanted to prolong her pleasure, so he eased the pressure of his tongue, licking just a little lighter. When her body relaxed and the taste subsided, he regained his momentum, bringing Lola back to her peak, then he pulled away again. On the third peak, "Oh, Nick!" Lola screamed repeatedly. Her secretions gushed like she was urinating but Nick knew that she wasn't. He'd helped Lola ejaculate a squirting G-spot orgasm.

Panting, she reached for him. If she'd pushed, that meant she wanted his head to stay between her legs. Lola wasn't pushing him at all. She was frantically grabbing at his shoulders trying to pull him up to her which meant she was silently begging for penetration.

Nick didn't start banging Lola like he had to prove his manhood. The way he'd treated her before laying her down on the bed made him the man. If he'd started out straight fucking her, the constant friction would've made Lola cum too soon and not in a good way. She would've been frustrated instead of happy. Nick wanted to prolong his ejaculation so he entered Lola's wetness with six shallow G-spot-stimulating strokes of his hard erection then one long, slow, and deep thrust pressing his dickhead all the way inside her. Pulling back but not all the way out, Nick gave Lola five shallow strokes and one deep one. Counting down from four to three to two to one shallow and one deep thrust, he alternated until they were both ready to explode.

Their bodies trembled together seemingly forever and then Lola gave him the most pleasant intangible surprise.

She gave Nick the ultimate gift of lovemaking that a woman gives a man who has given her a total body orgasm.

Lola cried.

Nick held her in his arms until she dozed off, then he eased out of bed. Walking over to his clothes, Nick dug deep inside his pocket, retrieved the ring he'd bought for Natalie, removed Lola's wedding ring, and slipped his ring on Lola's finger.

JEXCAPADE 14

Natalie

Having sex with Nick every day for three years straight never consumed but always complemented Natalie's life. Although she didn't have to, she could please herself just as well. But since sex for Natalie was 90 percent mental, her mind now was cluttered with so many issues there was zero capacity to concentrate on having an enjoyable orgasm.

It was six o'clock on hump day. The sun that had beamed bright in the day now hid behind a gloomy gray sky. Natalie was the last one in the office. The man she once knew had vacated the office next to hers hours ago. Natalie realized Nick had abandoned her to have sex with Lola in an attempt to get even because Natalie had had sex with DeVaughn. Nick's words and actions made it clear that he didn't want to touch Natalie's body since he could easily get his dick sucked and his needs met elsewhere. She hadn't expected Nick to be so cold, callous, and disrespectful with her in his office this morning. Natalie deserved better treatment.

Strange how a simple lie, the hidden truth, or an act of betrayal could trigger the demise of a relationship. Natalie couldn't say she was living by her number one rule. She wasn't much of a friend to Nick right now, especially not his best friend. Thinking about her reactions, oh, how easy it was for her to become defensive. She embraced her ego to justify her deception. She blamed Nick for doing what any other coworker competing for a seven-figure promotion would've done. The difference was because Natalie had sucked Nick's dick, she imposed restrictions upon him that she wouldn't have anticipated or expected from others.

Natalie's complete day seemed like a waste. DeVaughn hadn't returned either of her calls. Even after she'd left him a message saying she had his twenty-five grand in cash. Men weren't very creative and her instincts told her that DeVaughn had done to his wife the soul mating that Natalie had done with him. She also realized that Lola would willingly fuck Nick to get back at DeVaughn for him spending the night with her away from their home. Natalie couldn't say she blamed Lola for embracing her womanly motto of being equally yoked and equally stroked. There were too many men in the world for Natalie to waste time trying to make one man do the right thing. Respect her. But respect wasn't given it was earned. That meant she had to do her part too. Indirectly Nick had Natalie to thank for making his conquest fuck with Lola easier.

Their foursome quickly became a dangerous twister. No one would lose their life but by the time the web of deceit untangled all of their spirits will have transitioned love into hate and before she bailed out Natalie was getting ready to tie the knot tighter. If DeVaughn were tripping over Lola and Nick, Natalie wouldn't have to rethink her next request to DeVaughn. Fair exchange was no robbery. Asking DeVaughn to let her strap on and fuck him in the ass the same way he fucked her the other night wouldn't be necessary, Natalie would just do it. The way DeVaughn enjoyed having his asshole finger fucked was a clear indication he was wide open to deeper penetration and Natalie was definitely the woman to give it to him raw.

With Nick fucking Lola, Natalie doubted DeVaughn could get the information she needed. Shifting her thoughts toward her backup business plan, Natalie started typing. Her fingers raced across the keyboard with conviction and determination to succeed no matter what. All the ideas she envisioned for Divas Galore flooded the screen. From the models on the runway, to the waiters showcasing jewelry, to the private booths where small groups could have intimate business meetings, to Internet access at every table, text-messaging capabilities where diners could e-mail anyone in the restaurant and casually conference without leaving their tables, Natalie said aloud, "Oh my gosh, my state-of-the-art endless possibilities are overwhelming."

During the week she could host Happy Singles Hours. On Fantasy Fridays the models would role-play in outfits and accessories and her guests could order whatever items they wanted online from their seats using their Divas Galore credit cards. Divas Galore would become the five-star adult-members-only restaurant of choice for busy entrepreneurs living in and traveling to San Francisco, New York, Chicago, Atlanta, and New Orleans. Eventually Natalie would open a location in Paris next door to Dons and Divas so she could put Mr. Sexton and Flint out of business.

In that instant of embracing her wildest dream, her vision became clear along with her responsibilities. It didn't matter if she failed before succeeding. What mattered most was that she tried while she was alive. Not a lame attempt. Natalie had to commit to do her absolute best. Forget about the million-dollar promotion Flint dangled in front of her face. She'd make her own millions. Natalie didn't want to become a statistic between the lyrics of Langston Hughes's poem "Dream Deferred" because from what she'd heard action in the state of California was no longer affirmative.

Natalie said it aloud so she'd hear the commitment to herself. "Natalie Coleman, starting right now, not tomorrow, not next week or next month or next year. Today you will develop a plan to start your own business. Why work long hours investing in someone else? I'm smart. I'm intelligent. I have passion. I have loyalty and dedication. I have everything that successful people have. I've proven myself over and over again to others but this time I only have to prove myself to me. I've read Russell Simmons' book *Do You!* twice over and he's right. Successful people have visions. Successful people aren't afraid of failure. Successful people are successful because they are determined to succeed."

Natalie stood proud. Looking out the window, she couldn't see the San Francisco or the Oakland Bay Bridges. She took a deep breath. Beyond everything her eyes could see, having faith in the unknown, she firmly stated, "I quit." But not just yet. She had to know if the plan she received from DeVaughn was good enough to secure the promotion. If it was, she'd incorporate some of the concepts into her business.

An incoming call on her cell interrupted her thoughts. It was DeVaughn. Natalie debated on answering or ignoring his call. One ring prior to voice mail, she casually said, "Hello?"

"Hey, Natalie. What's up?"

"Not much. What's going on?"

"I'm just checking to see if you're ready to meet me. You know. So I can get that."

Natalie wasn't sure if DeVaughn was referring to the money or fucking but neither sex nor DeVaughn mattered. "This time of night?" she asked.

"Well, if you and Nick are busy, I can get that from you tomorrow."

So the truth slipped out. DeVaughn didn't know where his wife was and Natalie wasn't going to help him figure out Lola's whereabouts. "I'm busy. Let me call you in the morning," Natalie said, then hung up.

Saving her file, then shutting down her computer, she headed to the restroom. En route back to her office, Natalie overheard voices coming from Flint's office. Standing outside Flint's door, Natalie eavesdropped, hearing someone say, "How many times are we going to have to go over this. So what if I molested you as a child? You're a grown man now, get over it and suck my dick."

Flint responded, "I can't keep living this lie, man. You can have your fucking company and your daughter!"

"It sure would be a shame if anything happened to your grandmother."

What the hell? Natalie rattled her head in disbelief. That bastard. Mr. Sexton was threatening to do harm to Flint's grandmother and telling Flint to suck his wrinkled-ass dick? Natalie had never seen Mr. Sexton's dick but the way every visible skin cell on his body had given into gravity, she could only imagine how saggy his balls and his dick were, especially if he was uncircumcised. *Ew yuck.*

"Look, I already promised you that when Nick gets the promotion Natalie will replace you immediately. Come Monday evening you're free to do whatever you want. If you don't want to do me anymore after that, fine. But you leave my house and my company the same way you came, broke. Or you could suck my dick and everyone would be happy 'cause I'd keep my word and give you a generous severance package. Okay, a quickie in the ass and we can leave."

Natalie damn near fell on the doorknob when she heard Mr. Sexton weeping with pleasure. Was that dirty old bastard for real? Hell no! He'd preselected the position like Nick had said. But there was no way Natalie would fuck or work directly for Mr. Sexton.

"I'm cuming," Mr. Sexton said.

Who was doing whom? How many years had Flint been doing this? Now Natalie knew Flint wasn't serious about fucking her but she had no idea he was under that kind of pressure to perform. As sorry as Natalie felt for Flint, knowing what he had to do to earn his keep gave Natalie an advantage that would keep Nick from getting the job.

Walking to the water cooler for a much needed drink, Natalie was surprised to see Nick strutting back into the office at almost midnight. She hid beside the cooler until Nick closed his door.

The next door she heard was Flint's office door closing. Dropping to the floor, Natalie quietly crawled underneath Jonathan's desk, praying no one saw or heard her.

"One day you're gonna get yours," Flint said to Mr. Sexton.

"My son, I've already gotten mine. Good night, Nefertiti. Isn't she beautiful?" Mr. Sexton laughed, patting Flint on the ass as they left the office together.

Mr. Sexton couldn't have possibly seen her. What if he did know Natalie was hiding? She would be damned if she'd ever suck Mr. Sexton's dick. Tiptoeing by Nick's office back to her desk, she reflected on Nick's posture. Nick was happy when he'd skipped out for lunch but returning to the office he was the Nick she used to know. Confident. Arrogant. Manly. Sexy. And he had good energy surrounding him. That was the Nick Natalie needed to feel inside of her. Hell, if Mr. Sexton could get laid she could too.

Sitting at her desk, Natalie picked up the receiver and held the phone in her hand until the *bump bump bump bump* sound registered in her ears. Natalie hung up and did the same thing several times before placing the receiver on the hook. Was she losing her touch?

Walking over to Nick's office, she tapped on his door. "Mind if I come in?"

"Go away, Natalie," Nick yelled from afar. "This is all your fault!"

So typical and untrue, but Natalie wasn't giving up that easily. Repeatedly she tapped until finally Nick snatched opened his door.

"What do you want from me?" he asked between the gap.

"Nick, hear me out. Please. You were the one who started this between us. I'm the one who wants to make our lives whole again. Please, let me into your heart," Natalie said.

Nick stepped back without opening the door. When Natalie eased the door open, Nick stood at his window gazing out over the beautiful moonlit still waters of the bay. Natalie joined him in silence trying to listen to his thoughts.

As he loosened his tie, Nick's other palm slid from his forehead over his nose, then stopped, covering his mouth. Then dropping his hand alongside his thigh, Nick shook his head.

Natalie placed her hand on Nick's lower back. When he didn't respond, she gradually glided her palm up to the nape of his neck. He turned and faced her.

Somberly he asked, "Why, Natalie? Why?"

Why what? she thought, leaning her head into his chest. Gently Natalie hugged his waist.

Swiftly, Nick's hand raced across his ledge. Loose papers, pens, books, a coffee mug, and framed picture of the Effiel Tower went crashing to the floor!

Turning Natalie around, holding up her hair, Nick unzipped her dress, pulled out his dick, penetrated her pussy, and started fucking Natalie like he'd never fuck Lola. Nick didn't care how Natalie felt. She deserved his punishment.

Facing the window, she heard Nick say, "Natalie, all I ever wanted was to love you. To be with you. And you take that away from me every chance you get."

What was Nick so angry about? His hard throbbing dick banging deep inside her pussy made Natalie hot and wet. This was their first make-up sex session, so Natalie decided to play along. Holding on to the ledge, she thrust her hips backward into Nick's dick as hard as she could. It was like they were competing to see who could fuck the hardest.

"Nick, I miss you, daddy."

"You miss," Nick said, fucking her harder and harder. Natalie's head hit the window when he said, "You miss DeVaughn too?"

"You should be concerned about me!" Natalie shouted, bracing her hands on the ledge, aggressively pushing her hips back with all her strength. "If you would've never lied." Natalie started crying and couldn't stop.

"Ah yeah. I'm cuming, baby. Cum with me," Nick said, shooting his sperm deep inside her pussy.

Dirty bastard. "You came inside of me without a condom?" Natalie was too upset to have an orgasm. Speechless she stared out the window.

Nick pulled out. "I'm sorry, baby," he said, leaning his sweaty body over her soaked back, "but you leave me no choice." His foot spread her legs. His elbow wedged into the center of her spine. And his dick penetrated her ass.

Natalie screamed, "Ow! Nick, stop it!" Frantically whaling

her hands behind her, she tried to grab Nick's dick, hold on to his shirt, and scream for help but she couldn't. His pelvis was up against her ass so tight.

"Shut up, Natalie! Shut the fuck up!" Nick yelled, ramming his dick deeper inside of her.

Natalie was no longer crying tears of passion. She was in great pain. She pleaded, "Nick, please stop you're hurting me."

"You didn't deny DeVaughn and you'd better not deny me. This is my ass! You hear me! Mine!"

Natalie yelled back, "You don't fucking own me, my pussy, or my ass!"

Angrily Nick fucked her harder. Suddenly Natalie stopped crying and struggling and lay there. Her body flopped against the ledge every time Nick thrust his hard dick inside her. Nick continued fucking her until he came, this time he ejaculated all over her ass. "Satisfied. I pulled out this time."

Speechless, Natalie had nothing to say to him. Nothing at all.

Kissing the back of her head, Nick said, "I'm so sorry, baby. I don't know what's gotten into me. It's just that you drive me crazy and I was jealous when I saw you letting him fuck you in the ass and I was angry that I wasn't your first and hated myself for making love to you and Lola today without using a condom and I hate myself for loving you so damn much when I know I can't have you for myself. I'm so sorry, Natalie baby. I never meant to hurt you." Nick pressed his lips against the back of her head for an entire minute.

Natalie had counted every second to keep her mind off of

slamming her stiletto in the middle of his forehead for raping her. Listening to the zipper of his pants quickly close, Natalie wanted to hang Nick Thurston with the tie dangling around his sweaty neck. This was not what she had expected from him. He'd deliberately hurt her because he felt that she'd hurt him.

This was her pussy, her ass, her body and she was free to share it with whomever she damn well pleased without having to justify or explain anything to Nick. Where was that police officer when she needed him? What gave Nick the right to believe he was entitled to rape her? And he had the audacity to confess to having unprotected sex with Lola after having done the same with her. What if Lola's ass had some sort of disease?

Who was right? Who was wrong?

Nick said, "Please don't forget rule number one, best friends no matter what," then he left Natalie ass out sprawled across the ledge.

Nick may have been done but the incident was far from over.

Sexcapade 15

DeVaughn

DeVaughn paced the floors of the empty bedroom into the quiet living room, replaying his wife's voice in his head, "Honey, I'm home," but the problem was Lola wasn't with him. Traveling back and forth, he placed his palms over his temples. His fingertips touched as he held his head tight. Where was his wife? It was unlike her not to answer or return any of his calls. Was she okay? Had someone carjacked her? DeVaughn knew he shouldn't have let her buy that BMW 700 series. He wasn't a Christian but DeVaughn believed in the power of prayer, so he asked that his lovely wife safely return home.

The rising sun boiled his blood, increasing his pressure. If he didn't chill, he could die of a heart attack before Lola stepped her foot through the door. DeVaughn prayed for peace in the midst of his anger. His biggest fear was if his wife was all right that she was doing unto him what he'd done unto her.

Had Natalie said something to Lola to keep his beautiful wife out all night? Was Lola with Natalie? Doing Natalie? His heartbeat doubled, tripled, keeping pace with his feet until he finally heard the sound he'd been longing to hear. The garage door crept opened. Impatiently DeVaughn waited in the kitchen.

Lola entered with the grace of a goddess. The presence of a queen. A smile adorned her face as she peacefully greeted him, "Good morning, my love," wearing the same damn clothes she had on yesterday morning.

Blocking her path, DeVaughn frowned, then sternly asked, "Where in hell were you last night? I called you ten times. Where's your phone?"

Before his wife answered with a lie, he snatched her purse to investigate. Retrieving her phone DeVaughn scanned her received calls. "Why in the fuck was Nick calling you? Is that who you were with last night? Don't try to walk away from me. Answer me, Lola!"

Lola calmly stared at him and said, "Um, you see, DeVaughn, what had happened was my car broke down in the Montclair Hills. You know where that is don't cha? Of course you do, honey. Anyway, I knocked on a stranger's door but I wasn't as lucky as you. Can you believe nobody answered? So I slept in my car." Lola sighed, then continued, "You know how the story ends on Highway Thirteen. Don't cha, baby?" Lola's eyelashes flashed upward as she continued, "Anywhoo, everybody plays the fool, sweetie, and one of us has got to go to work and obviously that somebody ain't you. But while you're ranting all up in my face," Lola swiftly counterclockwise traced her hand in front of her forehead, cheek, chin, cheek, and back to her forehead, then asked, "Did you have enough time to come up with an answer for where in the hell you were all night the other night?"

DeVaughn's eyebrows drew closer together. Snatching Lola's wrist he questioned, "Where did this fucking ring come from? And where in the hell is your wedding ring?"

Lola stared at her hand in amazement. On the inside she was smiling, then answered, "I saw it, liked it, so I decided to keep it on. It's not like you ever buy me jewelry. I wanted a change."

Flinging Lola's hand against her breasts, DeVaughn said, "Fuck it." This was about her ass. He couldn't believe she was turning this on what he hadn't bought for her. Right or wrong he was the man of their house. "So is this what this is all about? Getting even. Fine." DeVaughn followed Lola to the bathroom. He stood in the doorway waiting for her to take off her clothes. "Take your ass to work but you might wanna call first before you come home."

"Um, hmm," Lola said, unfastening her bra. "You don't have the balls to disrespect our home. If I ever catch you, don't bother explaining, just pack your belongings and find some-place else to live, sweetie. Let some other woman support your unemployed behind."

DeVaughn's eyebrows touched, his lips tightened. As he watched his wife toss her panties in the laundry basket then turn on the shower, she refused to look at him. When Lola's right foot stepped under the steamy waters, DeVaughn ran to her, held her left leg, stuck his finger inside her pussy, then sniffed.

"Damn, Lola! Your smelly pussy is dripping with cum. Explain this," he said, shoving his finger in her nose. Slamming the shower door, his wife almost severed his wrist.

Singing, "Funny how one bad decision can change your life . . ." she ignored him.

DeVaughn wanted to sing the lyrics to Musiq Soulchild's "Betterman" but he was too pissed to remember the words, so he shouted, "Are you crazy!" not knowing what to do next. Thanks to Natalie, he'd had the best and the worst nights ever with his wife.

"Only for believing you'd always keep me first, DeVaughn. But nothing good lasts forever. Right?"

DeVaughn's neck stiffened like a beer bottle with a dickhead planted on top. Was that an indirect request for a divorce? Aw heck no. Lola wasn't going anywhere. Retreating to the bedroom, DeVaughn checked his voice mail. He'd missed several calls from Natalie, one mentioning she needed to talk with him first thing this morning and she wanted to bring him the twenty-five grand in cash. He wanted to call Natalie back but he didn't feel right because Lola was messing with his mind. Maybe he should take his wife on one of those seven-day cruises she loved so much. Lola shouldn't have to buy her own ring but there was no way he could afford the rock on her finger. DeVaughn didn't care how much that ring cost, Lola was putting on her wedding ring before she left the house.

Lola walked into the bedroom, removed the ring, put it in her purse, then she eased her wedding ring on without him having to make her. He watched her slip into an all-white suit with a short skirt and high heels, and then she left without saying one word to him. Lying across the bed, DeVaughn waited until nine before calling Natalie, hoping he'd catch her before any early Thursday morning meeting. After the first ring, her cell phone went straight to voice mail.

"I know she's not pressing the ignore button."

When he redialed her number, Natalie answered, "What, DeVaughn?"

"Whoa, what's up? Mrs. Attitude just walked out the door. I don't need this from you too. You hung up on me last night, remember, so I'm returning your calls."

"A little too late, don't you think. You didn't seem interested so——"

"Now wait a minute. I did exactly what you asked and Lola agreed," DeVaughn lied, "so can we hook up so I can get paid?" Desperately he had to do something major to regain his wife's trust and the extra money would help.

"Sure, I'll meet you at your place at noon," Natalie insisted.

"Naw, we'd better meet someplace public."

"Your place or no place. Call me back if you change your mind."

What was this, pussy liberation day? "Wait, it's cool. It's cool. I'll see you at noon," DeVaughn said, already regretting what he'd agreed to. What in the hell was he doing? Closer to the time Natalie was to arrive, DeVaughn dialed his wife to check her whereabouts.

"Hey, there," Lola moaned in the phone, and his dick instantly rose.

"Hey, baby. You still mad at me?" DeVaughn asked, looking

at the digital clock. Natalie would be at his place in less than two hours.

"You know I can't stay mad at you. But seriously we do need to talk. A lot has happened. Nothing has come between us before and we shouldn't let anyone else change the way we feel for one another. I've got a lunch meeting at two o'clock, then I'm headed straight home to you, baby. I can't stay angry with you. Oh, and so you'll know, I was able to reach the perfect person to have your plan ready by Friday."

"Damn, woman, you're the best. I'll see you this evening, baby."

Hanging up the phone, DeVaughn watched *Divorce Court, Moral Court,* and *The People's Court* while waiting for Natalie to arrive. He didn't prepare lunch or snacks, or do anything special for Natalie because just in case Lola came home early, Natalie had to be gone by two. Knowing a woman could smell when another woman had been in her house, DeVaughn prayed Lola wouldn't arrive before three.

DeVaughn heard Natalie's car pulling into the driveway, so he quickly put his sweatpants over his shorts, laced up his tennis shoes, slipped on a long T-shirt then his hooded sweatshirt, and met her at the door.

"Hey, come on in."

Natalie laughed, "You look like you're going out for an early-afternoon jog but I have to warn you you're overdressed. It's seventy-five degrees outside."

DeVaughn didn't care how hot it was outside or inside he was not taking off his clothes until Natalie was gone. "Yeah, gotta stay fit to keep up with a woman like you. You still got me thinking about our incredible night together." Until he got his hands on the twenty-five grand, he'd tell Natalie whatever he thought she wanted to hear.

Damn, Natalie looked great every time he saw her. Maybe DeVaughn could buy Lola some sexy outfits like Natalie's. Natalie wore a silk fuchsia short-sleeve dress that stopped midway on her thighs and a pink wrap hugged her shoulders and her waist. When she tossed her wrap onto the sofa, the scoop in the back smiled above the crack of her ass.

Natalie sat beside him and placed her purse and another bag on the floor. DeVaughn got excited about the twenty-five Gs and Natalie.

"DeVaughn," Natalie said.

"Yeah."

"Where's your bathroom?" Natalie asked, removing her white designer shoes with pink and blue symbols.

"First door on your right," he said, pointing behind him. "Take your shoes with you."

Picking up her purse, Natalie said, "Excuse me for a moment."

DeVaughn kept staring at the bag on the floor tempted to open it but he didn't want Natalie to change her mind about giving him the cash, so he waited. Plus, she was in his house and he didn't want any unnecessary disturbances in his peaceful neighborhood.

"DeVaughn," Natalie whispered.

"Yeah," he said, turning around. "Damn!" His eyes bucked and his tongue hung over his lip when he saw Natalie dressed in all black leather: bustier, garter, thong, with diamond-shaped fishnets. She strummed a black feather between her thighs.

"Come here, daddy. I miss you."

Something told him not to get up but his dick led the way. Stumbling over the case of money, DeVaughn walked up to Natalie. Their lips met. Hungrily he started kissing her, wishing she were his wife instead. The scent of Lola's pussy leaking with another man's cum made him seek revenge one last time before he'd make up with her. He stuck his tongue in Natalie's mouth while holding the back of her head.

Ripping away her Velcro thong, DeVaughn snatched off her garter, wondering what had gotten into him as he started chewing off Natalie's fishnets until he gnawed a hole large enough to put his hand in, then ripped them off.

Natalie pushed him to the living room floor. Grabbing her arms, he pulled her down with him as he scrambled for a few seconds removing all of his clothes. Rolling back and forth, they competed for the top position until DeVaughn pinned Natalie to the floor.

"Yeah, baby. You know you want this big delicious dick inside you," DeVaughn said, parting her thighs with his thigh. He shoved his dick inside her fast and as far as he could.

"Ou yes!" Natalie screamed. "Fuck me, motherfucka!"

Was it something he'd done? Natalie seemed angry. Volatile. Her energy exceeded his. This was not the Natalie he'd made love to night before last but that's what made Natalie so spectacular. Natalie was unpredictable. "Fuck me with your big black beautiful dick, you Mandingo motherfucka."

"You like this dick, huh?" DeVaughn asked, thrusting his dick harder and faster.

Each time he pounded that pussy, Natalie's back slid along the carpet. "I hate all of you," Natalie exhaled. Forcefully her hips started slamming into his. "Take this good pussy. Take it. That's all you want anyway, isn't it? Pussy. Pussy. Pussy."

At that point DeVaughn should've stopped. He realized that something was very wrong with Natalie. He pulled out, tossed her legs over her head, and started eating her sweet pussy and didn't stop until she came all over his face.

"Damn, you taste good, woman. Suck my dick. I want you to suck my dick right now."

"Yeah," Natalie moaned. "You don't give a fuck what I want. Have your way with me."

Crawling up to Natalie's face, DeVaughn stuck his dick in her mouth. "Aw yeah. That's it. That's it! Here it comes!" he yelled, stroking and squirting all over Natalie's face. He squeezed his dick from the base to the head several times trying to release every drop of cum until he collapsed facedown onto the carpet.

Natalie straddled his back and began massaging him with oils. Her touch felt so good DeVaughn dozed off to sleep until something strange awakened him.

"What the fuck?" he yelled, hoisting his ass in the air.

"Don't move. Damn you, I'm cuming," Natalie said, pushing her hips against his ass. Her hand wrapped around his side, gripped his dick, and started pumping up and down his shaft.

To DeVaughn's surprise, he was cuming too. "Aw shit! What the fuck are you doing to me?"

"Stroking your P-spot, daddy."

"My what?" DeVaughn asked, sprawled on the floor like a bear rug.

"Your P-spot. Your prostrate has the same sensation as my G-spot. The best way to stimulate it is with anal penetration."

DeVaughn couldn't admit it but that was the best nut he'd ever busted. When his body sunk into the carpet, he could not believe the incredible sensation he felt from his head to his toes. Glancing over his shoulder, he watched as Natalie pulled a black strap-on dildo out of his ass.

He stared at her in amazement. This woman had turned him out. He was glad that shit happened before he made up with his wife.

"I love you, DeVaughn," Natalie said, gently kissing his lips.

Unstrapping the harness, Natalie gathered her belongings and disappeared into bathroom. Be careful what you ask for, he thought. Did this mean he was gay or bi? Or was DeVaughn a straight freak?

He rolled over, his eyelids fluttered, then shut, until he heard "Baby, I'm home."

DeVaughn's heart raced with fear. Please don't let Natalie step out of that bathroom. How was he going to explain why the living room smelled exactly like his ass? Were the clothes lying next to him the first items he'd pack or the only clothing Lola would let him take before kicking him out?

DeVaughn cried, "Somebody please tell me I'm dreaming."

SEXCAPADE 16

Flint

For a man, every season was mating season pollinating the air with testosterone, filling Flint's dick with more sperm than he cared to have weighing down his nuts. "I hate him!" Flint yelled into the mirror, staring at himself. He went to the closet, retrieved the brown wicker picnic basket from the top shelf, held the gun in his hand, then pressed the cold steel into his temple.

"You can end this once and for all." Flint imagined Samantha skipping into their bedroom, seeing his body lying in a pool of blood and before she could scream she'd faint on top of him. If Samantha's father discovered Flint's body first, he'd probably cry over Flint's dead dick. A voice inside Flint's head said, "What are you afraid of? Pull the trigger, man."

Easing his finger in the hole, Flint touched the lever, opened his mouth, then closed his eyes. "I can't do this?" he cried. Walking over to the mirror, Flint felt helpless. How in this world could a grown man feel helpless? Flint understood how children felt helpless because they depended upon adults to provide for and protect them. Once a person turned twenty-one, there should be no excuses. Returning to the closet, Flint placed the gun back in the basket. There had to be a way for him to make his life better.

Flint hated Mr. Sexton but he loved his grandmother. Old and tired when she took him in, she could've said no. But after she'd said he could live with her, was his grandmother oblivious to all the sex acts Mr. Sexton forced Flint to perform when he was a child? Or was it easier for Flint's grandmother to pretend she didn't know? Was she worried more about her Christian reputation than his safety? Or were her religious beliefs so strong she thought Jesus would fix it by and by. Well, he didn't. That's why Flint stopped going to church years ago. Since Jesus hadn't shown him a way then, Flint had every right to do things his way.

Fuck it.

With a hard-on distracting him, Flint decided to live another day. He didn't want to jack off this morning before leaving the house, so he opted to host a Web mate at his place. A quick e-mail with his pic and his home phone number and his telephone rang moments later. Incredible. Was that guy so lonely that he was sitting by his computer waiting for the first offer?

On the third ring, Flint answered, "Hello?"

"Yeah, Justice, is this really you in the picture?" he asked.

Since most people knew him by Flint, it was easier for Flint to slightly alter his first name and eliminate using his last name when soliciting sex online. Interesting how prostitution was illegal but he could legally get his dick sucked for free by a complete stranger.

When the guy arrived about seven o'clock wearing a gray sweat suit and black shower shoes, Flint forgot all about his suicide attempt. Immediately he noticed the guy's impeccable pedicure. He was six foot two about 180 pounds with a well-trimmed goatee and full lips.

"Come on in, man," Flint said, leading him to the guest bedroom.

When he turned around, the guy was naked and his dick was hard. Flint untied his silk robe, releasing it to the floor. He stood before the guy, watching him as he dropped to his knees. Firmly gripping his dick, the guy sucked Flint's head into his strong wet mouth. Maybe the muscles in a man's mouth made men better dick suckers than women. Or perhaps it was the strength and roughness in a man's hand. Flint couldn't stand a woman pecking him on the head with her lips or scratching up his dick with her teeth. And he really didn't like the women who were afraid to grip his balls. Wasn't like his balls were going to fall off.

Sucking his head, "Mmm. Mmm. Mmm," the guy moaned with pleasure while stroking Flint's dick.

His masculine jaws tightened each time simulating swallowing Flint's dick. Forcing the entire shaft down his throat, the guy suctioned Flint like a vacuum. Flint's body trembled like a washer on spin cycle. He tried not to cum in the guy's mouth but the guy's hands palmed Flint's ass as he jammed Flint's dick to the back of his throat, refusing to let go. Flint felt cum shooting against his leg as he shot a full morning load straight toward the guy's stomach.

Pulling his limp dick out of the guy's mouth, Flint watched him lick his lips, ease on his sweats, and escort himself out the front door. What made some men such sexual animals? Flint knew how he'd gotten turned out at an early age against his will but lathering his body in the shower, he wondered who'd turned that brother out. What made him enjoy sucking a stranger's dick?

En route to the office, Flint chilled at a red light waiting for the signal to turn green. Glancing at the man seated in the car next to him instantly made Flint's dick hard. If that man knew the effect he had on Flint, would he beat Flint's ass or let Flint fuck him in his ass? Thinking about how soon he could jack off his next orgasm, Flint could tell this was going to be one of those fuck-a-thon days.

Entering the office, he passed Jonathan with a quick, "Good morning."

"Oh, Mr. Flint. Mr. Sexton called. He wants you to meet him at this restaurant for an important luncheon at noon."

Stuffing the paper into his pocket, Flint didn't bother checking the location. "Thanks," he said.

Jonathan was young, nice, attractive, well-dressed, and well-groomed every day. Why hadn't Mr. Sexton made an advance at him? Instead of going to his office, Flint headed into a private restroom stall, locked the door, and started stroking his dick while thinking about Nick. Flint swore he only stopped in the restroom to piss but this erection would not go away.

Spitting in his palm, Flint saturated his shaft. Closing his eyes, he stood over the commode, squeezing his balls at the base while rubbing his head. Forming a tunnel with his thumb and fingers, Flint envisioned sticking his head in Nick's ass.

Flint could bet that Nick's virgin butt was hot and tight. Flint slid his hand toward his other hand joining them at the base thrusting his dick all the way inside of Nick. As he held his dick like a sword, precum oozed out of the head. Flint wondered if Nick would let him lick his balls.

Flint imagined yelling, "Fuck this! I can't take it anymore! I'm getting ready to explode!" while fantasizing about pumping his dick hard and furiously inside of Nick. His sagging nuts were emptied, his dick was limp again, and he was still horny as hell. This shit just wasn't right. Flint needed professional help. Suppressing his sexual rage, Flint washed up, then tapped on Natalie's door. He didn't wait for her to respond, "Come, in," before opening her door, hoping he'd catch her masturbating or something.

Standing in Natalie's doorway, Flint said, "Get Nick and meet me in the conference room. I want an update on your business plans."

Sitting at the circular conference table in her office, Natalie glanced up from the stack of papers spread before her. Hesitantly she said, "But I won't have any information available for you until," Natalie's words trailed off as she glanced at her diamond wristwatch, then continued, "five o'clock this evening."

"You've got five minutes," Flint said.

"For what, to give you a reason to give Nick the job Mr. Sexton already promised him?"

Closing Natalie's door, Flint went to the conference room and waited. Natalie was right, so there was no point in debating with her and he gladly could give Natalie his job. Either way, both Nick's and Natalie's employment were secure. Flint could walk back out that front door and never see or do Mr. Sexton again. Easily he could give up all of the corporate nonsense for a normal life. But Flint wasn't normal.

Once molested, a child could never be normal. When Flint should've been deciding on whether to play football or basketball, or join the debate team, he was carrying his backpack filled with homework assignments to Mr. Sexton's home. Instead of focusing on making all A's or getting good enough grades to make the honor roll, as a preteen he was rolling around in bed with an old-ass pedophile. Flint had been mentally castrated. He'd become a recluse afraid to talk to his classmates, thinking his breath smelled like a dick.

Natalie strutted in and, for whatever reason, Natalie as fine as she was wasn't turning Flint on at the moment. When Nick walked in behind her Flint's eyes immediately fell to Nick's dick.

"Have a seat," Flint said without looking up. If Nick could suck his dick like that guy did this morning, Flint would dismiss Natalie from the meeting immediately.

"Um, um, um," Natalie whimpered, squirming her ass in the seat.

Chill bumps invaded Flint's body, his dick was soft, and a part of him became outraged at the undertone in Natalie's voice. Was that her way of indicating that she knew about his sexual preference? Nick's eyes softened, his head slightly hung as he stared at the table. Maybe Flint was paranoid about nothing.

"Natalie, you can start," Flint said.

Exhaling, Natalie said, "Flint, I just told you, I won't have anything available until five. Besides, you said we didn't have to give it to you until Monday." Boldly peering into his eyes, Natalie asked, "Is there really a job in Paris? The only one who seems to know about this new restaurant is you. Unless slick Nick knows but my investigative sources didn't discover any plans for a new Dons and Divas opening up anywhere."

How dare that bitch question him! Did she forget that he was married to the daughter of the owner of the entire chain? He had firsthand knowledge of everything before it material-ized. He was helping them out by giving them an upper hand by keeping the promotion in-house. Flint wasn't going to en-tertain Natalie. She'd been out of the office every day this week doing only God knows what.

"If you doubt there's a promotion, then I'll advertise over the weekend for outside applicants. Nick, do you have your plan?" Flint asked, trying to make his rising dick shrink.

Looking at Natalie, Nick answered, "I won't have it until five o'clock today. We can all meet then or we can wait until Monday."

Liar. Did they think he was stupid? Did they believe he didn't know what went on in the office between them after dark? For some odd reason, today Nick was Natalie's ass kisser in every possible way. Dismissing both of them, Flint said, "We'll meet on Monday as planned."

Watching Nick's round tight ass as he walked out of the room made Flint's dick harden again. Samantha was due home in the morning. God, he wasn't looking forward to her return. Flint needed his wife to hold him but right now Flint needed a man to wrap his lips around his dick and suck him unconscious.

Locking his office door, Flint logged on to www.craigslist .com and clicked on the men-seeking-men link and found an ad:

Looking to service some cock at lunch!!! 42yo, 160lbs, 5'7", blond, blue, masc, in-shape. 7.5thick . . . Looking to service one or more older top guys at lunch. Use my mouth and ass for your pleasure. Can host or travel.

Did he mean older or younger? Didn't matter. He was in search of too many dicks at one time Flint thought, then kept searching.

Black bottom guy 5'8" & 175lbs average build into sucking, rimming, and getting fucked. Looking for top guys 30 and over. Not hung up on race or body type just be hung, full of cum, and ready to have fun. I'm HIV and only play safe.

"Well, at least he was honest about his status. I've got enough issues of my own. I'll pass on that one."

Another click and Flint saw an ad from a black man with a thick dick that hung to his knees that read:

Black top here looking for a slim to medium build bottom (black men only!). I'm looking for something today and maybe on the regular.

Not with that elephant trunk dick! Flint thought, imagining having that guy's dickhead pushed in his ass then traveling through his intestines and popping out his mouth like a jack-in-the-box.

The next pick was it. This guy's side profile looked familiar. He was sitting at a table, gazing off into the distance over a glass of white wine, his eyes telling a story. Flint knew the look all too well. That guy had gotten turned out at an early age. The pictures of his naked plump ass turned Flint on. The guy's dick was the perfect size. But most important, he was a bottom looking for a topper.

Looking 2 be fucked starting slow . . . then rough and AG-GRESSIVE. Looking for today or another day . . . Not looking for a relationship. Looking 4 sex Only. I'm 31, 5'8", 185lbs, 8 cut, Negative, Drug & Disease Free, Ver/Top.

Flint e-mailed him right away, "R U Avail to host me now?"

Immediately the guy sent Flint the address and Flint was well on his way to Hunter's Point. When he arrived at a small but neat apartment, the guy handed him a glass of white wine. Flint took a sip, set the glass down, and removed his clothes, tossing everything on the loveseat. Missionary style, the guy sprawled onto the area rug, lifting his legs toward his head. Easing on a condom, Flint knelt before the guy's ass, fucked him slow, then aggressive like he'd fucked that bodybuilder at the gym. Remaining on his knees, Flint refused to lie chest to chest on top.

"Arrgh! Yeah. Fuck me a little harder," the guy begged, curling his lips away from his grinding teeth. His eyes were closed and his head leaned over his left shoulder.

Spreading the guy's cheeks, Flint dug deeper into his ass until the guy shot cum all over their stomachs. Flint's body trembled as he came long and hard. Opening a warming oven the size of a miniature microwave, he handed Flint a steamy white towel.

His eyes looked straight through Flint as his eyelids grew closer as if he suddenly remembered more than Flint's real name. He did. His pinkish center with chocolate outer covered lips never parted. His neck loosened and his head hung low. They didn't exchange any words. Flint didn't know what to say. Neither of them wanted to discuss their childhoods that were plagued by sexual abuse by Mr. Sexton.

Mr. Sexton was the person they should kill. The person who'd done all those horrible sex acts to them while they were so young, so innocent, so fucking foolish not to have told any adults. But they were children and they were scared. Back then Reverend Sexton threatened to kill anybody they told. He'd said even if they told someone no one would believe them over him. "I am the leader of an entire Christian congregation. Plus, if you tell, both of you will go straight to hell for ruining my church members' lives." The way everyone went to Reverend Sexton for advice, they believed him. He was upstanding in the community, righteous in the eyes of God, infallible in the eyes of man. So Reverend Sexton had done what he wanted to them. Every day that he wanted, he'd raped them.

Flint hurried the hell up, put on his suit, and left. Against their will, as young boys they were raped repeatedly and their lives had been changed forever. They suffered in silence among a world of empathetic strangers. Most people didn't want to hear the truth. If they did, they could've looked into their eyes when they were children and instantly known something was wrong. The eyes of children don't lie. But nowadays most individuals don't look one another in the eye. Maybe that's because everyone had a haunting secret buried deep within their souls. The defiant souls that are taught to place their faith in God not in man, but people do just the opposite.

Well, Flint wasn't sure whom to trust in anymore. Where was God when they needed him?

SEXCAPADE 17

Natalie

Thank goodness Friday was finally here and almost gone. This was the longest week of Natalie's career at Dons and Divas but it was also possibly her last. All day she debated about telling Nick she was quitting but her instincts told her to wait another two months until after Flint's test run of their plans at the restaurants.

Flint had flown out of the office before lunchtime and no one had heard from him since. Glancing at the clock, Natalie saw that it was 4:30 p.m. She could stay upset with Nick, forgive him, or get even with him for fucking her in the ass. She'd known Nick for four years, sexed him for three, and during that time Nick had never hit her, cursed her, or forced her to have sex with him. His random act of violent jealousy was an isolated uncharacteristic incident, so Natalie could find it in her heart to forgive him as long as he'd never treat her that way again.

It wasn't as though she didn't have her secret list of irrational things she'd done to some of the men she'd been with before Nick. Like the time she ran over one of her exes with her car. He shouldn't have broken her car window. Or like the time she poured gasoline outside another guy's front door, struck a match, and ran like hell when his home went up in flames. He should've let her in his house. Or the occasion where she'd taken over $100,000 worth of jewelry from one of her exes, placed his watches in a black satin bag, and donated them to the Salvation Army. He shouldn't have been so cheap when it came to spending money on her.

Natalie sympathized with Nick because each time she'd done something malicious, she'd justified her behavior saying, "I was young. I didn't know any better. He shouldn't have provoked me. He got what he deserved. That's what he gets for disrespecting me." The things Natalie had done were never her fault or as bad as the things other women had done to their men. Natalie was sane and everyone around her was straddling a straitjacket, teetering on falling into a mental institution.

If every friendship ended because of a major or simple misunderstanding, no one would have or be a friend. Nick was truly Natalie's best friend. Shutting down her computer, she needed to make something exciting happen to bring them closer.

Picking up the phone, Natalie dialed Nick's extension.

Flatly Nick answered, "What's up?"

"I wanted to thank you for supporting me earlier. You could've given Flint your proposal."

"Actually, no, I couldn't. I didn't have one to give him."

Politely Natalie asked, "Can you come to my office?"

"I'm on my way," Nick said, hanging up.

Natalie had thirty minutes to spare Nick before meeting DeVaughn at the bar inside Aqua Restaurant to pick up her marketing plan. If Mr. Sexton had decided to give Nick the position, then he'd have to do that because Natalie was not walking away from an opportunity to earn a million dollars a year.

Nick opened the door, walked over to her desk, and kissed her on the cheek. "Sorry about the other night. I left because I felt bad for treating you that way and I didn't know what to say to you afterward." Wrapping his arms around her, Nick hugged her tight. "Natalie, seriously, I am honestly sorry and I promise you and me nothing like that will ever happen again."

Natalie hugged Nick's waist. It felt good holding him in her arms. Not in a sexual way but in a caring sense. "That's behind us. We need to put a lot of things that transpired this week behind us. I forgive you."

"I forgive you too," Nick said with sincerity.

Forgive her. For what? What did she do? For a moment Natalie started getting angry. Men were the most self-righteous, self-centered inhumane beings on earth, always blaming their problems on women. Taking a deep breath, Natalie sat behind her desk and asked, "Do you have a plan for Flint on Monday?"

Nick nodded. "I do. And you?"

Natalie nodded in response. "So do you want to put aside our personal feelings, get down to business, and submit one plan? I think that was the purpose of this project. But honestly I don't think there's a million-dollar position waiting for either of us. I think we'll get huge bonuses but nowhere close to a mil."

Nick's eyes shifted to the corners. He pressed his lips together. After about two minutes his lips curved. "I have a better idea. Let's sleep on this."

Looking at him, Natalie smiled. "My place at ten tonight."

The moment Nick swaggered out of her office, Natalie phoned DeVaughn. "I'm on my way. I'll see you at five." If Natalie was going to work with Nick, she had to get her plan first.

Aqua was a short walk from her office but Natalie drove her car so Nick wouldn't get suspicious about her whereabouts if he saw her car in the garage but she was gone.

When she entered the restaurant, DeVaughn was already seated at the bar. His stool faced the door. Seeing the thick brown organizer on DeVaughn's lap made Natalie happier than seeing him.

"Hey, love. How are you?" Natalie asked, hugging DeVaughn's chest to her breasts. Softly she kissed his lips.

"Better now. And you?"

"I can't thank you enough for doing this for me," Natalie sincerely said.

"Well," DeVaughn said, frowning as he scratched the back of

his neck, "Don't thank me just yet. I have no idea what's in this envelope. After Lola——"

Natalie interrupted, "After Lola what?" motioning to the bartender to request a dirty martini.

DeVaughn exhaled, "After Lola heard about what we'd done, she suspected this plan was for you and——"

"And, what?" Natalie knew DeVaughn wasn't foolish enough to tell Lola she'd fucked him in the ass but she had to ask, "You told her what I did to you?"

"Let's just say I told my wife everything she needed to know. And you were wrong for leaving me on the floor ass up sound asleep. I dreamed Lola walked in on us. Luckily for me she didn't because I would've had to move in with you."

DeVaughn really shouldn't flatter himself believing that he could live with her. Men came up with some of the most ignorant things that they'd impose on women but let Natalie try to move up in his house and see how many different languages he can learn to say no in.

Staring at DeVaughn, Natalie asked, "Exactly what did you tell Lola?"

He looked into her eyes and softly said, "I came clean and told her I spent the night with you. I even told her about the strap-on. But I wasn't crazy enough to tell her that we had sex in her house. I also told Lola how I feel about you."

Feel about me? About what? Natalie could not believe what she'd heard. Either DeVaughn was lying or Lola was seriously about to put him out.

"And." DeVaughn smiled. "Lola wants us to meet her and

Nick at Tiburon Lodge tonight for a foursome. She wants you to teach her how to do a strap-on." DeVaughn winked at her.

Snatching the package from DeVaughn's lap, quietly Natalie sipped another martini to calm her nerves. Well, Lola was his wife and if it didn't bother her it shouldn't concern Natalie. "So does Nick know about tonight?"

"Aw yeah. Lola is meeting him there in a few minutes."

The bartender set a third martini in front of Natalie and whispered, "This one is on the house."

DeVaughn dragged her stool closer to him, then he placed his finger over her lips. The back of his hand stroked Natalie's cheek. "You've changed my life in so many ways. You have no idea."

Nor did she want to hear anything sentimental from DeVaughn at the moment. Had Nick known about this while they were in the office and not said anything even after Natalie invited him to her house?

Tossing a hundred-dollar bill on the bar, DeVaughn said, "Let's just go. And to answer the question on your face, no, Nick did not know. Lola just called him."

Standing at the parking valet, Natalie asked, "Then how do you know Nick is going to meet us there?"

DeVaughn clicked a few buttons on his cell phone, then showed Natalie the text. "Nick is in. What about Nat?"

Something in her gut didn't feel right but Natalie ignored the warning. She nodded, then followed DeVaughn on the thirty-mile drive from downtown San Francisco, over the Golden Gate Bridge, past Sausalito, and into Tiburon, praying this wasn't some sort of setup. If their night went well, maybe tomorrow morning they'd all take the short boat ride over to Angel Island and have breakfast.

When they arrived at the lodge, every cabin was dimly lit on the outside. The surroundings were peaceful. Maybe Natalie was worried about nothing. Since the six-million-dollar renovation, the lodge had converted all the theme rooms into upscale hotel rooms.

Retrieving her travel and sex toys goodie bags from the trunk of her Corvette, Natalie handed them to DeVaughn and strutted through the courtyard. Nick and Lola had started without them; they were relaxing outdoors in the wooden rocking chairs in front of the fireplace, drinking.

When Nick saw them, he removed his arm from around Lola's shoulder. Tossing a couple of cock rings, a set of nipple clips along with two clit stimulators on the table, Natalie ordered another martini which she really didn't need. Her pussy was pulsating and her heart racing, and she was ready to sex Nick, Lola, and DeVaughn like never before.

Sex for the four of them was more like starring in a porn film. They each became self-proclaimed A-list actors. This was the one time when each of them could imitate any person they wanted and do whatever they wanted without being judged. Whatever personal issues they had between one another were never addressed during sex.

"So, how was everyone's day?" Natalie asked seductively, looking at Lola.

Lola looked at her husband and answered, "Busy. Real busy. DeVaughn might be getting a big promotion."

A promotion? Wasn't that impossible without having a job?

Natalie stared at DeVaughn, frowning, on the verge of questioning him about the business plan he'd given her. Now she had to see what was inside that folder but she wouldn't find out until tomorrow. If DeVaughn had set her up, it was too late for her to complete her plan.

"Excellent," Nick said. "Right along with me. The men in this arena will be on top and in charge."

"Nick, you're always in charge," Lola said, kissing DeVaughn.

That idiot Nick. His ego was so huge it formed an eclipse over the possibility that DeVaughn might end up with his job. The energy zigzagging among all of them was hotter than the flames darting in the fireplace but Natalie's rising temperature wasn't sexual. She was pissed. Okay, Natalie had to take a deep breath and shift her frustrations to positive energy.

"DeVaughn, I wanna suck your dick. Get my bags and let's go. Or I could get started right here," Natalie said, massaging his hard-on.

Each of them raced upstairs to their suite like there was a prize for first place. Nick rinsed out the Jacuzzi, then filled it with water. Lola and Natalie undressed, then showered together while Nick and DeVaughn watched from the Jacuzzi.

Slowly Natalie lathered Lola's nipples, twirling them between mounds of suds, then slid her hand down to Lola's pussy. Lola eased her hands to Natalie's clit and stroked gently.

"Kiss!" DeVaughn yelled, standing up massaging his hard dick.

Lola's tongue glided over Natalie's lips. The water streamed over their faces and open mouths while their tongues danced where DeVaughn and Nick could see.

"Ou," Natalie moaned when Lola's finger penetrated her pussy. Natalie returned the favor, finger fucking Lola nice and slow.

"That's enough!" Nick shouted. "Bring those pussies over here."

Turning off the water, Natalie waited until Lola was in the Jacuzzi. Nick greeted her pussy with long loving strokes of his tongue. A little bit too loving if you asked Natalie but perhaps her escalated sensitivity to Nick having fucked Lola twice this week for lunch was to credit for Natalie's jealousy.

Opening her bag, Natalie tossed the electric penis pump on the dresser next to a set of blindfolds, vibrating nipple clamps, and a clit stimulator, and the strap-on dildo with a harness for Lola to do DeVaughn.

Flapping open the giant plastic dining tablecloth and spreading it over the floor, Natalie tossed three oil-filled water guns to Lola, Nick, DeVaughn and started blasting each of them with hers. Baby oil squirted everywhere as each of them hopped out of the tub dripping wet. DeVaughn was the first to slip, so Lola and Natalie double-teamed Nick. Lola swiped her foot under Nick's foot and Natalie went for his opposite leg.

Natalie blew on her gun while Lola braced her hands on her hips. Spreading their legs they stood over Nick, laughing when he landed on his ass. Tossing the guns aside they fell on top of DeVaughn and Nick and began wrestling. Natalie's slippery titties landed into DeVaughn's crotch when he shoved her shoulders. Natalie's hips bumped Lola's feet causing Lola's ass to slam against Natalie's back. Lola's pussy slid from Natalie's shoulders to her ass. With Lola and Natalie lying butt to butt, Nick started finger fucking them at the same time.

"Aw, Nick, lick my clit, baby." Lola moaned, tooting her ass in the air as she started sucking DeVaughn's dick.

This shit was not a figment of Natalie's imagination. Natalie stood waiting to see how Nick would respond. Over the last few days Lola had developed feelings for Nick. What had happened between them? There was nothing for Natalie to say but she wanted to tell Lola to focus on her husband, but DeVaughn was so busy enjoying getting his dick sucked his head was tilted backward and his eyes were shut so tight his face frowned.

Doggie style, Nick happily buried his face in Lola's ass and started licking her pussy.

Straddling Lola, Natalie assumed the doggie position too. Now Nick had two pussies in his face. Nick stopped doing Lola and thrust his dick inside of Natalie.

"Aw, damn, baby," Natalie moaned. "Your super dick feels so———"

Before Natalie could say, "Good," Nick pulled out of her and started fucking Lola as though he'd slipped his dick in the wrong pussy.

Sandwiched between Nick and Lola, Natalie pushed Nick aside. DeVaughn stopped stroking his dick and grunted, "Lola, get your strap-on, baby. I'm ready." DeVaughn should have been paying closer attention to Natalie but she hadn't figured out how to make that happen. Right now, she needed DeVaughn on her team.

Nick's hand froze in midair as though he'd changed his mind about spanking Lola's ass. "Man, did I hear you right? Say it isn't so." Staring at DeVaughn, Nick pulled his limp dick out of Lola. "Strap-ons are for ladies to fuck ladies, man."

Pointing toward the dresser, Natalie said, "Lola, it's over there."

"What's over there?" Nick asked, sitting up.

"The strap-on, man," DeVaughn answered. "Don't tell me Natalie never strapped on for you. That shit is explosive."

DeVaughn stroked his dick while Natalie joyfully helped Lola gear up for her first experience. This was Natalie's chance to get Lola away from Nick. Interlocking the harness around Lola thighs for a comfortable fit, Natalie stroked the perfectly erect five-inch dildo with one hand and held a set of vibrating dual silver bullets in her palm that would soon pulsate against Lola's clit and DeVaughn's prostate at the same time.

Tooting his ass high in the air, DeVaughn braced himself on his elbows. Kneeling behind her husband, Lola asked, "What do I do next?"

"Take that shit off, that's what!" Nick yelled.

Directing Lola's hips, Natalie told her, "Go slow. Everything is already slippery."

Nick got back in the Jacuzzi, watching in disbelief.

"Don't knock it until you've tried it, man," DeVaughn said. "Ou yeah, baby, a little deeper. Ou wee, that vibration is a bitch. Press it against my nuts and my . . . ass!" DeVaughn sang when Natalie slid underneath him and started sucking his dick.

"Um, um, um, I don't believe this shit," Nick said.

"Actually, Nick, I'm feeling rather empowered over here

doing DeVaughn in the ass. It feels really good to me," Lola admitted, fucking her husband harder. "I like this. I'm cuming and fucking. Now I understand why men wanna fuck so much. Come, do me in the ass, Nick," Lola said, fluttering her fingers over Natalie's clit.

Lola didn't have to ask Nick twice. Nick jumped out of the Jacuzzi dripping wet and slid right up against Lola's ass, bumping Natalie out of the way. Natalie's back slid from underneath DeVaughn.

Nick caressed Lola's breasts, kissed the nape of her neck, then gently held her hips. When he embraced her from behind, he closed his eyes as he penetrated her pussy, and Natalie couldn't believe the passion in his strokes and his touch. Lola closed her eyes and for a minute she stopped fucking her husband.

"Oh my gosh. Nick, say it isn't so. Are you making love with Lola?"

Natalie didn't realize she'd spoken aloud until DeVaughn looked over his shoulder and said, "What the fuck did you just say?"

$\int$ EXCAPADE 18

Flint

"What cha gon' do . . . with this pussy?"

Nothing. Not a damn thing Flint thought, flipping through cable television channels while listening to the radio in the background. It would be nice if Samantha moved out of his way. After all his favorite show, *Boston Legal,* was replaying from his TiVo. It was on three days ago but so much had transpired since Tuesday that he wished she'd kept her regular schedule of coming home on Saturday instead of showing up a day early. He really should be more careful of what he asked for.

Regardless if Samantha was home it wasn't like he could fly to New York and surprise her without getting chastised. She'd be everything except happy to see him step foot into her Manhattan penthouse unannounced. Now she was clamoring all over him like an octopussy in heat.

"Please stop, move. I've got a lot on my mind. I'll give you some attention when I'm ready," Flint said gently, moving his wife aside with the same lack of concern he had for her retrievers.

"Stop ignoring me," Samantha protested. "You've got to be gay not to want this pussy." She straddled his lap, rotating her hips on his uninterested dick, demanding his undivided attention.

Did she know about his relations with her father? Did she care? Why was it that when a woman said no, it meant no. But when a man pressured a woman into having sexual intercourse it equated to a criminal act. Sperm, pubic hairs, particles of skin under a fingernail or any DNA match could land an innocent man behind bars longer than a videotape of assault and battery. Flint would be better off beating the shit out of Samantha. At least then he'd get her attention. With less than 5 percent of reported rape cases being filed by men the statistics gave Flint one more reason why it was safer to have sex with a man.

Actually, if his wife were to ask him, "What's the show about?" he couldn't answer.

The visual before him wasn't the television or her; Flint vividly saw those haunting eyes. He wondered if the guy he'd fucked earlier was at this very moment sitting alone trying to piece his life together, drowning his sorrows in a bottle of chardonnay, fucking a woman, letting his woman suck his dick, or hosting another man to numb his pain.

Those empty corneas shielded sadness. The suppressed hatred resonating from that guy's eyes mirrored Flint's broken spirit.

Boom! If his wife didn't chill out, at any moment Flint could explode, kill her, then kill himself. But as usual Samantha was obsessed with fulfilling her desires. He was actually glad she was going back to New York early in the morning. He could stop being angry at her, appease her by fucking her to her specifications, or hold her in his arms all night, knowing that the dick that was on the tip of his tongue would be in his mouth tomorrow night.

Swish! Leather cattails swept across his face. Flint wiped his cheek as Samantha slapped him again and again. "I asked you a question," she said, bracing her palm in the center of his forehead. "Look at me when I'm talking to you."

Staring at his wife through narrowed eyes, he didn't bother saying, "No you didn't." Instead he answered, "What would you'd like me to do, mistress?"

"Submit to me right now," Samantha demanded.

Getting out of the bed, Flint squatted his ass on the carpet. His hands balled into tight fists pressing against the floor with his elbows touching the inside of his knees.

Yanking the collar she'd tied around his neck, she seemed glad to be home with her obedient husband. Next week she'd probably have him put on a dress, a wig, some makeup, and high heels. Being in control excited Samantha.

The one thing that disturbed her was her father. What had her father seen in Flint that made him insist she become Flint's wife when her father knew she had a fiancé in New York City? Sure they'd grown up together, gone to church together, sat in the same Sunday school class, but Flint couldn't have been more opposite of her.

He wasn't college educated. His mama died early in his life. His grandmother was more of a babysitter than a disciplinarian. He grew up poor. And his father, well, God only knew who that was.

At times Samantha felt he was the child she'd never had. Surely he was no businessman but her father insisted that he run the San Francisco location. On the surface that was. Those business plans due in for the opening of Dons and Divas in Paris would be reviewed by her. The selection would be made by her not her dad and definitely not Flint.

Samantha was partial to strong women, which meant selecting Natalie was easier than asking Flint for a divorce. She'd had enough of playing charades to keep her father happy. She was ready to move forward with her life, marry the man she was in love with, and in seven months give birth to the baby growing inside of her. No need to pretend her unborn child was for her husband because she made him wear condoms every time they had sex.

The heel of Samantha's black patent leather boot landed on the wooden treasure chest at the foot of their bed. "Lick this good pussy," she commanded, stuffing her clit into Flint's mouth.

His tongue lapped like a dog.

"You've been spending too much time with the Lab. Lick my pussy slower," she demanded, slashing the cattails across his ass.

"Yes, mistress," Flint answered, doing as he was told.

"Good boy. Mama loves you."

And she did love him. Not like a husband. More like he was an orphan. In some ways he was. She wondered what made him so sad all the time. So unhappy with his life. Maybe divorcing him would give him an opportunity to start over. And against her father's will, she'd find a way to give Flint a half million dollars of his own. Samantha's conscious wouldn't allow her to kick her husband out with no money.

Samantha knew Flint never wanted to marry her just like she didn't want to marry him, that they did it to satisfy her father. Her father was truly the only one who was happy.

"Get your ass up, put on this condom," Samantha demanded, tossing the gold packet in Flint's face, "And fuck the shit out of me!"

"Yes, mistress," Flint said, being obedient.

With her thigh boot still planted on the wooden chest, Samantha tilted her ass in his direction. His stiff dick penetrated her pussy and she went wild with pleasure, thrusting her ass against his pelvis.

"Yes, fuck me harder! Harder! Harder!" she yelled.

The slurping sounds coming from her pussy sounded like someone smacking gum with their mouth open. Samantha slapped those cattails against her clit and his balls until they both started screaming and cuming at the same time. Removing all her clothes, she tossed them to the floor and collapsed across the bed.

Letting the cattails whip fall to the floor, Samantha said, "Lie with me. I want you to hold me."

Flint hugged his wife's waist from behind as they lay in the spoon position. She couldn't stand to look at him, knowing this might be their last sexual encounter.

Quietly Samantha confessed, "I'm pregnant with someone else's baby, so I have to divorce you."

Flint replied, "Great. You've asked for what I've wanted from the day we stood at the altar. But before I sign the papers, you'll have to pay me a million dollars to walk, or I'm going to tell the whole world that your great Reverend father has molested me for years."

As she jumped on top of him Samantha's arms swung landing against his face, his chest, his head. "You fucking broke ass, dirty ass, conniving ass, lying son of a dead bitch!"

Tears streamed down her face because she didn't want to believe what she'd heard rumored at church. That was another reason why Samantha seldom came back to San Francisco. She wanted to escape the shame. But her husband didn't have to try to capitalize on those damn lies. Deep inside she'd had her own suspicions. Now everything made sense and Samantha hated her husband but she could never hate her father.

Holding Flint's face in her palms she replied, "I'll give you whatever you want if you promise to keep your mouth shut about my father. I'm so sorry. I knew something wasn't right. I didn't know what. Thanks for finally telling me the truth. Give me a week. I'll have my lawyer draw up the contract. You must leave the company but stay until I announce that Natalie's getting the job. Forget the trial periods. I'll fly in Monday and offer her the job by five o'clock."

"You are really fucked up! You think I'm stupid! You tell me you're marrying another man and you're pregnant like I don't mean shit to you!" Flint yelled with tears of hate pouring from his eyes. "Your father is fucked up too! That sick motherfucker!" Flint balled his fist and swung inches from Samantha's face. He had no intention of hitting her.

Dodging his fist, she screamed, "Aahhh!"

Flint would bet his entire million dollars that was probably the first time his wife feared for her life. Her ass wasn't so bad after all. But when she had that whip slapping him upside the head she didn't think twice about hitting him again and again. She didn't give a damn how her abusive role playing angered him. Well, if only for a few minutes, her ass knew what fear felt like.

"Call me a son of a dead bitch again and I'll kill you!" Flint yelled. "I just told you your father is a fucking molester and you're treating this like a business deal! I don't give a fuck who you give that job to. I don't give a fuck about you! Or your father! Or your crazy-ass mother who your father admitted into a fucking mental institution to keep her from exposing his dirty little secrets. And if you ever lay your motherfucking hands on me again, bitch, if you breathe or sneeze on me, I will kill you and your father."

Flint punched a hole in the headboard big enough to stick Samantha's head into.

She'd never had anyone threaten her life. But just in case Flint was serious, Samantha held her breath long enough to get the hell out of her house, wearing the first thing she'd grabbed, those thigh-high patent leather boots.

∫EXCAPADE 19

Nick

Nick had done all the right things. But he'd done them for the wrong woman.

The foursome was awesome. Cuddling Natalie in his arms while she slept, that Natalie was always full of surprises. Nick thought he'd never find another woman equally adventurous until he connected with Lola Davis. Prior to making love to Lola, he never appreciated her raw beauty because he saw her as off-limits since she was DeVaughn's wife. Lola helped him realize that a man should go after the woman he wanted regardless of whether or not she was married and let the woman decide if she wanted to be with that man. Many married women were unhappy but why should they be? Being married wasn't an entitlement that Lola should remain faithful to after saying "I do" if she didn't feel loved and honored by her husband, especially when she was the one paying all the bills.

Nick knew how to make Lola feel like a woman. If he could do for Lola the things he'd done for Natalie, there was no doubt she would reciprocate his generosity. He didn't complain, but a gift, one gift over the three to four years from Natalie, no matter how small, would've showed him, if only in that moment, she'd thought about him.

Last night Nick saw a different side of Natalie and DeVaughn . . . jealousy. If either of them had put more energy into the relationships they had instead of being so selfish, they wouldn't feel threatened. DeVaughn like too many other men was so busy drowning in sexual self-gratification that if Natalie hadn't opened her mouth, he would've never noticed Nick seriously making love to his wife.

After Lola came, Nick didn't care about DeVaughn squaring his shoulders, stomping around in circles, or shouting profanities with every other word out of his limited vocabulary. It wasn't like DeVaughn could kick his ass, which is why, Nick was certain, he didn't throw any punches. If DeVaughn was a real man, he'd take care of his wife instead of letting her get dressed for work five days a week while he lay up not even trying to find a job. In a way, Nick was relieved that DeVaughn knew because if he made one more wrong decision, Nick was stepping up his game with Lola.

Nick understood DeVaughn's bad temper. The one thing, the only thing that turned him off, was DeVaughn tooting his ass up in the air like a bitch. After last night, Nick would never see him the same. DeVaughn lost his hetero card for life. Once a man crossed over into anal penetration, it was just a matter of time before he wanted a real dick in his ass. Nick would find a way to convince Lola it was best if she divorced him immediately.

"Good morning," Natalie said, rolling toward Nick. Her arms stretched high in the air. "When did you and Lola get so close?"

Nick decided not to consider Natalie's feelings and answered, "About the same time you let DeVaughn fuck you in the ass. You see you and DeVaughn started what Lola and I are going to finish."

Natalie casually said, "It's probably best. Everything happens for a reason. I've got plans and whoever gets this promotion doesn't really matter because after the announcement is made there'll be no more us."

Natalie was right. There'd be no more them and no more Lola. Nick could be happy relocating to Paris without Natalie and all of her inconsiderate rules. They'd been together intimately for three years and they were still just friends. Definitely he'd miss Natalie but he had to find a way to take Lola with him. Maybe he could invite Lola on a trip to France, then convince her to stay.

"Where's Lola and DeVaughn?" Natalie asked.

"We're at my house and they're at home, I guess. I don't know," Nick said, getting out of bed. "I'm taking you to brunch, then I'll take you back to Tiburon to pick up your car."

"What, how'd we get to your place?"

"You had way too many martinis last night. I'm sure you

don't remember cursing out Lola and me either. Anyway, I drove us here. Now get up and let's get going before we miss our one o'clock reservation."

"Hmm," Natalie said, easing out of bed.

Natalie used Nick's bathroom while he showered in his guest bathroom to save time. Securing an oversized bath towel about his waist, Nick watched Natalie scan through her closet in the guest bedroom. She selected a casual mustard-colored pantsuit and brown open-toe shoes. Her hair naturally curled into a miniature afro and a smear of lip gloss was all the makeup she put on.

"You look beautiful," Nick told her as he heard his cell phone buzzing in the background.

Natalie followed him into his bedroom. Relocating away from her to the living room, Nick answered, "Hello?"

"Hey, Nick. It's Lola. Can you meet me a little earlier? Say around two o'clock to get your package? DeVaughn and I have plans later."

Swallowing the lump in his throat, Nick lowered his voice, then said, "Sure, where?"

"Jack London Starbucks inside Barnes and Noble."

"Oakland?"

"Sorry, Nick. I hope it's not too much of a problem but once we leave for Monterey we won't be back until late Sunday and . . . Nick, please. Just do it. I won't feel right keeping your money if you don't get what you paid for."

Intentionally leaving his plan in Lola's car yesterday was supposed to give Nick a reason to see her again for a few hours tonight. Tightening his lips, Nick asked, "Did you tell him the plan was for me?"

"I had to. I tell my husband everything. Nick, please keep what happened last night between us. I don't want any of my corporate partners to think differently about me or DeVaughn if I end up divorcing my husband. You know the running joke among other nationalities about how black folk can't get along not even in their own home. I don't want to be a statistic or the topic of conversation in the break room."

"So you'd rather stay married to a deadbeat?" Nick wasn't sure why but his heart hurt like hell. Disappointed, he said, "I'll see you there," and ended the call.

No sooner had Nick ended his call with Lola, when his cell phone buzzed again. All Nick thought was it had better not be DeVaughn calling trying to convince Nick to keep his mouth shut about what happened last night. DeVaughn had best be thankful Nick didn't have a video to put on YouTube.com. Obviously DeVaughn had gotten into Lola's head. Just as he was about to sit down, Natalie walked in and peeped around his shoulder. Shielding his caller ID, Nick said, "Since when did we become so inquisitive? You mind?"

Waiting for Natalie to leave, he answered, "Hello," walking around the coffee table so she wouldn't creep up on him again without him knowing.

"Yeah, Nick. I need to see you at my place today. Can you be here at two?"

Now Nick had a fucking three-way dilemma. Reschedule with Natalie and either miss picking up his business plan from Lola or miss a personal meeting with Flint to get this job.

Nick answered, "Let me call you back."

When he ended the call with Flint, Nick heard Natalie slam the door leading to his garage shouting, "Fuck you, Nick Thurston!"

What? What'd he do? Nick wasn't sure if he should've felt happy, scared, or pissed but he wasn't going to chase or call Natalie until tomorrow. "Shit!" Nick yelled, racing to the front door.

Blowing his horn, Natalie waved, driving off in his Bentley. As he ran after it barefoot in the middle of the street the towel fell from around his waist. With his dick flopping in the wind, Nick chased his car for an entire block, pleading, "Natalie come back!" He gave up when she skidded around the corner. Walking back home naked, Nick did the next best thing. He dialed a rental car company, reserved an SUV, and requested they deliver the car to him ASAP.

While waiting for his rental to be dropped off, Nick returned Flint's call.

"Hey, I'm glad you called back. So you can make it?"

"Is four okay?"

"See you then," Flint said.

Nick eased into a pair of black slacks, a silk short-sleeve button-down tan shirt, and his black leather slip-on sandals and headed to Oakland in a Ford Explorer. Barnes and Noble was buzzing with a group of junior high school students enthusiastically promoting an anthology they'd written.

"Mister, if you purchase our book today you'll save ten percent plus my school, St. Lawrence O'Toole, will receive a percentage of the proceeds plus I may earn a scholarship toward my tuition from the Lou Richie Foundation."

Proudly Nick looked at the young black man standing before him. He wasn't pushing drugs. He was articulate and he was a published author.

"How old are you?" Nick asked him, reaching for his wallet.

"Fourteen. We wrote our stories two years ago when I was in the sixth grade. My story was also published in a local newspaper. I want to write more stories. Will you please help us? If you don't buy it today, you can order it online at Amazon .com."

"Young man I'll take four copies if you promise to sign them."

Purchasing the autographed copies of *Diverse Stories: From the Imaginations of Sixth Graders*, presented by Mary B. Morrison, Nick congratulated the young man, then headed to the Starbucks café upstairs.

Texting Lola, he ordered a small coffee while thumbing through the thirty-three stories. A half hour later, exactly at two-thirty, Lola walked in late, placed the package on the small round table, and left without saying, "Hi," or "Bye."

"Lola, wait," Nick said, grabbing his bag and his package and leaving the coffee. Hurrying downstairs in front of the magazine section, Nick peered into Lola's sad eyes. "Lola, what's wrong? If I did something to hurt you, I apologize. I never want to hurt you. Lola, I love you."

A teardrop clung to Lola's eyelid as she turned away.

"Lola, please don't walk away from me like this. I deserve an explanation."

She stopped, turning toward him. Gazing into his eyes, Lola placed Nick's ring in his hand. Her lips trembled. "Nick, I'm pregnant," she said, then walked away.

Stretching out his arm to return the ring, Nick asked, "For who? For me? Is it my baby?" He followed Lola outside until he saw DeVaughn standing in front of Scott's Restaurant, motioning for Lola to come to him.

Nick's feet froze. The lump in his throat choked him so tight he felt like he'd swallowed his Adam's apple. Remembering the tiny handprints surrounding the title on the cover of the books in his hands, Nick wondered if the baby growing inside of Lola was his or her husband's. If she had no intention of telling DeVaughn that Nick might be the father, maybe going to Paris alone was best because if Nick stayed, there was no way he wouldn't demand a paternity test. Heading to the garage, Nick got in his SUV and drove to Flint's. The entire trip was a blur.

Flint opened the door, wearing knee-length basketball shorts, an extra-long T-shirt, and house slippers.

"Hey, come on in. I'm glad you could make it. I was just about to eat. You hungry?"

Holding back his tears, Nick said, "Famished," and followed Flint into the kitchen.

"You can have a seat in the entertainment room," Flint said, pointing toward the left. "I'll bring a plate to you. What would you like to drink, man? Wine, champagne, something harder?"

"Man, I need something stiff."

Flint smiled. "Not a problem. I've got you covered."

SEXCAPADE 20

Flint

Struggling to control the yearning sensation rising from his chest to his throat, Flint inhaled the lingering scent of Nick's masculine cologne. The tightness continued rising, blocking Flint's airway. Circling the island in his kitchen, Flint opened his mouth and began gulping oxygen. "Aw damn." Nick was actually in Flint's house, sitting in his entertainment room, waiting. Waiting to spend time with him.

I should've changed my clothes, Flint thought, rubbing his sweaty hands down his T-shirt to his shorts. If I change now, what will he think? Calm down. It's only Nick. Only? Damn. If Nick were his partner, Flint wouldn't have to fuck strange men or Samantha. Hopefully Samantha was on a plane flying through the air halfway to New York City. If Flint never laid eyes on that coldhearted woman again, that would be a well-deserved blessing. Flint had to make sure Samantha did not interfere with Nick getting that promotion Monday, then Flint would announce his resignation once human resources completed all of his paperwork. But tonight Flint wanted to make love to Nick.

"Your place is incredible," Nick shouted from the adjacent room.

Flint added a little extra base to his voice to conceal his excitement, "You can thank my wife's interior decorator. Make yourself comfortable. The Raiders are kicking ass, man. Sure hope they beat the hell out of the Chiefs."

Nick yelled, "What we need is a professional basketball team in San Francisco. But I'm pulling for Aaron Brooks for sho. The Raiders should've never let him go."

"I agree but sports and business are all about who's willing to work hard on the bottom long enough to be on top," Flint said, trying to give Nick a hint.

Flint poured two glasses of cognac and headed to the entertainment room. "Here you go," he said, handing a snifter with two shots to Nick.

"Man, this is the kind of spot I need. Six theater chairs, a movie projection screen, surround sound, damn! Where's your wife?"

"She was here last night. We had a great time but she's on her way back to New York as we speak," Flint said, sitting in the first row of three reclining vibrating chairs. He really wanted to sit next to Nick and inhale his manly scent but he used his better judgment and left an empty seat between them.

"I was looking forward to meeting her for the first time. What's up with old man Sexton? Is he planning on leaving you the company?" Nick asked as his cell phone rang. Checking his caller ID, Nick said, "Excuse me just a sec, I'ma take this."

Whoever it was Flint was thankful and hopeful that he wouldn't have to answer either of Nick's questions. Hearing Nick mention the two people he hated the most was altering Flint's good mood. Blowing out a puff of hot air, Flint rattled his head.

Bypassing the usual introductory greetings, Nick boldly asked, "Where's my car?" Sitting on the edge of his seat, he said, "Don't worry about where I am, woman, where's my damn car?"

Flint overheard Natalie's voice on the phone. "You're not slick, Nick. I know where you are. And if I were you, I'd be very careful. He's gay."

"Woman, you have gone fifty-one-fifty these last few days. Just bring me back my car. I'll call you when I'm on my way home. Good-bye." Nick ended the call, sighed heavily, then looked at Flint.

Flint sang, "If you got girl problems, I feel sorry for you, son."

Surprisingly, Nick chimed in with, "I've got ninety-nine problems but a bitch ain't one."

They laughed hard for about thirty seconds, then there was silence. Sexual thoughts of Nick crept into Flint's mind. Was Nick having similar thoughts?

With a shake of his head, Nick's smile abruptly disappeared as he commented, "I love women. I hate even saying the b-word because I'd never call my mother that. Right now I wished I could concur with Jay-Z's lyrics but I've got more female energy than I can balance."

A part of Flint wanted to ask Nick about his childhood but

he sensed Nick had had a good upbringing. On that note Flint stood and said, "Man, I'm going to fix our food."

Flint wasn't the best cook but he removed four southern fried chicken breasts from the deep fryer, and loaded them on their plates with homemade mashed potatoes with gravy and fresh stems of broccoli. For Flint, this was his first date. He'd never had a real date. Some may call it a blind date while others including Nick wouldn't see it as a date at all. Flint set both plates on a tray that stretched across the arms of the empty chair between them.

"Have you ever lived outside of the U.S.?" Flint asked.

"Never. But I've traveled to Paris, Amsterdam, Madrid, London, Trinidad, Brazil, Jamaica, Rome, you name it."

"Are you sure you want this job?"

"Positive. What is there not to love about Paris, right? I've been there three times and each time I've had a ball. I wish they didn't smoke so much but the women there are real women. They don't play games like the women here in the States. I can appreciate that. You know what I mean?"

Perhaps it was Flint's feelings of guilt after overhearing Natalie's comment but Nick asked as though he needed confirmation that Flint was straight. "How well do I know," Flint answered, then said, "How do you think Natalie will feel if you get this promotion?"

"I think she expects me to get it. Women and gay people are subservient to men like us. Wouldn't you agree?"

Not at all, Flint thought. Now he knew Nick was fishing, so he decided to throw him some bait. "Are you okay? Your mind seems to be someplace else. How would you feel about getting the job if I told you I was gay?"

Nick's eyebrows lifted as he held his breath. "I'm good, man. Women, you know. Going to Paris and all. That'll be perfect for me, um. Man, you're actually cooler than I thought but you're not really that way. Are you?" Nick asked, shoveling his potatoes back and forth like a hockey puck.

Flint decided not to answer him. "Yeah, women. My wife is wonderful but I can't figure her out," he said, letting him know he had his own problems with them too. "Seconds?"

"Naw, I'm full," Nick said, relaxing his shoulders. Most of Nick's food remained on his plate. "But I could use another drink."

Perfect. Flint needed Nick to get drunk before making his move. The only problem was Nick was clearly heterosexual. Fortunately gay bashing was something Flint hadn't encountered and he didn't plan on starting tonight. The game was coming on in a few minutes. He had to do something.

Standing in the kitchen filling two clean snifters, Flint got a brilliant idea. Hurrying to the bedroom, he opened the medicine cabinet in the master bathroom and smiled. Returning to the kitchen, he mixed Nick's drink half cognac, half gamma hydroxybutyrate or GHB, better known as the date rape drug.

"So how fast do you think you can learn to speak French?" Flint asked, handing Nick his glass.

"Yeah, I was surprised one of the criteria wasn't the ability to speak French," he said, sniffing his drink.

Loudly, Flint said, "Actually it is but until you speak fluently we're hiring a translator," trying to distract Nick from sipping his drink.

The liquid substance didn't have a smell but it was slightly salty. Flint knew because occasionally he would trade off with Samantha on taking it during sex.

"Well, I knew Natalie would have the upper hand if I included the French language as a requirement. I chose you because you'll get more respect in Paris than Natalie."

"I couldn't agree more. I can start taking classes ASAP," Nick said.

"A toast to your million-dollar promotion," Flint said, taking the lead on tossing back his double.

Nick opened his mouth, placed the glass against his lips, and swallowed the contents in one big gulp. "That tasted a little different, man. Yours?"

"Nope," Flint said, reaching for Nick's empty glass and setting it on the tray between them.

The date rape drug was potent and worked in minutes. Flint laughed and so did Nick until Nick held his head and said, "Man, my head is spinning. Maybe I shouldn't have started drinking after having so much alcohol last night."

"You okay?" Flint asked.

"Yeah, man. I'm cool but you're starting to look blurry."

"You don't look so cool. Let me get you some water," Flint offered.

"Naw, man. I got it," Nick said. When Nick stood his legs buckled beneath him.

Flint watched Nick lean like a falling stack of dominoes until his body hit the floor.

"What the fuck?" Nick's slurred speech resonated in slow motion. "I can barely feel anything below my waist. My arms are numb too, man. I think I'm having a heart attack. Call nine one one."

Reaching up toward Flint, Nick's arms collapsed, his eyes rolled backward, then closed. Falling to his knees, Flint slowly unzipped Nick's pants. His body may have been limp but his dick was just the way Flint wanted it, stiff. Bowing his face to Nick's dick, Flint sniffed his balls whispering, "I promise you'll get the promotion," but Nick couldn't hear him. Nick was passed out.

Flint imagined Nick protesting, "Fuck the promotion, let go of my dick."

Nick's delicious body was about to become Flint's dessert. Opening his mouth wide, Flint sucked Nick cleaner than he'd done the gristle connected to that chicken bone. His eyes rolled to the back of his head as Nick's head slid to the back of his throat massaging his tonsils. After Nick came in his mouth, Flint removed his shoes, unbuckled then removed his pants, rolled him over, lubricated his butt, and finally did what he'd dreamed about for a long time. Flint slipped his dick inside Nick's ass.

Gliding in and out of Nick's ass felt great. Why couldn't Flint have a man like Nick to call his own. "Damn, you're making me cum," Flint said, pressing his hard dick deep inside Nick.

With each wave of cum Flint pushed deeper until his dick went limp. Sliding out of Nick's ass, he whispered, "Fair exchange is no robbery. Consider this your million-dollar orgasm."

SEXCAPADE 21

Natalie

No two people were exactly the same.

Every individual's personality and sexuality was unique unto them. Not their parents, their pastor, or anybody else's. Molding individuals into social clones was as toxic as inhaling mold. But just like mildew spreading along bathroom ceilings, some parents never noticed the adverse impact of stifling their children's sexuality.

Natalie was blessed to have liberated parents, especially her mother. Natalie's mother shared with her many things that her mother hadn't discussed with her like puberty and sex, and Natalie heard the words "I love you" every day. Her mother didn't classify herself as Natalie's friend. Natalie was her daughter. And as candid as they were with one another, Natalie couldn't disclose her promiscuous behavior to her mom. Not because she was afraid. It just didn't seem right to say, "Mommy, guess whose pussy I licked today." Mothers were born to be held in the highest esteem, for solving problems, healing wounds, sharing love, giving invaluable advice, and imparting wisdom to their children that sustained generations to come.

When Natalie was growing up, her mother taught her that the body was a sexual canvas and she was an artist eternally in residence, constantly evolving into womanhood. Mama would say, "Womanhood is a journey, not a destination. Natalie, you must think before you speak. You must have faith in God and faith in yourself. Most important, my love, you must make time to sit still and listen."

To what, Natalie thought. What was she listening for?

Natalie remembered her mother saying, "Complaining to others transfers your negativity to them even if they don't realize it. And when you listen to others vent, each breath you inhale absorbs that negative energy. In order to be at peace, find a quiet space, align your head with the heavens, and let your feet rest upon the earth and your negative energy will transition from your body safely into the earth. God has given you everything you need to succeed."

Sometimes parents say things that at the time the words are spoken they're heard but not always understood. Now Natalie got it. She had to sit still for mental and spiritual clarity, and to listen to her inner voice. It was time for her to let go of her worries so she could grow.

Nick's car was parked in Natalie's garage because she was upset with him. But why? Knowing she wasn't accepting the promotion if it was offered to her should've been enough of a reason for her not to compete with Nick. She didn't have anything to prove to him or anyone else. Natalie had to let go of her jealousy that Lola and Flint had called Nick this morning but neither of them had called her. So what. She had one life and she refused to waste it trying to control someone else's destiny. Natalie had no control over others and nothing and no one on earth had power over her unless she relinquished her power to them.

If Natalie sat in a chair or lay still in her bed and created a desire to make love to herself or someone else, her passion drove her to orgasm each time. Like masturbating, she guessed that same level of harmony could overwhelm her in many other nonsexual ways. She needed something positive not someone negative to focus on. And since she was alone, well, it was time to do Natalie.

As she sat in her bedroom on the love-chaise she'd bought for herself, Natalie spread her legs, freeing her pussy to the fading sunset flickering through her skylight. Reclining, she braced one thigh against the side cushion, and let her other thigh rest flat while her foot touched the floor. She could meditate after this but right now she was ready to enjoy her body. No one could please her better than she pleasured herself. Not DeVaughn, not Lola, not even her best lover and questionable best friend, Nick.

Leaning her head back, Natalie closed her eyes and stroked her body with a gold feather. Starting at her feet, she immediately surrendered to the breath-holding sensation when the feather made contact with her toes. Ever so slowly, she swept the feather over her ankles, her legs, and her knees. Although the limited stroking was confined to certain areas, she was emotionally present with the arousal originating in her breasts and her neck, and the tingling in the crown of her head as the feather grazed her thighs.

Natalie breathed deep into her belly. In through her nose and out of her mouth, knowing she was a woman.

Stroking the feather higher up her thigh, she let the tip flutter against her pussy as she licked her lips. Now her toes were tingling and she wanted to scratch the itch below her shoulder blade but she resisted.

She breathed. Deeply into her belly and out once more. Natalie was a woman in control and at the same time not. She was afraid. Afraid of losing Nick. Afraid of losing herself in pursuit of her dreams.

Allowing herself to be vulnerable with herself instead of others piqued Natalie's passion and reinforced her female power. Dismissing the need to suppress her emotions or guide her thoughts during lovemaking freed her energy and her spirit.

Natalie was a woman welcoming new experiences, discovering new heightened levels of orgasms, pushing herself by herself to explore new territory. She needed people but more so Natalie realized she needed to stand up and not be accounted for but accountable.

She was a woman. A woman. Realizing if all women around the world refused to get pregnant and give life to a new generation, the world would cease to exist. Females' ability to reproduce was powerful beyond measure and if any man believed men rule the world, he was a very foolish man indeed.

Mentally Natalie scratched her itch. Not the one continuously nudging her in the back. She redirected that energy to her mouth and she licked her lips until she imagined having simultaneous orgasms with Nick—wherever he was—without either of them touching the other. Erasing thoughts of Nick from her canvas, Natalie didn't know why his energy kept resurging in the middle of her strokes. Gently zigzagging the feather across her abdomen, Natalie said aloud, "Natalie, I love you. This moment is yours and yours alone."

Her breasts begged for attention so she swished the feather over her nipples, "Ah, yes." Breasts are the best. Natalie loved the way the countless nerve endings could awaken her entire body. Touching or sometimes thinking about the stimulating sensations of her breasts made her cum. Her pussy pulsated in agreement. Natalie swished the feather over her collarbone and her neck and up to her face as she softly blew watching the hair stems flutter.

Natalie's nose tickled as she breathed. In and out. She sneezed. "God bless me," she whispered. Natalie was a woman in love with herself. Loving herself.

Laying the feather aside, she began to finger paint her body. Her canvas was blank. Her mind was open. Natalie was ready. She was ready to experience the unknown. Licking her middle finger, she created tiny little circles around her pearl until she created her own secretions.

"Ou yes," Natalie moaned with delight. "This feels so right.

Who could love me better?" she asked, smiling, then answered, "I can."

Now that she was nice and wet, she retrieved her toy. Before turning on the cordless eight-inch vibrator on low, Natalie saturated her toy with water-based lube. She closed her thighs, then rubbed the head along her shaft. That felt really good to her, so she opened her legs wider. Activating the slow rotation mode, the pearls inside the head danced in circles. Inserting the tip inside her wet pussy, she felt the vibrations and rotations celebrating her G-spot. Her body jerked with pleasure.

As she stopped the rotation and increased the vibration, the soft gel rabbit ears teased Natalie's clit as the pulsating head nestled inside her pussy pocket. She held the vibrator right there. "Yes, that's the spot."

Natalie breathed. In and out. Quietly, she came. There was no desire to scream or yell or lose control. She was at peace with herself. Natalie was loving herself. She was a woman who could pleasure herself. She exhaled. Her canvas for that moment was complete with every color of the rainbow and she had a pussy filled with gold.

Relaxing, her body sunk into the chaise's cushions. Her cell phone rang momentarily, interrupting her natural high. If she guessed correctly—based upon the position of the full moon shadowing her skylight—she'd say it was about eight o'clock, which meant the only person calling her would've been Nick.

Closing her eyes, Natalie ignored the annoying ring tone.

Natalie's phone rang again. "Nick, please. Whatever you have to say can wait until tomorrow."

Her phone rang again. The paint on her canvas was damp,

her rainbow was fading into her clouds of joy. Reluctantly, she retrieved her phone. Glancing at her caller ID, she was right.

Sighing into the phone, Natalie answered, "Yes, Nick?"

"Hey, Natalie, this is Flint."

Her heart pounded against her throat, choking out his name, "Flint? Why are you calling me from Nick's phone? Where's Nick?"

"Natalie, don't panic."

My God, those were the wrong words to say. "Don't what?" Natalie insisted. "Put Nick on the phone right now."

"Natalie, please, we don't have time for this. Take down my address. I need you to come to my house right now. Nick isn't breathing."

The phone dangled between her fingertips. Her body became numb.

"Natalie! Natalie! Natalie!"

"Flint, you have to calm down. If Nick isn't breathing, I don't have time to get to your address. He'll be dead by then. Do you know CPR?" she asked, trying not to pass out. Natalie had to do all she could to save Nick. She couldn't imagine her life without him in it. She was too afraid to have Flint dial 911, fearing by the time they asked several questions Nick might be dead.

Flint answered, "No, I don't."

$\mathcal{S}$EXCAPADE 22

Flint

Flint was scared shitless.

Dragging Nick's body from the entertainment room into his living room, he laid him in the middle of the floor on the Persian rug. Flint straightened Nick's shirt, buckled his pants, placed his arms at his sides, and picked the lint out of his hair. Later Flint would vacuum to erase the body tracks in the carpet, wash the dishes in the dishwasher, and dust every piece of furniture Nick had touched in case the crime scene investigators received a warrant to search his home. He'd cooperate with the authorities to the fullest extent but first Flint had to cover his ass.

The anger. The rage. The fire burning inside of him to kill Mr. Sexton or someone else was never intended for Nick. Flint had been so anxious to be inside of Nick that he hadn't both-

ered using a condom. His dick was hard, throbbing, and oozing with precum and he didn't know how much time he had
to fuck Nick before he regained consciousness so he had to do
back-to-back quickies.

Nick's dick tasted incredibly delicious like hot, creamy,
melt-in-the-mouth caramel. How could Flint convince the
police that this was an accident if they performed an autopsy
and found his sperm in Nick's ass? In retrospect the orgasms
weren't worth him harming Nick. If Flint could change
places with Nick, he swore he would in a heartbeat.

Rattling off directions to Natalie on how to get to his house,
he clearly remembered having read the side effects of the
date rape drug GHB which was ironically legal in the United
States to treat narcolepsy. They were drowsiness, dizziness,
nausea, problems seeing, unconsciousness, seizures, inability to
remember what happened while drugged, problems breathing, tremors, sweating, vomiting, slow heart rate, dreamlike
feeling, coma, or, in rare cases, death.

If doctors could prescribe GHB for patients, why couldn't
Flint give a dose to Nick? As with any medication, the problem was in this case Flint didn't know how much of the liquid
was lethal. And since the pharmaceutical industry was striving
to have every infant, child, and adult on meds, most of those
same side effects of GHB could've been stated on the extensive
A to Z list of drugs like Allegra, Amoxil, Botox, Valium, Valtrex,
Viagra, Vicodin, Xanax, or Zantac.

The only side effect Flint had hoped for was the "inability
to remember what happened while drugged" one. Actually he
prayed if Nick survived he would have absolutely no recollec-

tion of any parts of this incident. But just in case Nick did and threatened to kick his ass or kill him, Flint had taken pictures and recorded a video. With a click of a button Nick would be posted on www.YouTube.com for the entire world to see Flint sucking and fucking him. If he could get Nick out of his house fast enough, maybe he wouldn't recall coming over and they'd both move on with their seemingly flawless corporate careers.

Damn, the keys to Nick's rental car sitting in Flint's driveway were in the other room. Maybe he could return the SUV, have the charges billed to whatever credit card he had on file, take the rental car shuttle to the airport, then get in a taxi and come back home. Flint had to multitask like a magician and make some shit disappear. If he hadn't phoned Natalie, he could've buried Nick in the backyard. By the time the dogs would've dug up his body or the landscaper would've found his remains, Flint could've been living in Europe where natives were free to be openly gay.

"I'm getting in my car. I'm on my way," Natalie said, interrupting Flint's thoughts.

Yelling, Flint panicked, "No, please! Don't hang up on me!"

Natalie was his only witness that he'd tried to save Nick's life. He hadn't dialed 911 because he was afraid they'd suspect he had something to with Nick's accident and while the ambulance transported Nick to the hospital, the police would drive his ass to lockup. There was no way Flint was going to jail for having predatory sex or committing second-degree murder.

Natalie said, "I need you to calm down. I'm not hanging up. Just follow my instructions until I get there."

Since nothing serious ever happened to Flint when Samantha

gave him the drug, he figured nothing life threatening would happen to Nick. If it weren't for bad luck, he'd have none. Flint couldn't even cum without fucking things up.

"Does he have a pulse?" Natalie asked.

"I don't know," he answered, pacing around Nick's inert body.

"Place your pointing and middle fingers behind his ear at the back of his jawbone. Then I want you to slowly slide them underneath his jawbone an inch toward his chin and press upward into the crevice of his neck."

Flint's hand trembled like a leaf in gusty winds but he managed to do as he was told. "I've got a pulse!" he yelled. "Yes, I've got a pulse."

Natalie exhaled, "Thank God. I pray I won't have to walk you through doing chest compressions. Look at his chest. Is it rising and falling?"

Oh boy. More instructions? Sweat poured from Flint's forehead. "No, it's not."

"Place your ear to his nostrils and tell me if you can feel his breath."

"No. I don't feel a thing."

"Place your hand on Nick's chin and tilt his head back to open his airway. Now you're going to have to breathe for him. Continue holding his head back, open his mouth, and pinch his nose."

"Done."

"Now place your mouth over his."

Natalie was unbelievably calm. "Okay," Flint said.

There was nothing sexual about trying to save somebody's

life, especially if you were the one who'd placed their life in jeopardy. Flint's hands trembled as he listened to Natalie explain to him how to perform mouth to mouth, filling Nick's lungs by breathing into his body while watching his chest rise.

"You have to keep breathing for Nick and listening to me. I'm getting ready to conference call a 911 operator for an ambulance," Natalie said.

Flint wasn't sure what he would've done without Natalie guiding him through the process. Moments later the paramedics and Natalie were banging at his front door. The paramedics rushed over to Nick while Natalie hurried over to Flint.

"What the fuck did you do to him?" Natalie asked, standing inches in front of his face.

One of the paramedics momentarily looked at Flint as he took a step away from Natalie. What happened to being calm? Natalie eyes narrowed and her nose flared at the same time she squared her shoulders thrusting her breasts toward Flint.

He liftied his eyebrows, his eyes widened. "Listen, I thank you for helping walk me through this. I called you because you're the closest person to Nick that I know and since you guys are sex buddies, I figured you'd know if Nick had high blood pressure, high cholesterol, or some disease that could cause him to faint."

The expression on Natalie's face went from angry to tight lips and a cold stare. Wanting to get his facts on the record, Flint was satisfied when the two paramedics briefly glanced at one another like they too were fuck buddies.

The female paramedic asked, "Does he have any medical conditions?"

Abruptly, Natalie replied, "No. He's perfectly healthy."

When the female paramedic started taking Nick's vital signs the male ran outside.

Turning to Flint, Natalie said, "Oh, you don't want me to start talking about relationships——"

"Please, you guys. I'm trying to save a life here," the female paramedic said as the male rushed in with a gurney.

"Let's go into the next room," Flint suggested.

"Fuck you, Flint! If Nick dies, I'ma kill you!" Natalie cried. Her voice trembled as she asked the paramedics, "Is my baby going to be okay?"

Did she say, "my baby"? Flint was fishing for information but he didn't have any proof that Natalie had feelings for or had been sexually involved with Nick until now.

"Looks like it to me," the female paramedic said, staring up at Flint, "you did all you could. He's alive but we don't know if he's suffered brain damage due to the loss of oxygen. We're going to rush him to the hospital. You can meet us at San Francisco General."

Crying, Natalie stormed off into the kitchen and Flint followed her saying, "If I did anything, you heard her, I saved his life."

"Thanks to me," Natalie countered. "You didn't know where to check for a heartbeat. You don't even know CPR."

Okay, great. Kudos to Natalie. She knew a little something. Let's see if she'd respond to this. "So why did you call Nick your baby? You're sleeping with the wrong person to get the promotion."

Slap!

Natalie's hand landed across Flint's face. The stinging sensation lingered as he clinched his fist. For her sake, Flint hoped she didn't hit him again. He'd been abused enough in his lifetime and he wasn't about to add Natalie's name to the list. Flint knew he was wrong for thinking about hitting Natalie back but who cared about him when Samantha and Mr. Sexton abused his rights.

Flint's eyes bulged when Natalie grabbed the butcher's knife from the wooden stand on his countertop, and said, "Go ahead. Give me a reason."

Shit! Staring at the stainless steel blade, Flint didn't want to end up needing space in the ambulance next to Nick. Uncurling his fingers, he calmly said, "Look, Nick and I were having dinner and watching the game and the next thing I knew"—he paused, staring at the open bottle of GHB a little too long—"he passed out. I thought maybe Nick had a medical prob——"

Dropping the knife, Natalie yelled, "You fucking liar!" picking up the bottle. "You gave him this shit! You drugged my Nick?"

Speechless, Flint's mouth hung open as he tried to come up with another lie to cover the lie he'd already told.

Running into the living room, Natalie handed the paramedics the bottle and said, "Have them check his system for this. And if this date rape drug is in Nick Thurston's system," Natalie said, then pointed at Flint, "Justin Flint, the man standing right there, is solely responsible."

"Ouch," the male paramedic cringed, then asked, "Was this man raped? We see this more often than you'd believe in San Francisco. Problem is, most times it goes unreported. Understandably so. What guy wants to admit he's been raped?"

Natalie answered, "For Flint's sake, let's hope he didn't touch Nick. Because if he did, then Flint is going to be one dead man when Nick finds out. Nick is straight heterosexual, no doubts about it. He doesn't even like fingers in his asshole."

None of them responded to Natalie. The paramedics rolled Nick out on the gurney and Natalie headed toward the door behind them. Stopping Natalie in the doorway, Flint pleaded, "Wait a minute. You don't honestly think I raped Nick, do you?"

Natalie looked into his eyes. She didn't blink one time when she answered, "So what if I molested you as a child you're a grown man now, get over it and suck my dick."

Natalie cupped her pussy like she had balls and again Flint didn't know what to say.

Natalie continued, "I feel sorry for you, Flint, but to answer your question, yes, I do believe you raped Nick. Oh, and one last thing . . . I quit."

Flint didn't give a damn about Natalie quitting. Hell, he was resigning too. His bigger problem was he'd heard that men who went to jail for rape got group raped. Did that unwritten rule apply to a man that raped a man? If so, considering Flint was a topper, he was in deep trouble.

Chasing after Natalie, Flint jumped into his car and followed her to the hospital.

SEXCAPADE 23

DeVaughn

What would DeVaughn do with a million dollars?

Rubbing his palms together, he couldn't stop thinking about the endless possibilities. He could buy a whole new wardrobe, buy a bigger house on a higher hill, buy a BMW 700 series, put some twenty-fours on that bitch and get some serious slap in the trunk booming so hard that the people in the car next to him would feel his bass.

Life was short and DeVaughn was behind on getting his, so he didn't plan on wasting one minute. Putting things in perspective, this weekend he wanted to spoil his unborn baby and his wife. So for starters, he'd booked this fabulous suite at the Beach Resort Monterey since it was the only hotel there actually on the beach. From now on nothing but the best for his number one lady. DeVaughn had to use Lola's credit card for this trip but once he got that job, he was gonna retire his wife and pay for everything.

DeVaughn was excited beyond belief when Lola told him she was pregnant. She didn't act happy, perhaps because she was nervous wondering if having a baby would adversely impact her career and all but Lola didn't have a thing to worry about, not even Nick's feelings for her. That dude had a lot of nerve pushing up behind his wife at Tiburon like she was his woman.

Had DeVaughn been a violent person, Nick could've gotten himself killed or at a minimum gotten his ass kicked. He'd best not let the strap-on fool him. DeVaughn was all man. His jealous rage toward Nick dissipated when Lola reassured him, "DeVaughn, I'm married to you and you only."

Instantly his openness about sexually sharing his wife with Natalie and Nick changed. There'd be no more swinging, swapping, or foursomes. DeVaughn's love for Lola doubled knowing she was carrying his son. Did he have eyes yet, or a heartbeat? Did he have arms and legs or did he resemble that white thing clinging to an egg yolk. *Yes indeed I'm going to be a father.* Well, he hoped for a boy but a baby girl was cool too but he'd have to work 24–7 to do as Chris Rock said, "Keep her off the pole."

Natalie's twenty-five-thousand-dollar donation was nothing compared to the two hundred and fifty grand Nick gave Lola. Even if he didn't get the job or any job, Lola was going to finish what she'd started and drain Nick of the remaining seven hundred and fifty grand he claimed he was willing to invest. Yeah, he could comfortably become a stay-at-home dad driving around town with his mini-me in the backseat. For Nick's sake, DeVaughn really wanted him to get that position in Paris. That way DeVaughn could have his wife all to himself.

Lola wasn't happy when he insisted she meet Nick at Barnes and Noble for two minutes just long enough for her to walk in, handle their business, and walk out. Nick's behind was surprised when he came trailing Lola out of the bookstore and saw him. Nick should get accustomed to seeing more of DeVaughn and less of Lola, especially on Lola's lunch hour.

"Baby, why did you feel you had to sneak to be with Nick? You've never done that before."

Lola sat on the bed in their quaint hotel room gazing out the patio window, and said, "Why do we have to keep going over this? We discussed Nick and Natalie all the way here. Correction, you talked about them all the way here, through our entire dinner, while the movie *Love Trap* was playing, and now you're still hammering to death the same topic while I'm trying to relax and listen to the *Love Trap* soundtrack. I'm tired and aggravated, and I don't feel good. I need to get some rest."

Lola stretched across the bed as DeVaughn began rubbing her feet. She jerked, then curled into a fetal position, obviously not wanting him to touch her.

"Honey," DeVaughn explained, "I can't trust you. I want us to resolve this problem before we go home . . . we have to get on the same page. Here's what we're going to do. Nick's and Natalie's plans are due to Flint Monday. But Nick is going to need you to see him through implementation. We won't worry about Natalie." DeVaughn hadn't told Lola about the twenty-five grand. It wasn't that much money anyway and he'd planned on using it for a down payment on his new car. "We're going to orchestrate three more phases at two hundred and fifty grand apiece until we get the rest of his million dollars by the end of this week."

"DeVaughn shut the hell up! You're driving me crazy with your pathetic obsession about Nick's money. I can't do that to Nick."

He yelled back in her face, "You can! And you will do as I say! You are my wife!"

Lola stood, quietly picked up her purse, and headed toward the door.

"You're not walking out on me, Lola."

Tears clung to her eyelids. "DeVaughn, why do you always want something for nothing. Nick works long hard hours for his money. He's always buying Natalie expensive things all the time. He's a real man and he's a gentleman."

Looking into his wife's eyes, DeVaughn saw that she cared more about Nick than him. "So you wanna be with him? You think he's better than me? Is this what this is all about?" he asked, standing in front of the door. "You're not leaving me, you hear me, woman? You're not. That's final."

Lola walked over to the small desk and sat in the chair. Her cell phone rang. "Don't answer that while I'm talking to you," DeVaughn demanded, standing over his wife.

Checking her caller ID, Lola softly answered, "Yes."

After two seconds, Lola started crying.

Snatching the phone from her hand, DeVaughn asked, "What did you say to my wife?"

"DeVaughn, if I wanted to talk to you I would've called you. Put Lola back on the damn phone," Natalie said.

DeVaughn automatically assumed it was Nick since his name was on the caller ID. "Not until you tell me what you said to get my wife all upset."

"Nick is in trouble. I don't know who else to call. Please, DeVaughn, I need you and Lola to meet me at San Francisco General as soon as possible. Nick might not make it."

"You know whatever little game you're playing this time, leave us out of it. We're not meeting you at San Francisco General or any place else," DeVaughn said, ending the call.

Jumping from her seat, Lola cried louder, "Nick is in the hospital? We've got to go. DeVaughn, did you have anything do with Nick being in the hospital? Is this why we had to come to Monterey for the weekend? So I could be your alibi? I'm the one who can't trust you anymore. DeVaughn Davis." Lola stared him in his eyes, then said, "I want a divorce."

DeVaughn couldn't believe his fucking ears! "Forget that shit. That's what you're not getting from me. Besides, why in the hell would I want to hurt Nick? Lola, I'm serious, you're not leaving me with my baby inside of you. On second thought, if you want a divorce, fine. We can do that. But I won't sign anything until after you have my baby and give me full custody!"

Lola exhaled, "DeVaughn, it's not your baby, it's Nick's baby."

DeVaughn swore it took everything inside of him not to

hit Lola upside her head for her telling him some hurtful lying-ass shit like that when he was already pissed off, only making things between them worse. Whatever had happened to Nick, DeVaughn didn't give a damn. Nick could die for all he cared.

Walking out the door, Lola said, "You can drive me to San Francisco General or I'll drive myself."

It was well past midnight and DeVaughn wasn't letting his wife leave without him. Hell, she might pack his things, move him out, and move Nick into their house before he made it home.

They'd never unpacked, so DeVaughn grabbed their bags and followed Lola to the valet. The drive to the hospital was long for Lola because DeVaughn cursed her out all the way back to San Francisco.

SEXCAPADE 24

Natalie

What sense did it make living life without expressing love? All these years invested with Nick and all Natalie had ever done was suppress her true feelings for him. If he died in that emergency room, he'd never know how she honestly felt. The love she harbored would haunt her and she'd have no one to blame but herself.

Lola and DeVaughn probably wouldn't show up and she'd have no one to support her through her most challenging moment. Would she go into a depression? Would she lose her mind? Would she withdraw from society or give up on her dreams? Natalie had never lost anyone she'd deeply loved.

Natalie could practice expressing sincerity and forgiveness starting with Flint. Sitting next to him in the waiting room, she asked, "Did that really happen to you? How old were you? If you don't want to talk about it, I respect that."

Interlocking his fingers, Flint stared at the floor and spoke softly, "Yes, I was molested. I was nine years old. I was afraid and had no one to turn to. When I look back on things, Mr. Sexton was very methodical in his approach. He wasn't physically abusive. He took time to find out my favorite toys, food, and places to go in order to gain my trust. Then he'd buy me whatever I wanted. He'd cook pork chops and pork and beans for me, and he'd give me money to go see my favorite movies. After a while, each time he gave me something he'd have me sit next to him on the couch. Gradually he started touching me then kissing me in places where he shouldn't. The first time he made me cum I was embarrassed because I knew it was wrong but it felt so good. When I told him I wasn't coming by anymore, he'd said, 'It would be a shame if anything happened to your grandmother, because then you'd have no place to live, except with me.' You're the first person I've admitted this to. He's ruined my entire life to the point that I've thought about killing——"

"Natalie Coleman, come to the intake desk, please," resonated from the speakers.

"Sorry, Flint," Natalie abruptly said, giving him a hug. "That still didn't give you the right to rape Nick." Pausing, she waited for Flint to call her a liar, but he didn't.

All Flint said was, "You're right. But who gives a damn about me?"

"I've got to check on Nick. If he's conscious, the last person he'll want to see standing over his bedside is you. I think you should go."

In part, regardless of Nick's condition, Natalie wanted to be the first to tell Nick the bad news. When she approached the intake desk, the woman said, "He's going to be all right. He's asking for you. You can go in."

Flint's lips pressed together, then he asked, "Are you going to tell him what happened?"

"I have to tell Nick the truth," Natalie said, walking away.

There was no need for her to lie to the man she loved. Quietly she entered the room and stood by Nick's bedside. His eyes fluttered, "Why am I here?" Nick asked, stretching his arms over his head.

"Well, you won't be here much longer," the nurse said, checking Nick's blood pressure. "If your vital signs remain stable, you can go home in the morning."

Natalie waited until the nurse left, then she told Nick, "Baby, you're at the hospital because you had an incident."

"Don't you mean accident?" Nick asked, remotely adjusting his bed into a sitting position.

"No, baby. I wanted to be the one to tell you, you were raped."

"What the fuck!" Nick yelled, grabbing his ass. "Natalie don't play. Did I have some sort of prostate exam and you're fucking with me? You know how I feel about my ass."

Natalie chuckled but Nick didn't see the humor in her laughter, so she said, "Now you know how it feels for someone to violate you. Well, not really because you can't remember anything." Her jaws tightened, her lips shrank, as she stared at Nick. "Let's just say Flint did to you what you'd done to me in your office that day when you forced me to have anal sex."

SEXCAPADES

"You'd better be joking with me because if you're serious, I'm going to kick Flint's ass, then kill him."

"Why, Nick? You raped me. Should I kill you? Men rape women all day every day and get away with it. In fact, if women started strapping on, drugging, and date raping men maybe men would understand the ramifications, pun intended, of their actions."

Nick leaned against his pillow, "You know I didn't mean to hurt you."

"And I'm sure Flint didn't mean to fuck you in your ass. Look, Nick, what I've learned from all of this is . . . I love you. I was afraid you were going to die. I don't want to live my life without you. I don't have a ring to put on your finger, but, Nick Thurston, will you marry me?"

Nick's eyes filled with tears. "Natalie, don't play with my emotions. You know how I feel about you. Damn." Nick took a deep breath, then said, "I'm all choked up. But if you're serious, yes. I would love to marry you. Come here."

Natalie sat on the edge of the bed beside Nick. When Nick held her in his arms, her body melted into the warmth of his touch.

"I don't want the promotion, it's all yours. You can have it. I'm resigning on Monday," Natalie said, waiting for some sort of reaction from Nick, but she didn't get one.

Instead, Nick said, "I'm quitting too. I've decided to invest my money and open my own restaurant."

Kissing Nick's lips, Natalie said, "Me too! I'm opening Divas Galore," she said, hugging Nick's shoulders, then kissing his lips again and again. "You want to partner?"

Nick hesitated, then replied, "We partner on everything else, so if you're serious my answer is yes. We'll be husband and wife and business partners."

Natalie's lips pressed against Nick's seemingly for an eternity until DeVaughn entered the room and Lola walked in behind him and said, "Well, I guess the four of us will have to be partners and raise the baby I'm carrying because Nick is the father."

Lola stood on the opposite side of Nick's bed and held his hand. Natalie was too close to the two of them, so she stood up waiting for Nick to say something but he didn't.

Nick's eyes lit up when he looked at Lola, then he tried to blink away his excitement when he glanced at Natalie. DeVaughn quietly walked out of the room. In that instant DeVaughn must've realized what Natalie already knew, Nick was in love with both Lola and her but in very different ways. Natalie also knew Lola was lying about Nick being the father to expedite getting a divorce from DeVaughn.

Interrupting their bonding moment, Natalie said, "Well, in nine months, one way or another we'll all know the truth. And if by some small chance, Lola, you are pregnant with Nick's child the four of us will raise the baby because I am marrying Nick Thurston."

Lola gasped. "Nick, is this true?"

Natalie waited for Nick to say something, but when Nick picked up his pants, pulled out the ring Natalie had given back to him, and replaced Lola's wedding ring, Natalie didn't say a word.

Lola cried. "This time I promise I won't take your ring off."

$\int$EXCAPADE 25

Flint

Pacing the floor, Flint decided today was the day.

Being molested was one thing but raping Nick? What the hell was Flint thinking? Sitting on the side of the bed, he polished his gun. One by one he inserted bullets into the clip, shoved the clip into the shaft, and sat there. Did he really want to commit suicide? Or was he pleading for sympathy? Maybe if Mr. Sexton had apologized once or shown remorse for his sexual assaults Flint could've forgiven him. But how does one forgive someone who refuses to apologize?

Placing the gun inside his suit pocket, Flint went downstairs to their home office, pulled a few sheets of paper from the printer, placed a blue ink pen in his hand, and began to write.

"Why in the fuck did you rape me? Why did you make

me suck your nasty dick? Why do you still make me fuck you? You are a sick, demented individual. I hate you! I hate you because you've made me hate myself. When I was a child, instead of me playing with kids my age you stole my innocence.

"All of my adult life I've lived in shame. Hiding behind your money, your company, your daughter. I never had a life of my own. Never had a wife of my own. Not a real one anyway. No one to love me for me. Do you know what it feels like not to have anybody who loves you? I bet you don't. That's because you hide behind your pulpit and your congregation, concealing the fact that you can't even get a hard-on to fuck a woman. So you show up at my office and on my doorstep whenever you feel like it so I have to fuck you in the ass and make you cum.

"All these years I've questioned my sexuality because of you. I wish I could rip your heart out of your wrinkled-ass chest, splatter it all over the altar, then jump up and down on it 365 days a year and 366 during leap years. Not a day goes by I don't think about killing you. You deserve to die, you dirty old bastard. And today is your last day alive. I hope you've said your prayers during your sunrise service, repenting for all your sins because if not you're going straight to hell and I'm sending you there."

Folding the note, then sealing the envelope, Flint thought so what if he killed Mr. Sexton. He'd still had to live the rest of his life haunted by what Mr. Sexton had done to him. Bastard! Child molester! He didn't deserve to live. Better to go to jail for killing Mr. Sexton than for raping Nick. Either way, if Flint lived another day, his life was going to get a lot worse before it got better.

Staring in the mirror, he couldn't recognize the man before him. On the surface, he was handsome, well-built, nicely dressed with expensive clothes. A white gold-and-diamond watch circled his wrist. A platinum wedding ring curled around his finger. Money couldn't buy him love. Flint could fuck all day and night if he wanted to. With each orgasm, money bought lovers not love.

"You're just a faggot!" Flint yelled at his reflection, pressing his pointing finger against the image of his forehead.

Maybe he should live another day. Would serve Mr. Sexton and Samantha right. Flint hadn't heard from her since she'd left. Good. They didn't give a damn about him so, "Why should I give a fuck . . . about them!"

Flint got in his car and drove along the freeway. The sun was shining brightly. He could pull out his iPhone, go online, and find a masculine married man looking for a guy like himself to fuck him in the ass. The Bay Area was overflowing with married men on the down-low, especially in Flint's upscale neighborhood.

Nah, he'd better get this over with once and for all so he could stop fucking up other people's lives.

Exiting into the nice quiet community of Redwood City, Flint drove a mile or so, then parked his car. Silencing the ignition, he patted the gun in his pocket and stood before the doors of the church. Maybe he should go home. Maybe he should pray at the altar.

As he entered the church, the choir was singing "Just a Closer Walk with Thee."

Sitting in the back row, Flint bowed his head, then silently prayed, "Lord, please forgive me for what I'm about to do."

Was Flint wrong for not wanting to live his life like this anymore? Was he wrong for seeking revenge against a man who'd repeatedly abused him? Was he wrong for having a grandmother who cared more about her reputation than his health and safety?

Flint stood, walked up to the pulpit, and handed his grandmother the letter that he'd written for Reverend Sexton. Looking dead in Samantha's father's eyes, Flint eased his hand inside his jacket pocket, placed his finger on the trigger, pulled out the gun, and pointed it at Reverend Sexton's face.

His grandmother pleaded, "Justin, baby, what are doing?"

"Shut up, Granny! You knew what was happening to me. You didn't speak up for me then, so don't say a word in his defense now."

His grandmother sat in the front pew, hanging her head, praying, "Lord, please forgive him for he knows not what he's doing."

Yes, he did. Flint knew exactly what he was doing but once again his grandmother was trying to protect her reputation among the church members.

People continued to scramble while screaming and fighting for space under the pews. Colorful hats lined the aisles. Reverend Sexton stood there staring back at Flint as if Flint pulled the trigger he'd be doing him a favor. Well, Flint didn't come here to do him any favors. He came to church today to be saved. Contrary to popular belief, both suicide and homicide were forgivable sins. Flint simply had to repent before pulling the trigger. If there was anyone who could deliver him from the evils of that man's wicked molesting ways, it was God.

Flint set the gun on the altar, then dropped to his knees. Pressing his hands together, he prayed, "Lord forgive me for I have sinned."

The first thing Flint prayed for was forgiveness for screwing up Nick's and Natalie's lives. He'd fucked them over because all of his life he'd been fucked over by others. Before now Flint thought he was truly desensitized to caring for others but he couldn't bring himself to put a bullet in his head in front of the hundreds of women, men, and children. Nor could he shoot their minister.

Quietly Flint stood, exited the church, got in his car, and drove to the Golden Gate Bridge. Parking at Fort Point, he headed down the pedestrian bridge. Gazing down at the sail-boats floating atop the Pacific, he cried. Tears streamed along his cheeks, splattering on his collar. He'd embarrassed himself in church in front of an entire congregation. Everyone at that Sunday morning service knew his shame. They were probably gossiping, trying to figure out what makes a man want to have sex with another man or wondering what made him want to kill their pastor.

Flint would become one less man this hypercritical society would have to ridicule. What gave anyone the right to judge him? Raising his leg over the barrier, he leaned onto the rail, slowly rolling his other leg over the bar. His fingers locked onto the rail.

Filling his lungs with air, Flint closed his eyes. He leaned forward, his fingers loosened. He told himself in four seconds his life would be over. Hopefully, those rescuers heading his way wouldn't recover his body. Flint prayed he wouldn't become one of the three dozen or so jumpers who survived with broken bones and broken hearts. All he ever wanted was to be loved.

Exhaling his last breath, Flint let go.

Sexcapade 26

Nick

Two years later . . .

Honey. Wake up. The baby is asleep and we've got to get ready for our grand opening," Nick said, crawling out of bed and tiptoeing into his son's room.

Nicholas was sound asleep. Nick stared at him as his little man's chest rose and fell. Nicholas sighed, smiled, stretched, then briefly opened his eyes before closing them as he dozed into a peaceful rest.

Making his way back to the bedroom, Nick saw his wife was sound asleep. Quietly closing their bedroom door, he turned up the volume on the intercom to make sure they could hear Nicholas. He then retrieved the electrical clit massager, plugged it in, and placed it on the nightstand beside their bed.

Uncovering his wife's body, Nick spread her thighs, then whispered into her pussy, "Good afternoon, beautiful."

They'd learned to sleep when the baby slept but today was their last day as stay-at-home parents. Opening personal and business joint bank accounts had allowed them to take two years off from working while learning all they needed to know to start up their own business. They'd deposited enough money in their personal account to cover all of their monthly expenses for two years plus added an additional one-year reserve. Into their business account, they'd deposited enough funds to purchase their restaurant.

Gently placing his fingers against her inside lips, Nick stuck out his moist tongue, pressed it against his wife's warm clit, and slowly licked upward.

"Huh? Baby, what are you doing?" Startled, his wife rose to a sitting position. "I have to check on Nicholas."

Placing his hand between her breasts, Nick said, "Relax. He's fine. I just checked on him. We've got two hours before our grand opening and I want to make sure you're overly zealous for more reasons than one."

Admiring his wife lying back onto the pillow, Nick was relieved he'd married the right woman. Methodically his tongue stroked over her opening, teetered on her clit, then continued up her shaft. Pressing his lips softly against hers, he sucked, then said, "Spread this sweet pussy for your husband."

They'd been married a little over a year but everyday Nick was on his honeymoon. It wasn't that Nick didn't believe she was pregnant with his child, he wanted to make sure before investing his time and money into a lifelong commitment. From being by her side during the delivery of their son, to cradling his wife in his arms while she breastfed Nicholas, to never tiring of making love to her, Nick adored his wife.

"Anything for you, daddy," she agreed.

Placing her fingers at the top of her shaft, his wife pulled upward, exposing the most beautiful clit he'd seen. His mouth watered. His dick hardened.

"Yes, mama, hold my precious pearl right there."

Moving closer, Nick's mouth circled, then suctioned her clit. For a moment he flashed back to the pineapple, peppermint, brown sugar, and honey concoction Natalie had basted him with years ago and he smiled. Then he thought about the first night he'd made love to Lola and how she cried.

Turning on the clit massager, Nick carefully placed the vibrating tip close to but not on her wet clit. Watching his wife's clit protrude, Nick slightly moved the vibrator in half-circle motions along the left side of her shaft. He knew her body so well he didn't have to ask, "Am I pleasing you?" but he did.

"Ou yes. You know I love it when you give me a pussy massage."

Indeed. The pussy massage was all about pleasing his wife. He could get his later, after the grand opening of their restaurant. For the next hour, Nick played with his wife's pussy until she'd had five or six big orgasms.

Holding her in his arms, Nick asked, "Baby, are you happy?"

Softly, she whispered, "I've never been happier. Feels like I'm dreaming all the time. Baby, do I make you happy?"

Nick smiled, then answered, "You and Nicholas make me complete."

"I couldn't imagine life without my two favorite guys," his wife said, stumbling out of the bed.

"I feel the same way, baby, but where are you going?"

"We do have a son and we have a grand opening, remember?"

"I'll take care of Nicholas," Nick said. "You go shower and get dressed."

When he lightly stepped into his son's room, Nicholas's eyes were wide open. "Hey, man. How's daddy's fella?" Nick said, picking up his son.

Nicholas smiled, exposing his two bottom teeth. Nick sat in the rocking chair beside the crib for a quiet moment with their son. Cradling Nicholas in his arms, Nick said, "Daddy promises to always protect you and never harm you. I'll never leave you. And I'll never allow anyone else to mistreat you. I promise."

After Natalie had explained to Nick what had happened to Flint, Nick forgave Flint and they asked him to stand up in their wedding and their son's christening, and be the host at their new restaurant Nick and Nat. Old Mr. Sexton must've found religion when he wrote Flint a check for one million dollars. But Nick realized that the money couldn't buy Flint family and all Flint ever wanted was someone to care about him.

There were times when Nick reminisced about the good days when he and Natalie enjoyed swinging and swapping with DeVaughn and Lola. Thankfully Lola's baby was for her husband. Having a son made DeVaughn a better man. Nick was happy for them and at times he actually missed Lola and DeVaughn.

Rocking Nicholas, Nick said, "Son, some people will come into your life for a reason or a season but I'm here for you and your mother for my lifetime."

Book Club Questions

1. Have you or would you ever consider sleeping with your boss to receive a promotion? If you have, please describe your experience? If not, how far did you go. . . or would you go?

2. Would you be able to share your decision to sleep with your boss for advancement with your husband, wife, or significant other? What do you think their reaction would be? Would you jeopardize your relationship for a million dollars?

3. Would you sleep with your boss if you were the same sex?

4. Have you ever been involved in a swinging relationship? Would you host a swingers party for the experience and or for money?

5. Have you ever had anal sex with your partner, and, if so, did you enjoy it? If you've never had anal sex, would you like to?

6. Do you think a man who likes anal sex is headed toward being bisexual or gay? Would you penetrate your male or female partner if he or she requested it?

7. For the women in the group, have you ever fantasized about penetrating your partner, strapping on a dildo . . . or finger fucking your partner?

8. What would be your concerns about swinging or having sex with coworkers? Have you or would you have sex at work if you thought no one was watching?

9. Have you ever had sex with a stranger? Do you like having sex with strangers?

10. Have you ever posted an ad online or in the newspaper for a relationship or a sex partner? What was the outcome?

11. Have you ever answered an ad online or in the newspaper for a relationship or sex partner? If so, what happened?

12. Have you ever been rejected by your boss after attempting to sleep with him or her? How did this affect your working relationship?

13. Could you swing with your best friend and his or her partner?

Honey Bits

Common sense goes a long way. Drugs and sex have been around since the beginning of time. Mama used to say a lot of simple things that made plenty of sense. Here are a few things Mama used to say that you should always keep in mind:

- "Don't drink anything once you've put your glass down."
- "Always have enough money to get home."
- "Don't advertise what's not for sale."
- "Don't you rush to get old."
- "If it walks like a duck, clucks like a duck, it's a damn duck."

Aside from a woman losing her virginity, sex should be pleasurable and orgasmic. Realistically, sometimes it's not. I want women in particular to be smart and safe while being sexy.

- Do not readily trust men.
- Don't be afraid to ask the important questions upfront.

○ Do you have children? If so, how many?

○ Are you with their mother? If not, why?

○ Are you in a relationship? If not, when and how long was your last relationship? Why did the relationship end?

○ Where do you live?

○ Where do you work?

○ Do you have siblings? If so, how many? Where do they live?

○ What's your relationship like with your mother? Your father?

• Always be aware of your surroundings.

• Never drink from open beverage bowls or containers.

• Before going out on first dates, always text your mother, father, or girlfriend his phone number, license plate, address, etc., basically as much information as possible.

• Always let someone know where you are.

• Always use condoms. Keep at least two in your purse at all times.

Here are a few Web sites I visited while working on *Sexcapades* that may be of interest or benefit to you:

• www.RedCross.org and www.AmericanHeart.org: First, I'd like to recommend that everyone reading this, register and take a CPR (cardiopulmonary resuscitation) class through one of the professional organizations listed on the Web sites above.

I do know how to perform CPR. I've taken the class

twice and have passed both times. However, I must admit I haven't taken the class recently. When I was trained, mouth to mouth (MTM) and checking for a pulse were part of the process for laypersons. That has since changed and in some cases a 30:2 compression-ventilation ratio is recommended. Do not use the techniques provided in Chapter 22 of this novel as a guide to saving a person's life. This book is fictional.

- www.WomensHealth.gov and www.streetdrugs.org: Please, I urge you to learn about the effects of date rape drugs and educate your children.
  - ○ GHB (gamma hydroxybutyrate)
  - ○ Rohypnol aka Roofies
  - ○ ketamine (ketamine hydrochloride)

- www.RxList.com: Online listing of prescription drugs from A to Z with the side effects for each drug
- www.ncvc.org: National Center for Victims of Crime
- www.rainn.org: Rape, Abuse, and Incest National Network—they operate the National Sexual Assault Hotline, 1-800-656-HOPE
- www.mencanstoprape.org: Men Can Stop Rape
- www.craigslist.com: One of many Web sites where people of various sexual orientations advertise for sex; Craigslist is also a Web site to find great vacation rentals and much more

HoneyB Tips

SHAVING

Women with course hair should get waxed as opposed to shaving to reduce in-grown hairs. If you've never waxed, start with having your underarms, eyebrows, or legs done before waxing your pubic hairs. For shaving, both men and women can use Tend Skin to reduce or eliminate hair bumps. Tend Skin can be found at most beauty supply stores. If you use Tend Skin on your pubic area, avoid direct contact with your vagina.

WAXING

Waxing moist skin is always better than waxing dry skin. Wash your face and apply facial moisturizer before getting your eyebrows waxed. Soak in a tub of warm water before getting waxed below the waist.

INGROWN PUBIC HAIRS

Avoid ingrown pubic hairs by wearing panties or thongs with lace trim. Avoid wearing elastic-trimmed underwear. The elastic creates more friction while hugging and rubbing freshly shaved hairs into your skin, thereby not allowing the hair to grow outward. Soft nonelastic boy shorts, thongs, or underwear allow hairs to grow with minimal restrictions.

PEROXIDE

Three percent peroxide is safe for many things including using as a mouthwash. Simply mix peroxide with an equal part of water and rinse out your mouth one to two minutes, especially after oral sex.

ORAL SEXING HIM

Ladies, don't do anything that makes you uncomfortable. Don't ever put a dick in your mouth without inspecting it first. If it doesn't look, feel, and smell clean, give him a hand job not a blow job. Cleanliness, though, does not guarantee the person does not have an STD.

ORAL SEXING HER

Check for cleanliness. Sucking hard doesn't always feel good to every woman and by no means should you ever chew on a pussy. Listen to her body language. If she's pulling away from you, don't think you're the man and she's going wild for more. Ease up, and if she pushes the pussy back to you, suck softer.

As noted above, cleanliness does not guarantee the person does not have an STD.

SAFE SEX

Fuck responsibly. Always use condoms.

ALUM

It really does work. If you've never tried alum, it's better to use too little than too much. Women who have chronic yeast infections should not use alum or any other vaginal products that may cause irritations.

MONISTAT

Use a pea-size amount externally as needed. Listen to your body, ladies. If you feel a minor itch or irritation, address it early. Don't wait for the infection to escalate. Always keep Monistat in your supply cabinet.

SEX AND FRUITS

Fruity mixtures are great for added flavor during oral copulation. I don't recommend fruit concoctions for women who are prone to yeast infections. Be creative and remember, you can't go wrong with honey, honey.

HoneyB Safe: Don't Get Stung

To all my HoneyB doers, listen up. Can the HoneyB get stung? Can the HoneyB turn a toad into a prince? Keep on reading and judge for yourself.

On March 28, 2007, as we say in New Orleans, "Do what cha wanna." That's pretty much how I live my life. I went from a near-six-figure government job in 2000 to earning over a million dollars writing about sex and love and how the two impact our relationships. I definitely consider myself a savvy risk taker. I know how to do what pleases me on every level imaginable.

I actually live in Oakland, California, now but, anywhoo, back to my encounter. I was minding my own business. It was a beautiful sunny day in Oakland and I was headed to work on *Sexcapades* at my all-time favorite place to write, Starbucks.

My black laptop bag rested on one shoulder and my black leather handbag with my signature, Mary B. Morrison, embroidered in shimmering gold, hung on my other shoulder. As most of us do these days, I was multitasking, on my cell phone talking to my girlfriend who's an erotic romance author, and ordering my favorite drink, a grande soy, no water, no foam, extra hot chai, while requesting a bag of those wonderful roasted almonds Starbucks sells, but they were out of almonds. Quickly I made a decision to skip on my favorite bear claw pastry.

After ordering, I briefly looked for an available table but suddenly realized the background music that day at the Starbucks on Hegenberger Road was too loud and the temperature was way too cold for me to concentrate on writing. I love most things hot.

My body temperature went from 98.6 to 101 when out of nowhere a fine-ass brotha appeared standing in my three feet of personal space. He was the type of fine that made me say to myself, "A man that fine has done some time." But I like living on the edge, so I heard him out.

"Excuse me," he said. "I don't have a line or anything. I simply think you're beautiful and would love to take you out to lunch or dinner."

My saying is "A girl's gotta eat, so let the man treat," but I was slummin', y'all, wearing my personalized black zip-up sweat jacket, my Gap blue jeans, and my black and red Nike tennis shoes and I had on absolutely no makeup. None!

His crisp button-up long-sleeve pink shirt—I know what some of you are thinking, pink?—with gray and white vertical stripes and an all-white collar was wrinkle free. *Amen!* His tie was impeccably knotted and he had a nice pair of gray slacks flowing over his muscular thighs and nice firm ass. Oh, I can undress a man in seconds. This brotha's attire and approach warranted my attention but not nearly as much as his physique, his clean-shaven handsome masculine face, super full lips, perfect teeth, thick fingers, and nice-size feet.

Leaning into my Bluetooth, I said, "Girl, let me go."

"Huh? I didn't hear you. What was that?" she asked.

"Oh, I'm sorry," he said, "I didn't know you were on the phone."

Seductively holding up my pointing finger, I motioned for him to give me a moment, then said, "Girl, let me call you right back," and hung up before she could answer.

"Oh, I'm sorry. I didn't mean to interrupt. Like I said, I don't have a line. I simply think you're beautiful and would love to take you out. Here's my card. Please call me," he said before confidently strolling out of Starbucks.

I love confident borderline arrogant men. That shit turns me on! I glanced at his card, then stuck it in my back pocket, got my chai, and left. I headed to Coliseum Lexus to get my son's black 2006 ES330 washed and serviced. I love excellent service and the employees at Lexus near the Starbucks on Hegenberger are great, especially Nelson Peterson, a handsome brother who speaks seven different languages.

Off and on I occasionally thought about—I'll call him Triple A—throughout the day. Honestly I had words to write and had forgotten his card was in my pocket.

Later that night, I eased out of my clothes. Standing naked in my bedroom near my Cal-King bed, which needs a running start to jump into, I emptied my pocket and decided to call him up. We talked for a short, and I do mean brief, while. The next morning, something said to me, "Check out his company's Web site." So I did.

My intention for surfing the site was so I could speak intellectually and knowledgeably above the nice dick I envisioned was attached to the brotha. The Web site was informative and legit but I wasn't quite sold on the fact that he told me he went into the operating room to instruct the doctors on how to use his company's products. In my mind, I questioned if a surgeon with a patient lying on the operating table had time to consult with someone who wasn't a doctor on the use of a *product* during a surgical procedure. Hum? Maybe. I have to admit the Queen B of black erotica doesn't know it all, but, ladies, that was Red Flag #1, so I made a mental note to be on alert for unwarranted bullshit.

The same day, day two, he phoned that morning and invited me to lunch. I was reclining in my beige La-Z-Boy leather massage chair, munching on a whole wheat bagel with two scrambled eggs and four slices of bacon but managed to say, "Okay."

When I looked up at the clock on my wall it was almost eleven and we'd agreed to meet at one. Now, y'all, I really needed to be working on *Sexcapades* but I convinced myself to live in the moment, so I showered and got a little cuter than the day before but not over the top because I'm normally low key on my attire when I'm working.

I met Triple A at the restaurant inside the Hilton Hotel in Emeryville. If you haven't been there, FYI, it's one of those spots you know about but don't necessarily frequent.

While he ate his shrimp cocktail, I sipped on my favorite

adult beverage, a Grey Goose dirty martini straight up with olives. As we exchanged information through friendly conversation, I casually asked, "So where do you live?"

He answered, "Contra Costa."

Red Flag #2, y'all!

Contra Costa is a frickin' county not a city or a street, so I made a mental note of that too because I can't stand or tolerate evasive brothas. Don't try to get all up in my sweetness if you're not open to me stirring up in yours. Instantly I knew he was either married, cohabitating, or had something else to hide.

Keeping it moving, he went on to say, "I don't need a woman's money." He added that he owned six cars and was in an investment club that had grossed $12 million in 2006, making it notable that he was, as I say, "on the surface," financially well off. But this was Red Flag #3. Rich men do not disclose their assets. Most of the time if he's black you'll see his assets on his back, particularly in his car, jewelry, and overall grooming.

Triple A also mentioned, "I've been married for eighteen years. I'm single now but I like commitments. I like dating one woman at a time."

For the record, ladies, single does not mean divorced. I like keeping it real with as many men as I can feel. He'd just said he'd been married for eighteen years, so I started piecing together where he was going with his commitment stuff because the HoneyB knows that men say things they believe women want to hear.

I replied, "I could be married if I wanted to but I never want to get married again. Marriage is overrated. Maybe if I'd gotten remarried earlier in life or stayed married, I'd be married today."

Married folks like Triple A wanted to be single and single people, particularly women, fantasized about marriage and kids without genuinely assessing if they wanted a family because they felt it somehow validated or made them complete.

Women are naturally the most complete beings on earth. Just check out the nature channel and watch how the male species puts on a flamboyant show to get the females' attention. That means the male, in every aspect of nature, needs to prove himself worthy of the female he desires.

From all that I know firsthand of some married couples the union is synonymous with voluntarily committing oneself into a mental institution. I told Triple A, "Now that I'm established, I need a criminal background check, credit report, next of kin, blood sample, résumé, references, fingerprints . . ." then I laughed but I sure as hell wasn't joking.

Too many women trust that men are telling the truth when the fact is most men lie as naturally as they hold their dicks. Men will lie about anything whether it's their involvement with another woman or their financial status.

Eating his salmon, rice pilaf, and grilled asparagus, Triple A countered with, "I got my own. I'm not looking for anything from you."

While we were talking, I felt he should know, "I divorced my ex-husband because he hit me once. I'm from Louisiana, so I was actually doing my ex-husband a favor by leaving him." I know some shit that can have a brotha's dick in a twist if he fucked with me.

He looked surprised that I'd said that but I was indirectly letting him know if you're the type of man that has a tendency to hit a woman, you are not the man for me.

"Oh, I don't believe in hitting women," Triple A said, motioning for the waiter to take his plate.

We talked a little longer. I said to him, "What I want is a partner. A man who has ambition, passion, preferably his own business, money, loves to travel the world, money, a sense of humor, money, and good character."

He said he wanted the same but, "Every once in a while it would be nice if the woman paid."

Hold up, wait a minute. That might be cool, ladies, but just make certain your turn to pay isn't first, or second, or third. I've tried dating brothas who are still finding themselves and, trust me, most men don't know what they want. If Triple A was honestly coming out of a marriage of eighteen years where he professed to have never cheated on his wife, regardless of whether he was ending his marriage on an amicable note, as he'd said, or not, he needed time to heal emotionally. A man can't care for a woman for years, then keep it moving to the next woman like he's done with his wife and be honest.

When have you heard a man say, "Look, I'm getting divorced and all I want from you is occasional casual sex to keep my dick happy." The rebound woman seldom gets a commitment or has meaningful longevity in any relationship.

I won't date a man who has to decide whether to pay his child support, his rent, or his bills in order to take me out because I don't give a damn if he's totaling up in his head how much it's going to cost for all the dirty martinis I've had plus the appetizer, meal, and dessert. If he can't afford the meal, he doesn't deserve the thrill. But a girl's gotta feast, so I can do him if I choose . . . meaning I can take the dick and run and never call him again.

Triple A and I parted in the parking lot with our first hug and when his lips traveled toward mine, I glanced at them and let him kiss me on the cheek.

Later that night, my instincts told me to look this brotha up on www.zabasearch.com. I didn't do it but over the next few days my instincts kept nudging me in my side. I still didn't listen.

We had another date. I actually let him come to my condo to watch the NCAA Men's Basketball Finals between Florida and . . . damn, nobody remembers a loser, I can't remember who Florida beat that night. Anyway, we had a good time. I don't worry about uninvited guests because I live in a secure building so no one can show up at my front door unannounced.

Earlier, when we were making plans, we agreed that he'd bring the adult beverage and I'd order the food and he'd reimburse me when he arrived. I went to another one of my favorite restaurants, PF Chang's in Emeryville and ordered takeout. He showed up empty handed and almost immediately asked, "You have anything to drink?"

Red Flag #4. For me, the $55.00 I'd spent on food was the least of my concerns. Triple A wasn't a man of his word and I can't stand a liar. Can somebody please tell me why brothas lie for no apparent reasons? Ladies, men show us who they are early in relationships. Do not ignore the warning signs.

Triple A name-dropped on a few millionaires, saying, "You

just don't know, I have an A-list of numbers right here in my cell phone."

Red Flag #5.

Triple A didn't realize how small the world was. Some of the names he'd mentioned were also in my cell phone. And while I haven't fucked all the millionaires I know, I keep them close enough to get their cell phone numbers because a home number isn't close enough for me. I can reach a brotha even if he's at a hotel cheating on his wife . . . and have him answer the phone while he's knee-deep in pussy.

Overall the evening was decent. Triple A was doable but when I insisted on him using a condom, he protested. What was his problem? No condom. No sex. So he reluctantly put it on. But in the midst of our conversation I was elated that I didn't miss his mentioning of his middle names, which helped me a lot.

Triple A texted me the next morning, "Thank u. Thank u and thank u. The moon was so beautiful last nite did u notice? U were just as beautiful and warm and enticing. U r truly one of the most intriguing and beautiful woman I have ever met. I can't wait to see u again. (Did we ever eat?) . . ."

No, nigga, 'cause you never paid. I ate for days off of the food I'd bought.

His text message continued, ". . . Lol . . . I know I ate something that tasted like HONEY!!!!!! Plz have a safe and productive day . . . (That's a 10 page day right?!? Lol.")

That was a cool message but I'm not overly trusting of the flowery words. When I phoned him later that day, I had to ask again, "So where exactly do you live?"

He answered with that same ole tired response, "Contra Costa."

"Contra Costa is a county," I said, then asked, "Do you live with your wife or ex-wife? Why won't you say where you live?"

"Well, we have an in-law unit. I live in the back, that way I can see my two daughters. I let her have the house because I wanted to keep my girls in the lifestyle they were accustomed to."

Red Flag #6 . . . there were too many missing pieces to this brotha's puzzled life.

Okay, he'd mentioned the girls to me before but now things were becoming clearer. My decoding his message said to me, your wife put you out of the house but she's nice enough to let you stay in the in-law unit. Or you're completely lying and you live at home with your wife.

I said, "Let's talk later when we can meet face-to-face because I have lots of questions."

He agreed and we ended the conversation.

I love meeting different types of men. That's how I enhance my ability to develop great male characters. And I have truly met some characters in my lifetime.

Later that night, I was running my mouth on the phone with my girlfriend Vanessa. We've been friends since the third grade. In conversation, my instincts said, "Wait a minute. Didn't I tell you to check this brotha out? Do it now."

Logging on to www.zabasearch.com, I typed in Triple A's real name and an address in Alamo, California, and Antioch, California, came up along with a list of four relatives.

I have never paid for a report on anyone but I had to know more about Triple A, so I went to www.Intelius.com and paid $23.00 for his criminal background check for the state of California.

Here's what I found:

- Three complete addresses with phone numbers, for the house in Alamo, California, and Antioch, California, and a third in Hayward, California.
- Triple A didn't own any of the properties but his wife did. In fact, he'd signed an Interspousal Deed on April 1, 2005, relinquishing all of his legal entitlements to his wife as her sole property as a married woman. "I ain't mad at her and wish more women would protect their assets from men, especially women with children." His name was slashed out!
- A list of six other cities where he once lived.
- Four named relatives, one was later stated as his wife.
- Criminal Record A-01-42**** Offense date 08/27/1992— Contra Costa, Walnut Creek Municipal.
- Criminal Record 01-09**** Offense date 01/17/1995— Contra Costa, Walnut Creek Municipal.
- Criminal Record A 04-94**** Offense date 04/14/1999— Contra Costa, Pittsburg Municipal.
- Criminal Record A 04-98**** Offense date 06/01/2000— Contra Costa, Pittsburg Municipal.
- Criminal Record A 04-02**** Offense date 06/07/2001— Contra Costa, Pittsburg Municipal.

- Criminal Record A 04-09**** Offense date 07/23/2003—Contra Costa, Pittsburg Municipal.
- Criminal Record A 04-10**** Offense date 08/22/2003—Contra Costa, Pittsburg Municipal.
- Criminal Record A 01-95**** Offense date 05/30/2006—Contra Costa, Walnut Creek Municipal.

The report gives the complete record number, I just left it out, and I had to thank God for making me listen to my gut instincts. When I'd learned he'd been arrested for assault and battery, that was the part warning me not to deal with this brotha. I can't say it enough, "Ladies, listen up when your gut instincts are talking to you."

After sharing with my girlfriend what I found, I called my manager and told her. I forwarded the report to my manager and a few of my closest friends and I forwarded the report to Triple A that showed his first, middle, and last names with a note, "Is this you?"

He did live in Contra Costa after all.

He replied to my e-mail, "Was I that drunk? I don't remember giving you permission to pull my report." He continued, "I'm so disappointed in you. I agreed to talk with you and before we had a chance to speak you pull my report? I don't trust you."

I'm so fucking fed up with men who act like they are in control of women. Women rule this universe. Without women and the female species, everything would die, including men. And men need to start respecting women more but they won't unless women start speaking up and out about what they will and will not accept from men.

I told him, "Don't be disappointed in me. Anyone can do a background check on anybody without permission. If you weren't so evasive, I wouldn't have run the report. You've been to my house and you can't fuckin' tell me where you live." Fuck the dumb shit, he needed to get real with himself. That intimidation bullshit doesn't work with me at all. And you don't have to take my word for it. Ask any one of my exes and they'll all tell you the same. I say what I mean and I mean what I say. Maybe Triple A will be more honest with the next woman. Or I've made him, like some of the rest, smarter.

Just so you'll know, I could've paid $50.00 for all of the background information but I concluded I'd spent enough money on this brotha. This was my first time doing a background check, but considering the information provided, I'll investigate every strange guy I meet before inviting him to my home. I consider myself a good judge of character and most of the men I've dated are still my friends.

The HoneyB concludes, "You can't turn a toad into a prince but you can take the dick and run."

Ladies, have fun, be safe, and don't hesitate to . . . check him!

ACKNOWLEDGMENTS

First and foremost I thank the Creator for bestowing upon me many gifts. Having grown up financially poor in New Orleans, Louisiana, I treasure the teardrops I've shed en route to discovering my talent to write my first novel at the age of thirty-five. I'm now forty-three, and *Sexcapades* is my ninth novel. My other novels are written under my birth name, Mary B. Morrison. I'm striving not to take my blessings for granted or my greatness to my grave. I'd rather share my good fortune with the world and leave a legacy that documents my fingerprints having danced across the keyboard, stringing along words not people.

Spirit guides me with faith along an unmarked path that I cannot see. My Creator accepts me as I am; therefore, I do not seek nor do I need permission to express what is on my mind and in my heart in this or any other books I've written. I'm a grown woman and if you proceeded to read beyond page one, I hope you took this uncensored journey with a very open mind and a mature attitude about sex. I don't know what tomorrow has in store for me. Believing all I have for certain is each present moment, I have so many people I must make time to thank, so please be patient with me.

My heart smiles and shines through my eyes whenever I think of my one and only twenty-year-old, six foot nine, super-handsome, intelligent, and talented son, Jesse Bernard Byrd Jr. He's a young man of great character. I often say, "God gave me the right child." We never argue. My son never disrespects me. He gives me lots of hugs and kisses and frequently says, "I love you, Mom." Jesse is pursuing his dream of playing in the NBA. As part of his vision, he is transferring from the University of San Francisco to the University of California at Santa Barbara to proudly become a Gaucho.

My son's story resembles that of NBA player Mikey Moore. Moore gave back a reported $500,000 in order to transfer to a team where he'd have the chance to showcase his talents, skills, abilities, and his knowledge of basketball. Jesse gave up a $40,000 scholarship for the same reasons. I'm so proud of my son because he didn't allow a monetary eclipse or undesirable environment to overshadow his vision. Instead of relinquishing his power to an individual who had no control over him, Jesse consciously chose to step into the light God had shown him. My son's actions remind me of the hymn I grew up singing at St. Paul's A.M.E. Church in New Orleans, "This little light of mine, I'm gonna let it shine."

God gives each of us light so that we may shine in our darkest hour and so that we may selflessly see beyond our needs to brighten the lives of others. Throughout my success I've had individuals who have provided me life-altering opportunities and I'd like to thank Ken Nisewaner and Ricardo Rivas, may they rest in peace; Henry Dishroom; Lillie Zinnerman; Berry Gardner; Deanna Smith; Ernette Sterling; Jacqueline Mayo; Robert Lang; Joseph Smith; Yolanda Parks; Patrick Henry Bass; Eddie Murphy; author and the Bad Boy of radio Michael Baisden; poet Andrea Thompson from Canada; my first agent, Claudia Menza; and my mentor, Vyllorya A. Evans.

Obviously without my parents there'd be no me or my wonderful son. I'm eternally grateful to Elester Noel and Joseph Henry Morrison. Both of them have made their transitions into eternity, my mother when I was nine years old, and my father when I was twenty-four years old. For those of you who are blessed to still have your parents, give thanks. I wasn't fortunate to get to know my mother during her time on earth. I have no recollection of receiving a hug, a smile, a kiss, or the words "I love you" from my mother. My father was slightly more than a Holiday Dad during my childhood and at his peak of initiating bonding with us as adults he exhaled his last breath. Before passing, my father told me, "You do what you think is best at the time and if you live long enough you'll find you could've done better." Despite the love I feel I missed, I didn't overlook the fact that my parents loved me to the best of their abilities.

My parents also blessed me with the greatest siblings in the world—Wayne Morrison, Andrea Morrison, Derrick Morrison, Regina Morrison, Margie Rickerson, and Debra Noel. Man, I don't know what I'd do without them. My cousin Edward Allen is doing big thangs in the Big Easy with his record label. Much love to you, cuz. I also have a stepbrother, Bryan

Turner. I appreciate my great-aunt Ella Beatrice Turner and her husband, Willie Frinkle, for rearing me.

The Creator also blesses us with extended family. I want to thank my extended family for putting up with me. For those family members who truly know me, you know I strive for optimism; however, I can be a straight trip at times but you guys love me the same, and I appreciate Felicia Polk; Carmen Polk; Michaela Burnett; Margarita Maisonet; Koren McKenzie; Marilyn Edge; Vanessa Ibanitoru; Brenda Clark; my spiritual mother Barbara Cooper; Malissa LeBeau-Tafare-Walton; diva extraordinaire Onie Simpson; Brian "B. Sexy" Shaw; Chris Farr; my soul mate Pernell Bursey; Larry "Big D" Gurganious; Curtis Webster; Larry Addison; Howard and Ruth Kees; Timothy Kees; Denise Kees; my grown and sexy nieces Rachelle Davis, Angela Davis, Lauren Davis, and JoVante Morrison; and my grown nephews Janard Morrison, Roland Morrison, and Damien K. Aubrey, who's pursuing a degree in communications at Clark-Atlanta.

It's been a minute since I've met what I consider a manly man, so I'm giving mad props and much love to Daryl Battles. This writing business is what I live and breathe. When I need an author friend to bounce things off of I can always count on Carl Weber, E. Lynn Harris, Gloria Mallette, Marissa Monteilh, Naleighna Kai, Shannette Slaughter, Victor McGlothin, and Eric Pete. I want to send my love across the Pacific Ocean to Hawaii to a real woman, author, and friend, Tracy Price-Thompson, her husband, and her entire family for coming out to support my son, Jesse, in the Hawaiian Classic Basketball Tournament. Tracy and her husband have reared six children and when I say that each of their children are incredible individuals, I mean it. Keeping one child on track as my friend Gloria Mallette can attest to with her scintillating son, Jared, is a challenge in today's society but mainstreaming six outstanding progressive, high-achieving young men and women into society is priceless and commendable.

There are a handful of booksellers who opened their hearts and their doors, prominently placing me on their shelves when all I had was a poetry book back in 1999 and have carried me throughout my escalating career—Michele Lewis, Emma Rodgers, Vera Warren-Williams, Brother Simba, Brother Yao, Blanche Richardson, Karen Richardson, and Adeline Clark. In addition there are numerous booksellers who navigated my journey to the *New York Times, Wall Street Journal*, and number one *Essence* best-selling lists, and I want you to know while I may not know your names, I am grateful for your support.

Sean Bentley, the African American book buyer for Borders nationwide, and Pam Nelson of Levy Entertainment, I thank you for all you do not only for me but for each of the authors you promote.

Out of all the individuals I've thanked, my heart resides with you, the book clubs and readers who continuously buy my books. I've got to give props to Debra Burton, Taynay Matusumoto, and the entire Turning Pages Book Club; Lisa Johnson and Sisters on the Reading Edge; Bernard Henderson and Alexander Books Store and Club; Tee C. Royal; and RawSistahs.

Three angels sent from heaven have touched my life. Eve Lynne Robinson, my manager, wears so many hats I can't count them all but I can say she handles the details which allows me to focus on writing. Kim Mason, my Web designer and brander, is beautiful and brilliant. Don't take my word for it, check out her creations at www.MaryMorrison.com. And I have Mother Bolton, my reader who is soulful and sassy and embraces her sexuality. Any woman who can convert a pair of Pleasure Pearls into earrings is innovative. Imagine popping a pair of Pleasure Pearls off your ears into your vagina for daily exercise, then sanitizing and snapping them back on as earrings.

You can order your Pleasure Pearls and Ben-Wa Balls at www.MaryMorrison.com and let us know how creative you are. I'm so grateful these women have helped me transition into this new literary era with finesse.

We are working on getting my works into film. Believing the universe gives us what we consciously desire and articulate, I'm thanking in advance all of the individuals who'll become an intricate part of my vision to get *Soul Mates Dissipate* on the big screen. We're overdue for a real love story and with the help of the powers that be, we're going to bring drama, love, and sex to you like no other film has done.

Feel free to hit me up with a piece of your world at www.MaryMorrison.com. Peace and prosperity.